STAND IN THE SUN

Center Point
Large Print

**This Large Print Book carries the
Seal of Approval of N.A.V.H.**

STAND IN THE SUN

Max von Kreisler

CENTER POINT LARGE PRINT
THORNDIKE, MAINE

This Center Point Large Print edition is published
in the year 2013 by arrangement with
Golden West Literary Agency.

The text of this Large Print edition is unabridged.
In other aspects, this book may vary
from the original edition.
Printed in the United States of America
on permanent paper.
Set in 16-point Times New Roman type.

ISBN: 978-1-61173-897-1

Library of Congress Cataloging-in-Publication Data

Kreisler, Max von.
Stand in the sun / Max von Kreisler. — Center Point Large Print
  edition.
pages ; cm
ISBN 978-1-61173-897-1 (library binding : alk. paper)
1. Large type books. I. Title.
PS3572.O48S73 2013
813´.54—dc23
                                                    2013019179

To my beloved Jennie
In Memoriam

—for faith, hope and inspiration.

He took one last look at Adam Burgess, slumped forward in his chair, his chin resting upon the hilt of the knife in his throat, then quietly closed the door and moved with unhurried footsteps along the carpeted hallway.

Descending the stairs, he crossed the crowded lobby, his portmanteau banging against his legs. At the desk, he inquired if the stage to Julesburg had arrived.

"Should be here any minute, Mr. Marlin," the clerk said, handing him his receipt. "That is if it goes out tonight. What with the Sioux burning and killing everything that moves across the Plains, things are worse than they were last summer."

Resting his arms on the counter, he lowered his voice to a conspiratorial whisper. "Andy Girard down at the Overland office says that mail's piled up to the ceiling and no idea when they can start moving it. Tonight will be the first stage they've tried to run through to Julesburg in two weeks. It looks to me like—" He cleared his throat and stared over Marlin's shoulder with an odd, strained expression.

"Evening, Mrs. Slade."

"You'll never learn, will you, Herb?" a woman's voice said softly. "How many times has

Jack warned you not to gossip with Overland passengers?"

Marlin turned. His first impression was of a mass of long red hair, smoky eyes, and a too-red mouth. A fine body, stylishly dressed, although both body and dress were a trifle on the flamboyant side. He guessed her age at about thirty, give or take a couple of years.

A damned good-looking woman.

"You *are* an Overland passenger, aren't you, sir?"

"Yes, ma'am," he said. "If the Julesburg stage goes out tonight."

"It will." Smiling, she held out her hand. "I'm Virginia Dale Slade. My husband, Jack, is division superintendent of the Overland's Julesburg to Rocky Ridge Division. I'll be making the trip with you."

"My pleasure, ma'am," Marlin said. "I had not expected to be so fortunate."

"My God, a gentleman!" she breathed softly. "Only Major Beauchamp, the commandant of Camp Rankin, flatters a woman that way!"

"I've heard about Beauchamp," Marlin said. "What is a West Pointer doing here fighting Indians instead of picking up rank and glory with Grant in Virginia?"

Virginia Slade shrugged. "The Major's simply never learned to say, 'Yes, sir!' to his superiors without sounding insubordinate. Or when to keep quiet. He'll never make colonel and knows it. He'll finish out his service at one of the out-of-the-way posts like Camp Rankin, with no chance of—" She broke off as hoofs pounded down the street, followed by the sound of the Overland driver's post horn.

"Come on!" She took Marlin by the arm. "If that's Bob Ridley, he'll go off and leave us if we're not out there in a couple of minutes."

By the time they reached the street, a small crowd had gathered around the brilliant red-and-yellow Concord stage, shivering in the bitter cold as they joshed the impatient driver.

"Hey, Bob! You got your hair on good an' tight? I hear Bad Wound an' Pawnee Killer have been whettin' their scalpin' knives just for you!"

"Damned Oglala bastards!" The jehu spat and turned to his passengers. "I didn't know you was in Denver, Ginny," he said, heaving their baggage into the rear boot. "What you been up to?"

"Shopping and seeing the sights." She laid her hand on Marlin's arm. "Mr. Marlin, meet Bob Ridley, one of the best drivers in the West."

"Howdy." The jehu checked his passenger's ticket. "Julesburg, huh?"

"That's right."

"Well, let's hope we get there." He nodded to the Navy Colt at Marlin's hip. "You any good with that?"

"Good enough."

9

"You'll more'n likely have a chance to prove it," Ridley said curtly. He looked at Virginia Slade. "Well, get aboard, Ginny! I've got a schedule to keep."

As Marlin moved to help her, Virginia Slade paused on the iron step and smiled down at him. "Be careful or you will spoil me," she said. "And that could get us both in real trouble." Then, before he could answer, she ducked inside.

He barely had time to follow before Ridley released the brakes and sent the Concord spinning out of town. With the area swarming with hostiles, there was little likelihood that the journey would be monotonous. Settling beneath his buffalo robe, he relaxed.

From her corner, Virginia Slade smiled at him with bold, challenging eyes; and he wondered just how much, as Jack Slade's wife, she knew of what was going on in Julesburg and on the High Plains.

He dared not ask her.

The jingle of trace chains and the sound of voices snapped him awake. Raising the leather side curtains, he peered outside. Fifty feet away, lights glowed warmly in the darkness from a big sprawling building.

Across from him, Virginia Slade stirred beneath her buffalo robe and sat up. "Where are we?" she asked.

"Oak Springs, I think," Marlin replied. "How do you feel?"

"Like I've been drug over rocks!"

Bob Ridley, carrying a lantern, stuck his head inside. "Forty-five minutes for breakfast," he said and stomped into the big log home station, leaving the stock tender to care for the horses.

Half asleep and half frozen, Marlin and Virginia Slade stumbled after him, their breaths leaving a white vapor trail upon the still air.

In the dining room, a fire crackled warmly in a huge eight-foot fireplace. Bright curtains at the windows and clean white cloths created a home-like atmosphere.

A trim, black-haired girl, having breakfast alone before the fire, looked up as they entered.

"Hello, Virginia," she said. "You might as well sit here. I'm almost finished."

"Why, Susan!" Virginia Slade exclaimed. "How long have you been here?"

"Ten days," the girl said. "The whole area's swarming with Sioux and Cheyenne." She looked at Marlin with a disarming candor. "I'm Susan Ashley. Who are you?"

Her frankness intrigued Marlin. Seating Virginia Slade and then himself, he said, "I'm Kurt Marlin. I'm en route to Julesburg."

"Hello," she said and returned to her breakfast. After a moment, she paused, a faint smile warming her features. "I don't mean to be rude.

It's just that with home stations fifty miles apart, you get used to eating first and then socializing if there's any time left. Will you be staying in Julesburg long?"

"I can't say," Marlin answered. "It all depends upon whether I can find a challenging job there. It's not easy for an ex-Union cavalry officer to settle down to a routine life."

"You were a cavalry officer?" Susan Ashley's eyes lighted with quick interest. "What was your rank? Where were you wounded? How many battles were you in? Were you a hero? Tell me—I want to know!"

Marlin laughed; he couldn't help himself. She was the most refreshingly different person he'd met in years. "Can't a man have any secrets from you?"

"This is Union territory, Mr. Marlin." Susan Ashley observed him with a grave expression. "There's no need for secrecy."

"Believe me, there's no secrecy about me," Marlin said, smiling. "I'm thirty-seven years old. West Point, '44. Regular Army. A major with the Third Cavalry when war broke out. Fought from Bull Run to Gettysburg. As a lieutenant colonel, I commanded a squadron of cavalry, under Custer, in support of Sherman . . . until my luck ran out."

"Your head?" Susan Ashley asked, studying the great angry scar over his left temple.

Marlin nodded. "A musket ball," he said. "After three weeks, I convinced the doctors I was all right. I wasn't. During heavy action against the enemy at the battle of Woodstock, I passed out and fell off my horse. The squadron lost a dozen men rescuing me. It happened twice again after that. Even I knew it couldn't go on. Two months ago, I was invalided out of the service. Now I'm a man without a career, but not without ambition. It is my intention to build a new life for myself here on the Plains."

"So you're hunting the elephant," Susan Ashley replied quietly. "A lot of men are doing that these days. Coming west, seeking adventure and a future. But why Julesburg?"

The question surprised Marlin. "Don't you have any idea of just how much attention this Indian uprising and the raids on the Overland are getting in the East? It's drawn attention to the High Plains, fired people's imagination. As soon as the war is over, this country is going to grow, but slowly because it's not a place for the weak.

"Now I want to be a part of that growth. And with Julesburg a division headquarters for the Overland, as well as an outfitting center for emigrants, it seems a logical choice for both action and opportunity." He paused, spreading his hands in a gesture of completion. "There you have it; a thumbnail sketch of my life. Are you satisfied?"

"You've told me about Colonel Marlin, the officer," Susan Ashley said calmly. "When we have the time, I want to know about Kurt Marlin, the man. Now if you will excuse me, I have to get my things."

She was gone before Marlin could rise. He smiled wryly at Virginia Slade. "She certainly has a way of saying what she thinks!"

A thoughtful frown creased Virginia Slade's forehead. "You might as well get used to it," she said quietly. "Because you're going to be seeing plenty of her. You can run, but I doubt if it will do you any good."

He wanted to laugh; if it had been anyone else, he would have. But this woman across from him had done a lot of living; and she evidently knew Susan Ashley quite well.

"How old is she?" he asked.

"Twenty-six."

"She's an attractive woman," Marlin said. "Why hasn't she married?"

"She's had a dozen proposals," Virginia Slade replied. "Good men, too. But she knows what she wants. I suspect that she just may have found it." She smiled mischievously. "Well, now that I've spoiled your appetite, let's eat!"

A pleasant, gray-haired woman served them venison, fried potatoes, hot biscuits and honey, with plenty of strong coffee. They ate in silence, even Virginia Slade's cocky spirits drooping from

14

the combination of warmth, hot food and lack of sleep.

Bob Ridley, who had been in earnest conversation with Whitmore, the station agent, came over and sat down. His face was grave.

"A crotch-cloth party of twenty Oglalas was spotted near Thompson's Draw yesterday afternoon. Ginny, I think you an' Susan ought to stay here."

"Susan can stay if she wants," Virginia Slade said, "but I've got to get home. I have a husband to take care of."

"Dammit, I don't like . . . Oh, what's the use of arguing with you!" Defeated, Ridley turned to Marlin. "You got a beltful of ammunition for that pistol of yours?"

"About forty rounds," Marlin said.

"You ever fought Indians?"

Nettled by the jehu's harsh, abrupt manner, Marlin flushed. On the verge of a sharp retort, he caught himself, noting the lines of tension around Ridley's mouth and the concern in the man's eyes. With the safety of two women, plus Overland equipment and the precious mail for people along the far-flung, frontier, the jehu was under heavy pressure.

"I'm an ex-cavalry officer," he said. "I know how to fight."

"Well, you're likely to get a chance to prove it this trip." Ridley rose. "We'd best be on our way."

They crossed the frozen yard to the stables, Ridley's lantern a feeble eye in the darkness. As Marlin helped Virginia Slade aboard, Susan Ashley hurried up, carrying a small reticule.

Lifting her inside, Marlin was surprised at the firm lightness of her slim body and disturbed by the quickening of his pulse as the warmth of her came through to his hands.

"Thank you," she said in a low voice.

He took the "backward" seat, facing the women. A moment later, they were under way, the warm glow of the station's lights giving way to star sheen.

With the side curtains drawn against the cold, Marlin sat silent, listening to the gentle breathing of the sleeping women, while his mind sought to unravel the events of the past twenty-four hours.

One thought kept nagging him. Someone in Washington had betrayed him and Adam Burgess. Yet only three men—President Lincoln, Secretary of War Edwin Stanton, and Postmaster-General Montgomery Blair—had known of their mission.

No, he thought. Only three of whom he had known. The fourth man, whoever he was, was a traitor. An enemy to whom he, Marlin, was already known; but whose identity he could not even guess.

He wondered if Adam Burgess' murderer had been the spy in Washington, and if the man would follow him to Julesburg, or whether someone else would take over from there. That they meant to kill him was a foregone conclusion. For if he remained alive, sooner or later, he would uncover the truth of what he had been sent here to find out . . . whether Makpiya Luta, Red Cloud, and Tashunko Witko, Crazy Horse, were leading the tribes in a general uprising against the hated *Wasicun*, whites. Or whether the chiefs were simply pawns in a much bigger game with the true color of the enemy Confederate gray.

Somewhere in Julesburg lay the answer to that question. If he died before he could relay that information to President Lincoln, the Union could, even at this late date, lose the West to the Confederacy and the High Plains to the Sioux, Cheyennes, and Arapahos. To stay alive had now become a matter of moral commitment. All the more so since he had been personally selected for this mission by the President himself.

Even now, sitting in the darkened, lurching coach, Marlin could vividly recall that moment when a military aide had ushered him into the President's private quarters; and he had stood rigidly at attention until the President said quietly, "At ease, Colonel. And sit down. You must learn, like me, to relax whenever you can."

Silently, Marlin obeyed.

For some moments, the President sat motionless, his head resting against the high-backed

17

chair, his fine, deeply set eyes scrutinizing Marlin with an intense appraisal. And meeting that penetrating gaze, Marlin had the odd feeling that this tall, lank man, with the homely, fatigue-drawn face, knew more about him than he knew about himself.

"Well, Colonel," the President said gravely, "no doubt you're wondering just why you're here. I'll be brief and to the point. You are familiar with the widespread Indian uprising throughout the Central Plains? And with the serious charges made by Senator Conness against Mr. Ben Holladay, president of the Overland Mail and Stage Line? I should be surprised, Colonel, if you were not, since the matter seems to be the favorite subject of both the newspapers and the man in the street."

"There were newspapers in the hospital, Mr. President," Marlin replied. "I have read the journalists' accounts of the situation."

Nodding, Lincoln leaned back in his chair, his face grave. "Senator Conness' charges disturb me a great deal," he said. "If those charges are true—and, to date, I've no proof one way or the other—then Mr. Holladay is guilty of conspiracy against the U.S. mails, of the robbery and murder of Overland passengers by lawless men acting under his orders—and of hampering the war effort. This would place both Postmaster-General Montgomery Blair and myself in the embarrassing position of having granted mail contracts to such a man. And I've troubles enough already."

Marlin remained respectfully silent, wondering just what the President was leading up to. After a moment, Lincoln continued.

"What concerns me even more, however, is Mr. Holladay's countercharges that the Indian uprising and, specifically, the attacks upon the Overland are part of a Confederate conspiracy to destroy communications between the Union and the West. Such charges, if true, could have a disastrous effect upon westward emigration—and might possibly prolong the war as much as an additional six months. God knows how many lives would be needlessly lost."

He paused to leaf through a folder spread out in front of him on the desk. Then pushing the folder aside, he studied Marlin with a thoughtful expression. "Your service dossier is quite impressive, Colonel. West Point, '44. Cadet Corps commander. Graduated first in your class. Cavalry. A brilliant strategist, a bold, daring field officer, War College material . . . The Army has lost a fine officer, sir." Lincoln's fine, grave eyes shadowed.

"I know it is not easy, Colonel, for a man whose life has been spent in the service to have his career wiped out by a single musket ball. But the nation demands great sacrifices of its fighting men, sir—from some, much more than others."

The President lapsed into word-gathering silence.

Quietly, Marlin waited, his mind busy with what had been said. This war-harried President had not called an invalided-out-of-service-cavalry colonel here to the White House just to extend his sympathy. There had to be a deeper, more important motive. Perhaps . . . His pulse quickened.

As though reading his mind, the President smiled faintly. Then the smile vanished; the hollow-cheeked face took on a somber, almost stern cast.

"You were ordered here, Colonel, for a special Presidential assignment. Your mission: to determine if, as Mr. Holladay claims, a Confederate conspiracy is linked with the Indian uprising. And if such a conspiracy does exist, you are to seek out and destroy the Confederate spy directing it."

Suddenly, all the bitter frustration that had been building up in Marlin during the empty weeks since his separation from service flowed out of him. He stared at the President, unable to believe that this thing was actually happening to him. He had thought he was through. Now, miraculously . . .

"Mr. President," he exclaimed, "that is a mission of the greatest importance! Why *me,* sir, of all the officers in the Army, for the job?"

"It's all here in your dossier, Colonel," the President replied. "Born in unorganized territory a hundred miles east of Julesburg. Freighting experience on the Sante Fe trail in your youth. A knowledge of Indians gained from fighting them during that period. A cavalryman, used to traveling long distance on horseback. A brilliant mind; a knowledge of men.

"And perhaps even more important"—Lincoln's face warmed with the words—"a man who chose to remain loyal to the Union, even though it meant losing the love of his family. You are uniquely qualified for this assignment, Colonel; and I have every confidence in your ability to complete it, one way or the other." He straightened in his chair, his manner becoming suddenly brisk.

"You are to depart immediately for Denver, Colorado Territory, and, thence, to Julesburg, a division headquarters of the Overland Mail and Stage Line. There you will present your credentials to the commander of Camp Rankin, a short distance away, and inform him of the nature of your mission. You are authorized to request such military assistance from him as you may require in the execution of your operation. Now do you have any questions so far?"

"No, Mr. President," Marlin said, still trying to adjust to the situation, "No questions."

For a moment, the President studied him without speaking. When he did break the silence, Lincoln's voice carried a new, grim note.

"Other than you and me and the commander

of Camp Rankin," he said, "only three other men will have knowledge of your assignment. Secretary of War Edwin Stanton, Postmaster-General Montgomery Blair and Mr. Adam Burgess, a postal inspector being dispatched by Mr. Blair to investigate Senator Conness' charges that the Overland is mishandling U.S. mails.

"Mr. Burgess will accompany you as far as Denver, where you will split up. From there, each of you will carry out his own mission independently of the other. You will communicate with me by special code through James Henderson, an Army intelligence agent in Atchinson. Henderson will pass your messages to an agent in Washington, who will then hand-deliver them to me. Now do you have any final questions? If not . . ." The President rose, tall, rawboned, shoulders slumped from a chronic weariness. "I cannot stress the importance of your mission enough, Colonel. I can only say that if there *is* a Confederate conspiracy out there on the Plains, thousands of lives may be saved if you destroy it. Good luck, Colonel."

Saluting smartly, Marlin left the quiet, lamp-lit study, carrying with him the unforgettable memory of President Lincoln standing tall and gaunt beside the desk, both face and figure bespeaking the dignity, the character, and the spiritual strength of the man himself.

Now, relaxed beneath the buffalo robe, listening

to the gentle breathing of the two women sleeping opposite him, Marlin remembered that moment and drew both comfort and strength from the memory. If the President of the United States believed in you, then you had to believe in yourself—and in your ability to get the job done.

Leaning his head back against the seat, Marlin fell asleep.

Danger, a solid reality crowding in upon him, snapped him awake. For a moment, he remained motionless, listening to the thrumming hoofs of the chestnut racers beating out a staccato rhythm through the predawn silence, feeling the bitter cold seeking him out even beneath the buffalo robe.

"Hiii-yiiii-haaaaa!"

High and keening as a northern wind, it cut through the early-dawn silence, chilling his mind as the bitter cold had chilled his body. Twice before, between Atchinson and Denver, he had heard that dread Sioux war cry; and both times men had died, arrow-studded and bullet-riddled. Now if this was the band of Oglalas that had been spotted near Thompson's Draw . . .

As he threw back the buffalo robe, he heard the crack of Ridley's nine-foot whip; and then he felt the Concord pick up speed, the team's drumming hoofs thundering over the yellow, rolling Platte hills.

"Hiii-yiiii-haaaaa!"

Like a slicing blade, it parted the sleep layers of the two women dozing fitfully under the dim glow of the interior lights. They sat up, staring at him with wide, not-yet-awake eyes.

"My God!" Virginia Slade cried. "What was that?"

"Sioux," Marlin said quietly, not wanting to alarm them, yet not knowing how to avoid it. "You'd better blow out your lamps. If they're riding captured Overland racers, we're in for a running fight."

"Why did they have to be Sioux?" Virginia Slade said bitterly. "They'll chase us right up to the gates of Camp Rankin!"

Checking his Colt, Marlin punched a handful of cartridges from his gun belt and laid them on the seat beside him. Across the lamp flame, Susan Ashley's eyes met his with frank candor. He wondered if she was aware of what might happen to her; and then he realized that, as the daughter of an Overland station agent, she had probably grown up under the dark shadow of the Indian threat.

Something of his thoughts must have shown on his face for opening her reticule, she drew out a double-barreled .38 derringer and a small bag of cartridges. Then she looked at him and said calmly, "Are you afraid?"

About to raise the side curtain, Marlin paused

24

and stared at her. She had a disconcerting way of saying what other people simply thought. Finally, he said, "If I let myself, I probably would be."

A faint smile warmed the graveness of the girl's face. She blew out the lamp with a gentle breath.

Marlin raised the side curtain, letting in a rush of icy air. In the pale winter dawn, he caught his first glimpse of the enemy—a score of riders a hundred yards behind, spreading out and closing in fast, waving rifles and pennoned lances and shredding the air with their chilling war cries.

Overhead, a rifle cut loose. And now the Sioux began firing, their bullets thudding into the Concord's heavy poplar and basswood body. The stage careened around a bend, skidded wildly, and almost overturned as Ridley gave the team free rein.

From topside, Marlin heard the shotgun boom twice; and then he saw the messenger's arrow-quilled body hit the spinning front wheel, bounce off and out of sight.

A rider raced alongside, his face black-and-ocher daubed, his eyes glaring straight at Marlin. Marlin fired and the dark, twisted face fell away, only to be immediately replaced by others. He kept firing, aware that the Henry .44 and the .38 had joined in to help clear away the danger.

An arrow *thunked* into the wood paneling inches from his head. As he swung to meet this new threat, a big Sioux in a full-length war bonnet shot him in the chest. The force of the bullet slammed him back hard against the seat. He felt no pain, only a momentary sense of suffocation.

He put the last shot in the Colt in just below the chief's heart. The Sioux dropped his Spencer, shouted, "*H'g'un!*" the Sioux courage word, and, swerving his pony in close, threw himself half through the stage window. Marlin laid the barrel of his empty pistol across the Sioux's temple. The chief coughed, vomited blood, and fell beneath the spinning wheels.

"Red bastard!" Virginia Slade cried. "He tried to kill me!"

"He was a chief and a brave man," Marlin said, watching the riders suddenly fall back. "With him dead, they are giving up."

"He was a dirty, stinking savage!" Virginia Slade cried passionately. "I don't understand you. You shoot Indians like they were buffalo; and then you feel sorry for them!"

The pain was beginning to come now, dull, heavy, but coming just the same. "You don't have to hate something to kill it," he said, hearing his voice calm and just a little sad, from a long way off. "You only have to realize that it's dangerous to you."

Again, he was conscious of Susan Ashley's fleeting smile and could not help but note how it transformed the grave, still features.

Beside him, Virginia Slade sat silently a moment, swaying against him as the stage rocked around a bend. Then she said, "Wait until you see what they do to white men."

Slowly, he turned his head and looked at her in the growing dawn light. "I've seen what white men can do to white men," he said in a flat voice. "No Indian can come even close to it."

Pain had hold of him now. Pain and a bubbling froth held back by a tightly clenched mouth. Throwing back the buffalo robe, he opened the door, grabbed the iron side railing and climbed topside.

He barely made it.

As he dropped heavily on the seat beside Bob Ridley, the jehu turned a still gray face toward him. "We damn near lost our hair that time," Ridley said. "I reckon we would have, after Lew got quilled, if it hadn't been for you. You're right handy with that gun, mister." He leaned forward and spat a thin, brown stream of tobacco juice over the foot dash. "The women all right?"

"Yes," Marlin said and vomited blood over the buffalo robe.

"Hey!" Ridley reached out and steadied him, his voice sharpening with alarm. "You're hit!"

"And bad, I'm afraid," Marlin managed. "But don't let the women know."

"Hell, you got no business up here!" The jehu

27

halted the string. "Ginny! Susan! Give me a hand! Marlin's hit!"

Somehow, with Ridley's help, Marlin made it to the ground. By then the women had let down the "backward" seat, turning the stage's interior into a large bed. He crawled inside and collapsed. Once, he roused long enough to realize that he was lying between Virginia Slade and Susan Ashley with their close-pressed bodies cushioning him against the pitch and roll of the fast-moving Concord.

And then consciousness began to unwind itself, faster and faster, from the guarded spindle of his mind until there was no more left.

It was nearing six o'clock, with dusk shadows already darkening Julesburg's boardwalks, as Kurt Marlin turned his horse over to the hostler at the livery stable and walked slowly toward the hotel. He had just been given his final clearance by Captain Bowers, the post surgeon at Camp Rankin.

Although the supper hour, he had to shoulder his way through the crowd jamming the walks and flowing out into the rutted street. Yells, drunken laughter, and off-key singing, competing with the discordant music of out-of-tune pianos, blasted his ears from saloons and dance halls. And on the outskirts of town, thousands of horses and mules jamming the dust-roiled corrals, kicking and fighting and braying, added to the incessant noise.

One of the Overland's most important division headquarters, as well as a major freighting terminal, Julesburg handled three thousand freighters every year. Now, with both stage and freighting travel across the Plains at a virtual standstill, scores of men were more or less marooned in the town.

Pausing in an empty doorway, Marlin studied the sea of faces under the light from the swinging doors. Somewhere in this shifting mass was the man who had murdered Adam Burgess; and who had probably been assigned to kill him as well.

A thin-edged frustration sliced his nerves. In the three weeks since Bob Ridley had brought him in, badly wounded, he had uncovered nothing. He still had no idea as to why Adam Burgess had died; or who had been behind the postal inspector's death. He had only a lot of unanswered questions plaguing him.

For instance, was Holladay, as Senator Conness claimed, robbing his own stages and mishandling the mails? And had Adam Burgess been murdered to forestall any investigation of the Overland? Or were the Indian uprisings Confederate instigated, as Holladay insisted, with a Confederate spy even now operating inside the town?

He was no closer to the truth than he had been in Denver. Yet his period of convalescence had not been entirely wasted. For one thing, he had established a reputation of sorts. Word of his part in the running battle with the Sioux had spread quickly. Bob Ridley, Virginia Slade, and Susan Ashley had seen to that. Within twenty-four hours, everyone in Julesburg knew all about him, including his war background.

At the Ashley home, where Susan had insisted that he convalesce, he had been quietly drawn into the warm circle of their lives. In Ed and Emma Ashley, he had found staunch, loyal friends. And in Susan . . . His mind slid away from the thought now, half afraid of what he might find there.

Ed Ashley, the Overland's assistant station agent, he had found to be an experienced, highly competent man working under constant frustrations—a situation that would not change as long as Jules Reni remained in charge. According to Ashley, Julesburg was run by Reni, the degenerate French-Canadian station agent, who had founded the town. Reni was strongly suspected of working hand-in-hand with the outlaw element who used the town as a base of operations against the Overland itself.

But outlaws were not the only threat to Julesburg. As Marlin had improved, he had also seen arrow-studded, bullet-riddled stages racing into town with dead messengers and wounded drivers and gut-shot horses. The Indian raids, he was now convinced, were real and steadily mounting in intensity.

Other than what Ashley had told him, however, his Overland contacts had yielded him nothing of value. He had talked to Jack Slade, the division superintendent, a couple of times. Despite the ugly rumors he had heard about the man, Slade's driving energy had impressed him. Whatever else he might be, Jack Slade was ruthlessly efficient.

Major Beauchamp, to whom he needed to present his credentials as a Presidential agent on "special assignment," was in Denver and was not expected back for another day.

Slade, Ashley, Beauchamp—these were the people with whom he had to develop day-to-day associations in order to get a clearer picture of the overall situation. These, and Ben Holladay. For he had the distinct feeling that one of them, consciously or unconsciously, held the key to the truth behind the Indian uprising.

A drunk staggered out of the saloon, brushing Marlin aside and reminding him of where he was. As he stepped out onto the boardwalk, he collided with a big, bull-necked man heading in the same direction.

"Marlin!" the big man exclaimed. "I was looking for you."

"Hello, Slade," Marlin replied. "I just got back from the fort." He studied the Overland super-intendent with a professional appraisal.

Medium height, weighing one hundred eighty pounds, well-dressed, soft-spoken, affable, it was hard to believe that Jack Slade had killed more than twenty men. Or that he was the most-efficient, most-feared, and most-hated employee in the entire Overland system. Yet it was rumored that not even Mark Twain had been able to escape the man's personal magnetism.

"Emma Ashley told me you'd ridden out to the post surgeon's office for a final check-up," Slade said, his handclasp firm, friendly. "What was Bowers' verdict?"

"To use the Captain's own words," Marlin replied, *"Discharged. Return to active duty."*

Slade grinned. "That's Bowers, all right." He grew suddenly serious. "If you've got the time, there's something I'd like to discuss with you."

Something in the man's voice, perhaps a faint trace of worry creeping in to deepen it, caused Marlin to cast him a quick, sharp glance.

"I was about to have supper," he said casually. "Why not join me? I think Emma Ashley must run the best hotel-dining room accommodations between Atchinson and San Francisco. Where else can you find bright curtains at the windows, flowers on clean tablecloths, and fine food for a dollar and a half?"

"No, thanks," Slade said. "I've already eaten. But I will have coffee with you."

They shouldered their way through the roistering crowd to the two blocks to the hotel, their shoulders hunched against the chill wind sweeping in from the northwest.

The hotel lobby was deserted, but the dining

room was well filled. Shucking their heavy coats, they took a table near the huge fireplace. Ordering a steak, Marlin leaned back and studied the diners around him, seeking, as always, some clue in a covert look, an unguarded word.

Across the room, he spotted Ed Ashley visiting with friends. Ashley smiled, rose, and came over. A small, wiry man in his early fifties, he had, according to Slade, switched over to the Overland when Holladay had taken over the then crumbling Russell, Majors and Waddell outfit and reorganized it into the largest stagecoach venture in the world.

"Well," Ashley said. "What did Bowers have to say?"

"A routine recovery," Marlin replied. "No complications. He also said that there was an excellent chance that, in time, I might fully recover from the head wound. In other words, no blackouts, headaches, or double vision."

"That *is* good news!" Ashley puffed on his battered pipe a moment. "Susan and Emma were worried about you. Why don't you drop by later and tell them about it? Say around nine o'clock?"

"Thanks," Marlin said. "I'd like that."

"Good," Ashley replied. "Then we'll be expecting you."

"You're making friends fast," Slade remarked as Ashley moved away. "You know you've made quite an impression around here. A fighting cavalry officer who's already done his part in the war. A man who helped stand off a Sioux stagecoach attack and saved two women, including my wife. Yes, I'd say you're off to a good start. And Ed's a good man to know. He'll be taking over soon as stationmaster."

"What about Jules Reni?" Marlin asked. "I've heard a lot of rumors about him."

Slade scowled. "They're not just rumors," he said. "Reni's been robbing the Overland blind for the past two years. We suspect he's working with half a dozen outlaw bands; but we haven't been able to prove it. Holladay's warned him to clean up the town or get out. He's done nothing. Now he's through."

Watching him closely, Marlin could detect no sign of deception in either voice or manner. Slade's concern and anger seemed genuine; and his charges against Jules Reni reflected public opinion in general. If the charges were true, then Senator Conness' case against Holladay would be seriously weakened. Perhaps even totally disproved.

"Tell me—" Marlin broke off as the waitress served him. When she had gone, he continued. "How do these outlaw bands operate?"

The Overland superintendent's face darkened with angry frustration. "Stagecoach raids for gold and registered mail. Robbery and murder en route and at way stations. Theft of Overland racers worth three and four hundred dollars apiece. When we offer a reward, the horses are 'found' and the reward claimed. A week later, the same horses may be stolen again. And it's all being blamed on the Sioux."

Marlin glanced up quickly. "You don't believe Indians are responsible?"

"I didn't say that," Slade countered. "There's no question about this Indian uprising. Hell, they're on the warpath from Kansas to the Rockies. But some of these raids are white men's work. Or, at least, a white man's behind them."

For a moment, Marlin gave his attention to his food, his mind absorbing this sudden and unexpected flow of information. Slade was a shrewd man; if he had anything to hide, he wouldn't be talking this freely. Normally, he wouldn't be so frank under any circumstances. Why now? Unless—

Laying down his fork, he asked casually, "I know this sounds far-fetched, but could Jules Reni be behind this Indian uprising?"

Slade brushed his chin with tentative fingers, then shook his head. "He could maybe be mixed up in it; but he's not behind it. He hasn't got the brains or the confidence of the chiefs for any-thing like that."

"Then who?" Marlin asked cautiously, wanting to know more but not wanting to arouse suspicion.

"Ben thinks it's the Confederacy," Slade replied. "It's a known fact that if the Overland doesn't get the mail through and keep people informed of what's going on, the Union could lose the whole West. That's what the Rebs want."

Thrusting back his plate, Marlin regarded Slade thoughtfully. "I don't think either side, the Union or the Confederacy, has been able to persuade a single Indian nation to align itself in our war. Individual bands, perhaps, but not an entire nation."

"Oh, I'll agree with you there," Slade replied. "The Sioux, especially, hate us because the Overland passes through their finest hunting grounds. If they can use the Confederacy to destroy the Overland, they'll do it."

"Do you think that's what they're doing now?" Marlin asked. "Playing on a desperate South's hope of gaining the West and prolonging the war if these raids continue?"

The other man shrugged. "Probably," he said. "And, no doubt, the Confederacy's making the chiefs believe that if they can wipe out the Overland, white emigration will stop, and they can go back to the old ways. Hell, I don't know." A baffled expression darkened his face.

"All I know is that, somehow, the Indians are getting hold of Spencer repeating rifles, more and better ammunition, whiskey . . . and that they're learning to break up a cavalry charge before it can form. Now you add to this the fact that the Sioux are among the finest horsemen in the world, that Tashunko Witko, Crazy Horse, is a brilliant military strategist, that Makpiya Luta, Red Cloud, is a bold, natural leader and that Tatanka Yotanka, young Sitting Bull, makes powerful medicine and, friend, you've got a pretty good idea of what we're up against here on the Plains."

He ran a hand through his thick, black hair, his mouth thinning into a grim line. "Hell, you've seen the beating the Overland's taking, especially this division. It's got to stop. That's why I'm here to try and clean up the mess."

He put down his coffee cup and level-eyed Marlin. "Tell me. Now that Captain Bowers has given you a clean bill of health, what are your plans? You still intend to stay in Julesburg?"

Marlin shrugged. "Why not?" he said. "There's a real challenge here. If someone offers me the right kind of job, yes, I'll stay."

Tilting his chair until it teetered on its back legs, Slade linked his hands behind his head and measured Marlin with a long, steady look.

"You know when you first came here, I figured you as a man with a definite purpose. Hunting another man, maybe a woman. A Pinkerton detective, a bounty hunter." His face altered subtly. "It even occurred to me that you might be that damn Reb spy."

"And what made you change your mind?"

Marlin asked, hiding the on-guard tension within him.

A faint smile warmed Slade's eyes. He settled his chair back on all fours and unclasped his hands from behind his head. "I telegraphed Holladay to check on you with the War Department," he said. "You're not only clear; you were a natural leader, a resourceful commander." He leaned forward, his manner suddenly businesslike.

"I've been doing a lot of thinking since Ridley brought you in three weeks ago. I need someone to help me clean up this town, start the stages rolling and pin this conspiracy business on the Confederacy. Maybe it won't stop the raids; but at least it will take some of the pressure off Ben in Washington.

"With your background, you would be the ideal man for the job. Besides, you saved Ginny's life. I figure I can pay a debt and help myself at the same time. What about it? The pay would be good. Three hundred a month, plus room and board at the hotel."

Marlin chewed on the idea a moment, not hurrying his decision. As a trouble-shooter, he would be free to make inquiries, have access to company records and the unquestioned right to range over the division's six hundred miles of road, seeking firsthand evidence of a conspiracy. Evidence that he must have and could probably secure no other way.

"That sounds like a big, dangerous order," he said.

Slade's eyes met his steadily. "Danger is no stranger to you. Nor have you ever been one to run away from it."

For a moment, Marlin measured Slade in silence, sizing him up, feeling him out for some sign of deception. Then, satisfied, he said, "You realize I don't know anything about running a stage line."

"You're not expected to," Slade said. "What we need is your brain and your ability to take care of situations as they come up. Most of all, we need you to get to the heart of this conspiracy."

"All right," Marlin said. "We'll give it a try. When do I go to work?"

Slade's face relaxed, his whole personality suddenly warming. "Take another day or so to get your strength back," he said. "Talk to Ed Ashley and Bob Ridley. Get the general picture from them. Then report to me on Monday morning. Meanwhile"—he rose and thrust out his hand—"welcome to the Overland!"

Watching Slade work his way across the crowded dining room, Marlin found it hard to believe the chilling stories he had heard about the man. Yet there was no doubt but that Jack Slade was a dangerous, unpredictable individual; and that many of the stories were true.

As true, Marlin thought, as those which he

had heard about Virginia Dale Slade, a bold, uninhibited spirit. An ex-bordello girl whom Slade had taken as a common-law wife, she was hot-tempered, headstrong, and, in her own way, as unpredictable as her husband. Yet, for all that, Marlin found her an intensely human person, attractive, witty, and generous.

Finishing his coffee, he went out into the lobby. A score of stranded guests sat around the big potbellied stove. With the stages not running, every room was taken. He nodded to the desk clerk and went upstairs to his room. A while still to wait before he called on the Ashleys, he sat down on the bed to think.

For the first time since his arrival, he felt relaxed. The weeks of tense waiting were over. He had accomplished his first objective—a job with the Overland that gave him a reason for staying in Julesburg, as well as great flexibility of movement. Now, if there was in fact a conspiracy, his next move would be to flush the enemy into the open.

He fell asleep.

The sound of a bugle awakened him. Stumbling over to the window, he stared down into the street. An Overland coach, flanked by two squads of cavalry, was just rolling past, headed for Camp Rankin. Evidently, Major Stephen Beauchamp and his wife had returned.

He moved away from the window, feeling a great sense of relief. Henceforth, he would know that only a couple of miles away there was a Union garrison commanded by a fellow West Pointer. If he had to have help, it would be there. The first thing Monday morning, he thought, he would call on Beauchamp and present his credentials as a special agent on a Presidential mission.

He filled the washbasin with water from the hand-painted pitcher, splashed the last of the sleep from his brain, and dressed. He went downstairs and across the heat-filled lobby and out into the icy street.

Promptly at nine o'clock, he knocked on the door of the Ashley home near the edge of town.

Susan Ashley admitted him. "Come in, Kurt." Her gray eyes warmed with pleasure. "I'm so glad to see you."

He stood motionless, staring at her. The burgundy dress, with its low-cut bodice and slim waist, fell gracefully to her feet. Her rounded shoulders, golden tan like her face, glowed warmly under the kerosene lamps. A cameo necklace nestled between her breasts. Falling naturally to her shoulders, her long black hair contrasted startlingly with the calm, gray eyes.

She was not merely beautiful, he thought; she was something more. She reminded him of the hills behind his parents' home in Kansas, strong, enduring . . . of a young pine thrusting eagerly upward to the sun . . . of a quiet meadow and clear deep water. She was—*different.*

Half-smiling, Susan Ashley regarded him with a quizzical expression. "Is there something wrong with me?"

Marlin's eyes ranged over her face, feature by feature. "No," he said. "It's just that I have the distinct feeling that I'll never meet another you."

Her eyes leveled with his in perfect under-standing. "Why, that's the nicest thing any man ever said to me! I hope you never repeat it to another woman."

"Susan, I thought I heard—" Emma Ashley, a pleasant woman in her late forties, came into the hall. At sight of Marlin, she broke off and moved quickly forward to greet him.

"Hello, Kurt," she said. "Here, give me your coat. Susan, don't just stand there! Take him into the parlor so he can get warm."

Seated before a big, wood-burning fireplace, Ed Ashley rose and shook hands as Marlin entered. "Make yourself at home. Like a drink? I can offer you good Bourbon. Or Scotch, if you'd rather."

"No, thanks." Marlin chose a comfortable chair near the fire and held his numbed hands out to the dancing flames. "I had dinner with Jack Slade tonight," he began.

Carefully, Ashley loaded his battered pipe, lit it,

and puffed thoughtfully a moment. "What did Jack have to say?"

Sitting back in his chair, Marlin looked at the little group, all watching him with a quiet expectancy.

"Why," he said, smiling, "Slade offered me a job as the division's trouble-shooter."

"Did you take it?" Susan Ashley asked quickly. "Oh, I do hope you took it!"

"Susan!" Emma Ashley exclaimed. "You've no right to get so personal!"

A faint smile curved Susan Ashley's mouth. "I've every right," she said calmly.

"I think you should explain yourself, young lady!" her mother replied, half exasperated.

"You'll know when the time comes." Quietly and with conviction.

"Susan, I just plain don't understand you!" Emma Ashley sighed. "Don't pay any attention to her, Kurt. She's always been like this, even as a little girl. Always living in some secret world of her own. Saying the oddest things."

"It's all right." Marlin paused, then addressed himself to Susan, who sat watching him with parted lips. "I go to work Monday morning."

A warm glow lighted Susan Ashley's fine gray eyes, and he felt some of that warmth reaching out to him with a sweet intimacy.

"Well, now, Susan," Emma Ashley said. "Are you satisfied?"

"Isn't it what we've all been hoping he would do?" Susan countered. "Help to open up the stage line and to make this town a decent place to live in again?"

"You're right, of course, Susan," Ed Ashley admitted. "And now, once we get rid of Jules Reni, perhaps we can do just that."

"Jack tells me you're due to take over from Reni as soon as Holladay arrives," Marlin said. "When do you expect him to get here?"

"Sometime this month," Ashley replied. "Hopefully within the next ten days."

"Do you think Reni will make trouble?" Marlin asked, stretching his feet toward the warmth of the fire.

Ashley shot him a surprised glance. "I thought you knew there was bad blood between Reni and Slade. When Holladay fires Reni, it will be Slade's job to run him out of town. And Reni's already sworn that if Slade tries it, he'll kill him. Yes, there will be trouble. You can count on it."

"Tell me, Ed," Marlin asked, "just what kind of man is Jack Slade? I've heard a lot of ugly rumors about him; but he just doesn't seem to fit the picture."

Ashley puffed thoughtfully on his pipe. Then he said slowly, as though not liking the subject.

"Jack Slade is a natural killer, Kurt, probably one of the most dangerous, unpredictable men in the West. If he's in the mood, he'll kill you whether you're armed or not. I remember once, when he was with Russell, Majors and Waddell, him and a teamster tangled over a woman. It ended in a Mexican standoff. Jack convinced the teamster that they should drop their guns and go at it with their fists. When the teamster threw down his gun, Jack just stood there laughing while he shot the fool."

Marlin sat silent, waiting, while Ashley paused to fire up his dead pipe. When he had it going again, Ashley continued.

"If you forget everything else, remember that teamster. Because what happened to him can happen to anyone who crosses Jack Slade. He can't be trusted, Kurt. Not even if he likes you. When he's sober, he's courteous, friendly, and hard working. But when he's drunk—and he's drinking more all the time—he's a fiend. He goes around shooting up the town and anyone who gets in his way. When he sobers up, he usually apologizes, pays damages, and buries the victim at his own expense. He's killed more than twenty men. Before he dies, he'll kill a lot more."

"I don't understand it," Marlin said, shaking his head. "Why does Holladay keep him around?"

"You've got to understand, Kurt, that this is wild, rough country," Ashley replied. "And that the men who work for the Overland are, for the most part, just as wild and rough. It takes a man like Slade to handle them. However, there's more to it than that. Ben Holladay and Jack have a lot in common. They both fought in the Mexican war, freighted on the plains, like women, gambling, and fighting. They're both ruthless, fearless, and have a fanatical love for the Overland. Save for the killings, I guess you could say that they're two of a kind. Anyway, Holladay's backed Jack a hundred per cent so far. It's my opinion, though, that, unless Jack cuts out his heavy drinking and shooting sprees, Holladay will sooner or later have to fire him. It's causing trouble with businessmen and giving the entire division a bad name."

Sitting there before the fire, comfortable, relaxed, listening to Ed Ashley's quiet, impersonal description of Jack Slade, Marlin found it difficult to reconcile his own impression of the man with the proved reality. Yet he knew that Ashley was not the kind to exaggerate. Around Jack Slade, men walked carefully.

"How do you and Slade get along?" he asked. "Have you ever had any trouble with him?"

"No." Ashley shook his head. "We came over from Russell, Majors and Waddell together when Holladay took over the line. I guess you could say I know Jack as well as anyone living, except Virginia Slade; but he's still a mystery to me. He's a killer, yet he has two loves. Virginia, his wife, and the Overland. You saved the life of the one, and you fought to protect the other. He'll not forget that."

"And yet"—Marlin straightened in his chair, drawing his now warmed feet away from the fire—"you say I'm not to trust him."

Ashley hesitated. "If his mind is clear, yes. But if he's sick or drunk, not even I trust him. Like I told you, remember that teamster. The best advice I can give you is to stay away from Jack when he's drinking.

"Well—" He rose and turned to his wife. "Emma, how about some coffee and a piece of that chocolate cake of yours? Come on. I'll give you a hand."

When they had disappeared into the kitchen, Susan Ashley turned to Marlin with a grave expression. "I'm so glad you're here," she said. "Dad has needed someone he could depend upon so badly. Now, perhaps"—her eyes lowered—"I, too, can have someone to turn to, to talk to. It's . . . it's been very lonely out here."

She was not flirting, Marlin realized, but simply expressing the need of an intelligent young woman in a land not noted for the finer things in life. He sensed that her very nature put up a barrier between her and others—and that what she saw around her provided no incentive to remove that barrier.

"Tell me about yourself," he said, smiling.

"There's nothing to tell," she replied quietly. "Born in St. Louis where Mother ran a boarding house while Dad worked as a teamster in the

Sante Fe trade. After the war with Mexico, when the trade began to dwindle, he drove a stage for a small feeder line. In '56 or '57, he joined with Butterfield, first as a driver, then as a station manager for smaller way stations. From there to Russell, Majors and Waddell as assistant station manager at Denver. He's good!" Her voice filled with pride.

"When Ben Holladay took over the line from Russell, Majors and Waddell, Dad was one of the first men he asked to come over to him, along with Jack Slade. Dad could have stayed at Denver; but he was needed here, and he knew it. So—"

"No, no!" Marlin broke in, laughing. "I know about your father. Now I want to know about *you!*"

Susan Ashley stared at him, startled. "But I'm telling you about *me!* Westward, always westward. Educated on wheels, for the most part. If not, then in one-room schools. Rough towns, rough people. As a matter of fact, I guess you could say wheels have been my life—for wherever wheels have replaced pony tracks, my family has followed. Someday, I suppose we'll be following the iron wheels.

"Tell me"—she looked at him, her face eager, alive with curiosity—"what's it like on the other side of the Missouri? I mean . . . Chicago and New Orleans and New York and places like that.

"Would you believe it? My father works for the Overland—and the Overland connects with practically the whole world—yet I've never even been to San Francisco! Whenever Notley Ann, Ben Holladay's wife, visits here, she makes me feel so, so provincial! You should hear all about those big parties she gives in her mansions in New York and San Francisco and that fabled *Ophir* estate in Portland, Oregon! Champagne and caviar and beautiful music and famous, intelligent people and—" She broke off and, as suddenly as it had appeared, the glow faded from her eyes, and she regarded him once more with her grave, quiet expression. "I'm a romantic little fool, aren't I?"

"Because you dream?" Marlin said gently. "No. The West is being tamed by people with dreams—and the courage and foresight to make those dreams a reality. You dream of mansions and champagne and caviar and Viennese waltzes—and, in New York and Massachusetts and Louisiana, people dream of cowboys and Indians and miners in red shirts and fabulous gold strikes like the Ophir mine.

"And some of those people, because you and your kind have already led the way, will come out here seeking new horizons and your dreams will mingle and from them will emerge a new West in which each of you will find what you seek. No; I don't think . . ." He stopped, flushing.

"I must sound like some sort of preacher or a dime novelist."

Susan Ashley lifted her face to him, her eyes holding steady, and said softly, "You sound exactly as I knew you would from the moment I first saw you. That's why"—she spread her hands in a wordless gesture—"why I want to know more about Kurt Marlin, the *man*."

Watching her, listening to the earnestness in her voice, Marlin felt himself drawn to her as he had never been drawn by any other woman. The others had been interested only in the epaulets on his shoulders, in the fact that he would make brigadier by the time he was forty-five, and that he knew all the correct social graces. Susan Ashley seemed not to care what kind of future lay ahead for him. To her, he was a man, a human being—something he had never been to anyone else in his life. It touched him deeply, broke down the bars of his natural reticence. A slow smile spread over his face, giving to the high forehead, the piercing eyes and the high-bridged nose an unaccustomed gentleness.

"What is there to know about a man who's spent practically his whole life in the Army?" he said. "You wonder why I came to Julesburg? I was born about a hundred miles due east of here in unorganized territory. My father was a sergeant at Fort Leavenworth. Before that, in '21, he was with Captain William Becknell when Becknell took a pack train across the country to the Arkansas, followed the river northwestward to the Rockies, and then struck southward to Sante Fe.

"The next year, when Becknell returned with wagons and blazed a new, more direct route to Sante Fe, my father was with him again. This time Becknell left the Arkansas near Cimarron. So, you see, your father followed the trails that my father helped to establish."

"Go on!" Susan Ashley urged. "I want to know all about you. Your mother, your brothers, and sisters—everything!"

Marlin hesitated; he had never been one to talk about himself. But her interest was so genuine that he could not refuse her.

"I guess we must have moved around as much as you did," he said. "First one Army post, then another. A lot of the enlisted men's wives served as laundresses. My father would never let my mother do that. She had been a schoolteacher before they married. She saw to it that I got a proper education. Her heart gave out when she was barely thirty-nine. I was sixteen. You remind me a great deal of her. She was a dreamer, too; but she was also a woman of courage and had a great capacity for love. She loved my father very much. Enough to follow him all over the country.

"After her death, my father left the Army and sent my three brothers and two sisters back to live with relatives in Independence. He went back into the Sante Fe trade, like your dad; and I went along with him, doing a man's work, for almost three years. He was killed on the trail by Cheyennes in the summer of '44. But he had lived long enough to somehow get me an appointment to West Point. I entered the Academy that fall."

Marlin fell silent, staring into the flickering fire, feeling, for the first time in years, a nostalgia for the past.

"What about your brothers and sisters?" Susan Ashley asked quietly.

A shadow passed over Marlin's features. "One brother was killed at Bull Run. The other two are fighting with Lee in Virginia. My sisters do not write to me. Perhaps it is just as well."

"I'm sorry." Reaching out, Susan Ashley laid her hand on his arm. "It takes a great deal of courage to make that kind of decision."

"We weren't always a divided family," Marlin said. "When we were growing up, we raided watermelon patches, tried chewing tobacco and drinking Taos 'lightning,' went to pie suppers and square dances, courted the girls, and beat up any boy who made eyes at our sisters. In between times, we kept in shape by beating up one another."

The memories came flooding through his mind, strong and good, and suddenly he was laughing, and the tears were running down his face and he was not ashamed but glad because he knew that Susan Ashley understood. And then his laughter stilled and he was looking at her and her eyes were shining in a way that made him warm and complete.

"Well . . . ," he said awkwardly, "now you know everything about me. Are you satisfied?"

"Just one more question." Susan Ashley turned until she was facing him squarely. "Are you married?"

He had known that sooner or later she would ask him that and he was halfway prepared for it. "No, I'm not married," he said. "Maybe it's selfishness, a fear of losing my personal freedom. Maybe it's just that I couldn't drag a woman from a pillar to post the way my father did my mother. Or it could be that I've simply never met the right woman. I don't know."

"If you ever do meet her"—Susan Ashley's hand tightened on his arm—"will you let me know?"

Gravely, Marlin searched her candid gray eyes. "I promise," he said, "you'll be the first to know."

They were sitting quietly when Ed and Emma Ashley returned with cake and coffee.

Soon afterwards, Marlin returned to the hotel through the bitter cold night. The hotel lobby was deserted save for the clerk and a couple of dozing guests beside the cherry-red stove. He nodded to the clerk and went upstairs.

In his room, Marlin undressed in the darkness. Sliding between the chilly sheets, he relaxed, reviewing the events of the day. For the first time, the lethargy which had dulled his spirit for the past two months lifted. Perhaps it was the challenge of his assignment; the knowledge that, although the Army no longer considered him physically fit for active combat, he had been chosen by President Lincoln, himself, for this hazardous special mission. Certainly it made him feel still useful, still a part of the war. And yet he knew that it had nothing to do with the change that was taking place inside him.

The real reason was Susan Ashley. She radiated a warmth, an integrity, a candid frankness that drew him strongly to her. There was between them an affinity that required no words to express their innermost thoughts. Tonight, she had stirred his emotions, come closer to him than he cared to admit. Resolutely, he thrust the image of her from his mind. Until his mission was completed, there was no place for Susan Ashley or any other woman in his life.

With an effort, he concentrated upon his conversation with Jack Slade earlier in the evening. That talk had yielded some valuable bits of information and had substantiated more acquired from other sources. Slade's sincerity he did not doubt. And Slade, as well as Ben Holladay, believed that the Indian uprising involved a Confederate conspiracy, with the Overland the prime target. Destroy it and the vital link between the Union and the West was broken.

To complicate the Overland's difficulties, Jules Reni, as station agent, was robbing the company blind and was prepared to fight to hold his advantage. Reni was suspected of being connected with a half a dozen outlaw bands in the area. There was also the possibility that the Frenchman might be the Reb spy, although Jack Slade did not think so.

Propping himself up in bed, Marlin stared thoughtfully into the darkness. Could Slade be wrong about Reni? Was the Frenchman his man? He doubted it. Jules Reni lacked the intelligence, the leadership, and the respect of important white men and war chiefs like Crazy Horse, Red Cloud, and Spotted Tail.

The Confederate spy behind the scene, *if* he existed, would definitely not reveal himself. He would operate through others. And his lieutenant would be a man on a much higher scale than Jules Reni. This should help to narrow the search, for such a man could not help but stand forth among the rough, uncouth crowd in Julesburg.

Methodically, Marlin's mind began to sift the various professions, weighing, evaluating each in turn.

Banker? Such a man would have the money and the intelligence to finance and direct such an operation.

Lawyer? An attorney would know how far he could go within the framework of the law, have a keen knowledge of men, and the necessary contacts with the criminals he defended.

Merchant? Money, the advantage of being able to haul contraband such as guns, ammunition, and whiskey without arousing suspicion, as well as knowing tribal chiefs with whom he might have traded before they planted the lance.

Some of Marlin's optimism faded. Even such a narrowed-down category could apply to at least a hundred men; and he did not have the time to check out a hundred men. Already, he had wasted two valuable weeks because of his Sioux battle wound.

On the bright side of the picture, however, was his new job with the Overland. As a trouble-shooter, he would be free to make inquiries, have access to Overland personnel and the unquestioned right to range over the division's six hundred miles of road, seeking firsthand evidence.

If he could eliminate or at least isolate Holladay's activities from the overall carnage on the Plains, he would then have established two vital facts. One, that there *was* a Confederate spy directing the conspiracy. For that reason, he looked forward to Ben Holladay's arrival. He had to know exactly who and what he was fighting. And time was running out on him; the uprising was spreading, the tribes becoming more confident that they could drive the hated Wasicun from their lands.

Soberly, Marlin turned his head and stared at the moonlight seeping in through the frosted window panes—and some of that cold chilled his mind, his heart. It was a big job. One which, if he failed to accomplish it, could cost the Union the West even at this late date. And even if he did succeed, it would not quell the Indian uprising—only render it a little less effective. Yet that marginal difference, however small, could relieve the Army of having to transfer troops from combat areas in the East for frontier service.

Tomorrow, he decided, he would call upon Major Stephen Beauchamp, present his Presidential credentials, ask for the Major's view of the uprising and what the Major was doing in the Julesburg area to combat it.

Sun, melting the frost upon the window panes and laying brightly across his face, awakened Marlin. He rose, dressed quickly, and went down to the dining room for Emma Ashley's Sunday morning "special"—griddle cakes, sausage, eggs, hot biscuits, honey, and steaming coffee.

Already, the dining room was well filled. At a corner table, Jules Reni breakfasted alone in sullen silence. Across the room, Jack and Virginia Slade were just ordering. And, seated near the fireplace, a Union cavalry major and a slim, blond-haired woman with her back partially to Marlin.

So this, he thought, was Stephen Beauchamp, the man upon whom he would have to depend for help in an emergency. Ramrod straight, even seated; well-built, medium height, black hair, an intense face, and a confident bearing that must have set many a fellow officer's teeth on edge. It was not hard to understand why Virginia Slade had said of the man, "The Major's never learned to say 'Yes, sir!' to a superior officer without sounding insubordinate." Co-operation from Beauchamp would require tact and diplomacy, rather than pulling rank on him.

As Marlin looked about for an empty table, he spotted Jack Slade motioning him over. Threading his way among the diners, he said, "Good morning."

"Sit down," Slade invited. "You might as well eat with us. Besides, I need to talk to you."

Ordering the "special," Marlin relaxed and smiled at Virginia Slade, stunning in a fashionable dark blue, watered-silk creation. "My compliments, ma'am," he said. "You look very beautiful this morning."

"Well, thank you, sir!" Virginia Slade's eyes sparkled with pleasure. "You do know how to start a woman's day off right! As I told you before, Major Beauchamp—incidentally, that's him and his wife over there by the fireplace—is the only other man in the Territory to compliment a woman that way."

"Arrogant bastard!" Slade growled. "We've

been pressuring him for weeks to provide stages with cavalry escorts. He keeps holding back."

With a frown, Marlin put down his coffee cup. "I thought the Army was under orders to provide the Overland protection."

"It is," Slade answered sourly. "But Beauchamp has a way of ignoring orders he doesn't like. That's why he's here instead of earning rank and glory with Grant or Sherman."

"Why haven't you lodged a complaint with his superiors?" Marlin asked. "Or, if necessary, with the War Department?"

"That takes time." The lines around Slade's mouth deepened into angry furrows. "We haven't got time. I'm sending you to Salt Lake in the morning with a couple of 'messenger' stages. That means you'll be carrying mail and specie only— no passengers. I've got no choice. Either we open up the route west, or the Overland could lose its mail contracts. That just might put Ben under. And, by God, that's not going to happen!"

Laying down his fork, Marlin stared at Slade, speechless. He had planned on working in the Julesburg area for the next few weeks. But this unexpected turn of events threatened his whole mission. Under the circumstances, he did the only thing he could do—protest.

"Salt Lake!" he exclaimed. "You expect me to take two stages across four hundred miles of rugged, Indian-infested country in midwinter without an escort? Why, not even a company of cavalry could survive out there!"

Subtly, Slade's features altered, losing their warmth and taking on a dangerous cast. "What do you think I hired you for?" he said. "To hang around here all winter, complimenting my wife while you draw top wages. Now either you take those stages out in the morning—or you're through. Do you understand?"

Go to hell, you fanatic son of a bitch, Marlin thought. *If you want to get yourself quilled like a porcupine with Sioux arrows, that's your business. But don't expect me to do it. I'm not that much in love with the Overland.*

He thought it; but he didn't say it. He would do what he had to do—take it in silence, for the moment. To lose his job with the Overland would virtually end his mission. Slade would not tolerate him around Julesburg once he was fired. And he could not operate without the town as a base. Still pride and self-respect would not let him yield to threats.

"If I take them out, Slade," he said evenly, "it will be with an escort. Otherwise, you can go out there and get yourself killed and to hell with your job! I'm not one of your two-dollar-a-day teamsters. Now do *you* understand me?"

A grudging admiration relaxed Slade's face; and Marlin knew that he had judged his man correctly. Weakness was one thing Jack Slade could not tolerate in others. If you stood up and fought him, you had a chance.

"All right." Slade shoved back his chair and rose. "Come on. I'll get you a damned escort. If I can't, then I'll give you a dozen of the best Indian fighters in the Territory." He motioned to his wife. "You stay here, Ginny."

Rising, Marlin followed Slade across the dining room. As they approached the Beauchamps' table, he saw the Major put down his coffee cup with a frown—and sensed that Slade's dislike of Beauchamp was reciprocated.

"Good morning, Major," Slade said civilly. "Good morning, ma'am." He bowed to the slim, honey-blond woman beside Beauchamp. "I hope you'll forgive the intrusion; but with your permission, I'd like a word with your husband."

Janet Beauchamp tilted her head, her long blond hair glowing under the lamplight and, for just an instant, her exotic green eyes flicked to Marlin and she smiled and she was, he thought, very beautiful. Then she turned her attention to Slade and replied in a cool, formal voice, "You don't need my permission, Mr. Slade; you need my husband's. So why not ask him?"

Slade flushed, and his big shoulders squared in unconscious aggression. "I'll do that, ma'am," he said, his tone matching the woman's in coldness. "Major, I have a matter of great importance to—"

"Mr. Slade . . . ," Beauchamp interrupted curtly,

"I do not discuss business on Sundays, during meals, or in my wife's presence. Whatever business you have to take up with me will have to wait until tomorrow morning."

For an instant, Marlin, watching, saw Slade's face whiten with anger. Then it passed. "Sorry, but I'm afraid the matter won't wait, Major. I need an escort for two stages to Salt Lake in the morning."

"Salt Lake!" Beachamp stared at him, unbelieving. "Why, man, you'd lose those stages in the first seventy-five miles!"

"That's a risk we'll have to take, Major."

"You can take it," Beauchamp snapped. "But I'll not send troopers out on a suicide run!"

Nettled, Slade came close to losing his own temper. "Now just a minute, Major," he said. "You're under orders from General Mitchell to furnish cavalry escorts to the Overland upon request."

Beauchamp's face whitened with anger. "An order," he whipped back, "which I carry out when I consider it in the best interests of the Territory."

"You don't make Army policy, Major; you simply carry it out." A deepening note crept into Slade's voice. "But you seem to have trouble remembering that."

"You run the Overland, Slade," Beauchamp flared. "And I'll run my command—without any help from you!"

"I wish you would, Major. It's about time."

"By God, sir, I resent that!"

Slade's smile was polite, deadly. "Major, I'm not going to quarrel with you in front of your wife. Nor can I do what I'd like to do without antagonizing the Army. But, some day—"

"Gentlemen, please!" Janet Beauchamp's voice, cool, demanding, silenced Slade and made Stephen Beauchamp sink back in his chair. "If there is one thing I detest it's public scenes! Now, Mr. Slade, will you please leave?

"And you, sir"—the green eyes sought Marlin's—"you've said nothing at all. I think you should introduce yourself."

Waiting until Slade walked angrily back to his table, Marlin said smoothly, "I am Kurt Marlin, ex-Colonel, U. S. Cavalry, recently invalided out of the service. As of yesterday, I am the Overland's chief trouble-shooter for this division. But may I make it clear that I am not responsible for Mr. Slade's conduct."

"Colonel Marlin!" Janet Beauchamp's eyes widened with pleasure. "But, of course! Captain Bowers told us about you upon our return from Denver." Smiling, she extended a slim, white hand. "I'm Janet Beauchamp. Welcome to Julesburg, sir!"

"Thank you, ma'am." Marlin swung his attention to Beauchamp. "Major, may I speak to you in private? It concerns a matter of the greatest importance."

Rising, Beauchamp offered his hand. "Of course, Colonel. But whatever it is, I'm sure it can wait until we've had dinner. After all, I don't meet a fellow West Pointer every day in the week on this Godforsaken frontier." He smiled and immediately looked ten years younger. "Sit down, sir, and bring us up to date on what's happening in the East. In turn, I'll tell you what I've learned about the Indian country. Although I doubt it will compare with your experiences."

Envy clouded Beauchamp's voice; and Marlin read in the man's eyes a hunger for the war and the glory and the opportunity to be a part of it as he, Marlin, had been.

Lonely, Martin thought. *Lonely and frustrated despite the poised, self-confident manner. A man who would not be pushed but who might, if handled right, be led to co-operate.*

"Please do join us," Janet Beauchamp urged, "if only for a cup of coffee. We're so isolated out here, it's seldom we get the chance to talk to an intelligent person."

In her voice, Marlin sensed the same desperate loneliness, the almost pathetic eagerness to recapture the world from which she and her husband had been separated for so long.

"I don't mean to be rude," he apologized, "but I have a great many things to do. We'll be leaving before dawn. But may I have the pleasure of calling when I return?"

"Of course." Janet Beauchamp tried unsuccessfully to conceal her disappointment. "Why not for dinner some evening? I'm an excellent cook; and Stephen can guarantee you some very fine brandy." She smiled wryly. "It's one of the few luxuries we permit ourselves."

"I'll look forward to it," Marlin assured her. "And now, Major, may we have that talk? It will take no more than ten or fifteen minutes. You'll excuse us, ma'am?"

"Certainly." Janet Beauchamp tilted her blond head and smiled up at him. "It's all right, Stephen. I'll wait here for you."

As Marlin and Beauchamp passed the Slades' table, Marlin paused briefly. "I'll be back in a few minutes," he said. "Stick around."

Following Beauchamp into the lobby, he led the way upstairs to his room.

"Well, Colonel." Beauchamp sat down in the golden-oak rocking chair, crossed his legs, and smiled inquiringly at Marlin. "What's this important matter you wished to discuss?"

"First," Marlin began, "let me say I'm sorry for Slade's actions. I realize that you can't very well back down from your decision—and yet that is exactly what I must ask you to do."

The smile vanished from Beauchamp's lips. "If you have brought me here, Colonel, to discuss those escorts, you're wasting your time and mine.

I was led to believe that the matter was of the greatest importance."

"Keeping the Overland route open to California *is* of the greatest importance, Major," Marlin replied. "No, wait!" as Beauchamp started to rise. "I am here on official business."

Slowly, Beauchamp sank back in the rocker, his eyes narrowing. "I should have known that a West Point colonel, with a war record such as yours, wouldn't be out here taking the risks you're taking just for money. Whom do you represent, sir . . . General Mitchell or the War Department?"

"I am a Presidential agent, Major, sent here to investigate a rumored Confederate conspiracy linked to this Indian uprising. Apparently, its purpose is to destroy the Overland and thus disrupt communications with the West in the hope of winning that area over to the South. A last desperate effort to stave off surrender for a few more months . . . at a senseless cost of thousands of lives."

"A Confederate conspiracy here on the Plains!" Beauchamp stared at him incredulously. "I don't believe it! Holladay's been shouting that propaganda for weeks. I think the real truth lies in Senator Conness' charges that Holladay is raiding his own stages for his own profit!"

"The President is inclined to believe Mr. Holladay," Marlin replied dryly. "However, he's keeping an open mind regarding the matter. My assignment is to uncover this conspiracy, if it exists, and to destroy it. I am authorized to request such assistance from you as I may need in carrying out my assignment. Having briefed you on the situation, I'm counting on your co-operation."

Beauchamp leaned back, laced his hands behind his head, and studied Marlin with a troubled expression.

"Colonel, as a cavalry officer and a fellow West Pointer, I am sure you can appreciate my position here. I have a hundred and twenty inexperienced Iowa Volunteers to protect an area swarming with a thousand Sioux, Cheyennes, and Arapahos. As commander of Camp Rankin, my primary duty is to protect Julesburg, a major emigrant-outfitting center, and the settlers in the region from Indian attack. That is a responsibility I can neither ignore nor neglect.

"Although I have reluctantly furnished escorts for special mail and gold shipments in the past, I feel that it is no longer feasible. I can only say that I will provide such men as I can spare without weakening my garrison."

A man who cannot be pushed, Marlin reminded himself. *But a man who, with tactful handling, might possibly be led to co-operate.*

"If the matter were still open to discussion, Major," he said reasonably, "I might perhaps sympathize with your views. But you have been ordered by General Mitchell to furnish the

Overland escorts; you now have no alternative but to carry out that order."

Color flooded Beauchamp's face. He unclasped his hands from behind his head and placed them, palms down, fingers widespread, tips whitening from the downward pressure, on the desk.

"Colonel, if I obey that order to the letter," he said, "half of my entire force will be in the field at all times. I can't seem to make you understand, sir, that I have a responsibility to the people of—"

"Major, the President has relieved you of any responsibility in this matter," Marlin interrupted. "However, I assure you I have no intention of stripping Julesburg of its defenses—although I doubt frankly that, if the town should come under attack, you could do more than defend the fort and such townspeople and settlers as might seek shelter here. You have my word that I will ask for no more men than you can reasonably spare."

With open reluctance, Beauchamp yielded. "I cannot argue with the President of the United States," he said. "Certainly no sane man wants the war to continue one single day longer than is necessary. But I will *not* reverse my stand regarding those Salt Lake escorts." His mouth set stubbornly. "No hired killer like Slade is going to intimidate me, Colonel. However, when you return, we'll work out a schedule."

"Fine." Marlin rose. "As a matter of fact, I was going to advise against any immediate action.

Slade might figure you were up to something. And as unpredictable as he is, no telling what he might do. I think an escort the first week after I return would be good. Then we can begin to increase them.

"Now, one more thing. Have any of your patrols reported running into traders, whiskey peddlers, or other suspicious characters recently?"

"No." Beauchamp's tone was positive. "Ever since Holladay began making those wild charges, I've questioned patrols who have been out on scouts. Not one of them has ever reported seeing a white man with the Indians, or run across anything to suggest a spy operating in the area. With the war already lost, a conspiracy just doesn't make sense."

"War never makes sense," Marlin replied with a grim smile, "but still men wage it . . . and, sometimes, don't know when to quit. Well . . . I'd better let you get back to your wife. Please give her my apologizes and tell her I'm looking forward to visiting you soon."

Beauchamp stood up, the rocking chair bumping gently against the back of his legs. "Aren't you coming?"

"I think it would salve Slade's ego if you went down alone," Marlin said. "I'll follow in about ten minutes."

With a nod, Beauchamp left, closing the door behind him.

Walking over to the window, Marlin stared down upon the dusk-dimmed street. He could not help but feel a certain satisfaction at the way he had handled the situation. Slade's aggressiveness had come very close to ruining his chances of gaining Beauchamp's voluntary co-operation. Only a common denominator, West Point, had kept him from being drawn into the feud. Fortunately, this bond, plus his Presidential authority, had now assured him of the Major's help without first going to General Mitchell.

When he returned to the dining room ten minutes later, the Beauchamps had gone; but Jack and Virginia Slade were still lingering over coffee.

"Well," Slade demanded darkly as Marlin eased into a chair, "what was all that secret talk about?"

"I was trying to repair the fences that you tore down," Marlin retorted. "If you'll just leave the Major to me, I think I can guarantee those escorts within a couple of weeks. One thing I can tell you—you won't get them by threatening Beauchamp."

Slade's cold eyes rested appraisingly upon Marlin a moment. Then he made up his mind.

"All right," he agreed. "Handle it your way. But one of these days, I may have to kill that son of a bitch." Abruptly, he shoved back his chair. "Come on, Ginny. Let's get out of here." The black mood was on him and Virginia, recognizing it, obeyed silently. Marlin followed suit.

In the lobby, the three of them paused, little currents of emotion swirling among them. Then Slade said, "You'd better catch up on your sleep, Marlin. You'll be pulling out before dawn."

"With an escort," Marlin stated evenly.

Slade sucked in his breath; and when he spoke, the air made a little whistling sound between his teeth. "With your damned escort."

Nodding, Marlin smiled at Virginia Slade, said, "Good night, ma'am," and walked away, feeling Slade's angry eyes following him . . . and knowing that the man's anger had nothing to do with the escort, but in the way Virginia Slade had looked at him, Marlin.

She could, he mused, get him killed.

At four o'clock the following morning, Marlin held a last-minute "war conference" with Slade, Ashley, and Bob Ridley in the hotel dining room. Behind drawn curtains, Emma Ashley and Susan served them breakfast by the light of low-turned lamps. With Major Beauchamp adamantly refusing a cavalry escort, Slade was taking no chances of word leaking out about this "crash through" messenger trip to Salt Lake. If a shoot-out with bandits or Confederate-informed Sioux could be avoided, the stages just might make it.

Quietly, Marlin sat back and listened to Slade's

final instructions. The Overland super's manner was grim and he minced no words.

"I want a complete report on conditions between here and Salt Lake," he said. "Indian and bandit activity and where it's worst. Inefficiency at swing and home stations. Mail and stock losses. Employee casualties. Conditions of roads, bridges, ferries, and telegraph . . . everything. The technical details Bob Ridley can help you with.

"All decisions, however, will be yours. And remember, from Atchinson to California, the Overland is the Law and you're it's on-the-spot representative . . . judge, jury, and executioner. The men going with you are under orders to back you to the limit."

He swallowed a mouthful of beefsteak and eggs and washed it down with hot coffee; and Marlin, watching him, thought that whatever the Overland's crimes, they would not be laid to Jack Slade. The man's dedication to the Overland showed itself in everything he did.

"One more thing," Slade said, setting down his cup. "When you reach Salt Lake—Deseret, the Mormons call it—report to Joe Holladay. He's Ben's brother and the chief agent there.

"Then go see Brigham Young. Him and Ben have been close friends since '38 when Ben was Colonel Doniphan's courier during the trouble at Far West."

"Far West?" Marlin frowned, trying to associate

the name with history. "Wasn't that where twenty Mormons were killed at what they called the 'Massacre of Huan's Hill'? I think Colonel Doniphan was called in to arrest Joseph Smith and some others?"

"That's right!" Slade shot him a surprised glance. "Six thousand troops, under General Lucas, had the town surrounded. That was when Ben, as Doniphan's messenger, scuttled back and forth between the lines with secret dispatches from Doniphan to Joseph Smith, trying to get the Saints to negotiate. Later, when Doniphan refused to carry out Lucas's execution order for Smith and four other Saints, it was Ben who carried Doniphan's refusal to Lucas. By God, with tempers the way they were, that was a brave thing to do!" A bright, proud flame burned in the Overland super's eyes.

"The Mormons never forgot. Ten years later, when Ben Holladay gambled every dollar he had on a freighting venture to Salt Lake, Brigham Young remembered. With just eight words— *'Brother Holladay is a trusted and honorable man'*—he started Holladay toward becoming what he is today. The Saints bought everything Holladay had and asked him to come back with more." Slade shoved back his plate, wiped his mouth and swept the group around the table with sharp eyes.

"Show Young and his people every respect. Salt

Lake is the western hub of our operation. We have to keep the good will of the Mormons. That may not be easy. They haven't forgotten '57, when the government sent troops into Utah. But do your best. If you get into trouble or need service, wire me if the lines are not down. If they are, you're strictly on your own. Any questions?"

Marlin shook his head. "No."

"All right." Slade rose and the rest followed. "Then get started. I want you back here in two weeks. Just remember—don't stop for anything. Sioux, bandits, or the Devil—run over them, through them or under them, but *run*. We can't afford to lose that mail or what's in those boots."

After the others had gone, Marlin went into the kitchen where Emma Ashley was busy over the big wood-burning range. She looked up, her face shadowing. He knew what she was thinking and countered with a quick smile.

"Don't worry," he said. "I'll be back. You just keep a pot of coffee on the stove for me." He glanced around the kitchen. "Where's Susan? I wanted to ask her if she needed anything from Salt Lake."

"Why, I don't know," Emma Ashley said. "She was here just a few minutes ago."

"Well," Marlin said lamely, "tell her I said good-bye."

It surprised him that he should feel such a rich mixture of emotions—resentment, disappointment, and, yes, injured ego—because she had not waited to see him off. The memory of those moments spent with her at the Ashley home had given him the impression that she was interested in him. It would seem that he had been wrong.

"Well," he said again, "good-bye, Emma."

In the dining room, he slipped into his heavy wolfskin coat and checked Colt and rifle. As he turned to leave, he collided with Virginia Slade. She was breathing heavily and her face was devoid of its usual devil-may-care expression.

"I ran half a mile," she said. "I was afraid I'd miss you. And I didn't want you to leave without this." She handed him the twin of his own Navy Colt, along with holster and belt. "Now you can be a two-gun man! Only bring it back to me in person, damn you!"

She started to kiss him, shook her head ruefully, and stepped away. "If Jack ever found out, he'd kill us both! Go on—get out of here before I do something stupid!"

A raw wind stiffened Marlin's face as he crossed the darkened compound toward the waiting stages. Drivers and shotgun messengers hunched impatiently on their seats, stomping their feet against the numbing cold. In the baggage boots was a quarter of a million dollars in gold, as well as twenty thousand pieces of mail.

Unconsciously, Marlin's shoulders squared. It was a heavy responsibility and one which he wondered whether he was capable of handling. Driving an ox team to Sante Fe at sixteen was one thing; commanding cavalry against Confederate troops was still another. But running two stage-coaches through four hundred miles of bandit- and Indian-infested country during an uprising was something else again.

He had almost reached the lead coach when Susan Ashley caught up with him. With her face a white blur in the darkness, she laid her hand on his arm, and he could feel the trembling of her body beneath her heavy coat.

"You shouldn't have come out in this cold, Susan," he said. "It's close to zero."

"I had to see you off." Her voice was quiet, calm. "And to let you know I'll be praying for you. Be careful, Kurt—and come back, please!" Her lips brushed his lightly, then she was gone.

"For Christ sake, Marlin!" Bob Ridley cried. "Let's get going!"

Climbing aboard the stage, Marlin settled himself beside Ridley. The jehu spoke his string in a low voice. Iron-tired wheels turned on well-greased axles. Muffled hoofs crunched dully over frozen puddles. Silently, the stages rolled through the town. Past the Ashley home. Out past Camp Rankin. Then only the open country ahead.

Four days later, Marlin rolled his bullet-holed, arrow-studded stages over the snow-capped

Wasatch range and down onto the sweeping plain approaching Deseret—the City of Great Salt Lake—five hundred and sixteen miles from Denver.

Racing westward, he had crossed the Platte at Latham and snaked on to Virginia Dale, the second division point. From there, they had pounded across the Laramie plains, across Bridger's Pass and the Continental Divide . . . Ham's Fork, Fort Bridger, over the Wasatch range, and now onto the plateau.

With the jehus laying the leather to their strings, the stages rocked down Deseret's wide streets and pulled up before the Overland freight dock, their post horns sounding their arrival.

A crowd quickly gathered. This was the first mail stage to break through in weeks, and the Saints welcomed it as only those cut off from the rest of the world can—with an eager excitement.

As Marlin climbed stiffly down from the high seat and stood stomping his feet to restore circulation, a medium-sized man with sandy hair and an intense face stepped out of the office and walked quickly toward him.

"I'm Joe Holladay," the man said, shaking hands. "You must be Marlin, the new trouble-shooter Jack Slade wired me about. I don't mind saying I'm damned glad to see you."

Carefully, Marlin studied this man about whom

Ed Ashley had told him a great deal. Wild, reckless, and hot-headed, Joe Holladay had matured under the heavy load of responsibility placed upon him by his famous brother. Well-liked and respected by the Mormons, he was industrious and levelheaded, with but little time for anything except the Overland. A bachelor, he lived and ate his meals at the National Hotel.

"And I'm glad to be here—alive," Marlin replied. "It took a bit of doing. I lost one man and have three badly wounded."

"Bob—" Holladay called to Ridley. "Get those wounded men to the hospital. Then report back to me."

He turned his attention back to Marlin. "Although these people are our friends, there's been some outspoken criticism over our failure to get the mail through lately. Even freighters are having to fight their way through. Your arrival will quiet the critics for a while anyway." He had reason to be pleased and obviously was.

"That's good," Marlin said. "Now if you don't mind, I'd like a bath and twelve hours sleep."

"I'll see that you get both as soon as possible," Holladay assured him. "Right after you give me a general idea of the situation between here and Julesburg. You can do that while you're eating. Later, I'll want a more detailed report.

"Herb!" He called to a middle-aged man supervising the unloading of the stages. "Separate the

Salt Lake stuff from those sacks and transfer the rest to new coaches. Tell Rattlesnake Pete and Fiddler Jim I want them rolling in an hour. If you need me for anything, I'll be at the National."

Wearily, Marlin followed Holladay down the wide, pleasant street, admiring the ten-acre blocks laid out by Brigham Young's orders, caught a glimpse of the as yet uncompleted six-spired Temple in the Square—and intently searched the faces of the men and women who had pushed worldly possessions in handcarts across two thousand miles of wintry, Indian-infested country eighteen years before. People not to be reckoned lightly, Marlin thought, nor to be dealt with unfairly.

Although the National's dining room was well filled, Joe Holladay managed a table for Marlin and himself. Then while Marlin ate, the Salt Lake agent plied him with short, terse questions.

"How widespread are the Indian attacks?"

"The route's swarming with Sioux," Marlin replied. "And some Arapaho."

"Where did you lose your men?"

"This side of Fort Laramie. About a hundred Sioux jumped us. We killed fifteen or twenty before they broke off."

"Did they have rifles?"

Marlin nodded. "Sharps, Henrys, some Springfields, and a few Spencers. And from the way they were wasting it, they had plenty of ammunition."

"That fits in with what Ben claims," Joe Holladay said. "That the Rebs are getting guns and ammunition to the tribes and stirring them up with whiskey."

"Maybe," Marlin replied.

Joe Holladay's face darkened. "Where else could the red bastards be getting the stuff?"

"Free traders, possibly."

"Free traders, my ass!" Holladay retorted. "No trader could get his hands on that much stuff without getting caught."

"All right, then," Marlin suggested. "Suppose an organized band is raiding Army ordnance trains, and then giving it to the tribes."

The Overland agent's eyes narrowed thoughtfully. "There *have* been Army losses," he admitted. "But General Price won't say just how much. You think that could be the answer?"

"It could be."

"Can you prove it?"

"No."

"Then we're no better off than before."

"I wouldn't say that," Marlin countered. "We've gotten two stages through. At least, it's a beginning."

Joe Holladay shook his head impatiently. "It won't get Ben off the hook in Washington. That damned Conness is screaming louder than ever. Even those yellow-rag newspapers in Denver are demanding Ben's hide. With our mail contracts coming up for renewal—and Wells-Fargo and Butterfield both eager for a chance at them—we've got to come up with hard-core proof."

Lighting a cheroot, Marlin drew on it until he had it burning evenly. Despite himself, he felt some of Joe Holladay's frustration and personal anger against the Overland's enemies also infecting him. He had come here to investigate charges against Ben Holladay, among other things; yet, more and more, he was becoming involved in Holladay's interests.

"If Conness wants the truth," he said, "let the fool come out and see for himself. The proof is here on the Plains."

"Conness isn't interested in the truth," Holladay replied bitterly. "He has a fanatic hatred for Wells-Fargo; and he's lumped Ben and the Overland in with them. Especially Ben. I've never seen anyone envy and want to destroy a man as much as Conness wants to destroy Ben. No, you couldn't drag the Senator out here."

He drained his cup and smiled grimly at Marlin. "That's the Overland's worry and your special headache. Prove Ben right—uncover a Confederate conspiracy—and you've got the world on a platter. Fail and no one will blame you very much. After all, we haven't done any better." He pushed back his chair and rose.

"Finish your breakfast and then get some sleep," he said. "I've got to get back to the office.

Tomorrow, I want you to call on Brigham Young."

After the station agent had gone, Marlin checked into his room and fell across the bed, fully clothed.

Sun splashing across his face awakened him. He had slept fourteen hours. Hurriedly, he shaved and changed into fresh clothing and left the hotel.

At the Overland office, he was told that Joe Holladay had left on a road inspection tour and was not expected back for several days.

"Joe said you were to leave for Julesburg before dawn tomorrow," Webber, the assistant station agent, informed him. "And that he wished you luck."

"Tomorrow!" Exhaustion, built-up tension from the long journey suddenly caught up with Marlin. "He's got to be out of his mind! That gives us only one day's rest! Even Jack Slade expected us to lay over for four days."

"I can't help that," Webber retorted, flushing. "I'm just passing on orders. But try and understand Joe's position. How would you feel if the whole country was cutting your own brother to pieces—and him doing the best he could to keep the Overland's routes open?"

"I wouldn't know," Marlin snapped. "But I wouldn't throw away other men's lives to save him!"

"Look," Webber said, his voice taking on a

placating note. "With that mail you brought in now racing toward California, Joe figures that if he can also push a stage *eastward*—and get it through—it just might still the clamor long enough for the Postmaster-General to renew the Overland's million-dollar-plus mail contract. If Ben Holladay loses that contract . . ." Webber spread his hands in a resigned gesture.

"All right," Marlin said, knowing he really had no choice. If he refused to take the stages out, Joe Holladay would fire him, or wire Slade to have him fired. "All right. We'll be on our way before dawn."

Angrily, he left the office and headed toward the Square. He still had to see Brigham Young.

The Mormon leader received him in a small, bare room as austere as a monk's cell. Rising from his chair, Brigham Young extended a big hand in greeting.

"Welcome to Deseret, sir!" he said warmly. "Your arrival could not have come at a better time. My people were hungry for news and mail. We are grateful." He motioned Marlin to a chair beside his desk. "Sit down."

"Thank you." Across the desk, Marlin categorized the Mormon with a quick, all-encompassing glance. A big man with deep-set, penetrating eyes, a full, sensuous lower lip, a heavy, determined chin covered by a carefully groomed beard, Brigham Young reminded him more of a politician, a banker-merchant, or a soldier out of uniform rather than the spiritual leader of some twenty thousand Mormons in Deseret. On second thought, Marlin amended, Young was probably all those things, among many others, since he was also Deseret's temporal authority.

A faint smile spread the Mormon's lips. "Don't be embarrassed, Mr. Marlin," he said, and Marlin knew that the man had read his mind perfectly. "Many people expect me to either look like St. Peter—or the Devil with horns, a forked tail, and a pitchfork. But you can see for yourself, sir, that I am only a man." Abruptly, he changed the subject.

"They tell me you were attacked several times en route, and that you lost some of your escort. I'm sorry to hear that. Just how bad is the situation?"

"A nightmare," Marlin said succinctly. "Way stations burned to the ground, stock tenders killed and scalped, thoroughbred racers stolen, mail destroyed, and Sioux and Arapaho everywhere. General Mitchell can't handle it; he simply hasn't got the men—and the ones he has are Irregulars who know nothing about Indian fighting."

Brigham Young shook his head. "You paint a mighty dark picture, Mr. Marlin."

"And one which is bound to grow darker,"

Marlin replied. "The Army can't spare seasoned troops from the eastern front for service here. We can expect no help from anyone but ourselves."

The Mormon leader regarded him thoughtfully. "I know that Ben Holladay thinks this uprising is being helped by whites," he said. "Do you agree with him that the Confederacy is involved?"

"I've no proof of it as yet," Marlin answered carefully. "But it is my frank opinion that there is a conspiracy with operations extending from the Capitol to Utah. I believe that if it is not crushed, settlement of the High Plains and the Pacific Northwest may be set back a quarter of a century. At best, the war could drag on for perhaps another full year."

"Tell me, Mr. Marlin . . ." Brigham Young concentrated on his blunt, spatulate fingers. "Are you a Union man?"

It was a delicate question. Recalling the trouble in the past between the Mormons and the Federal government because of this man's introduction of polygamy among his people, Marlin hesitated. Then returning Young's steady gaze, he said quietly, "Are you, sir?"

Brigham Young smiled at the riposte. "Utah is not unsympathetic to the Union cause, sir, despite Secretary of War Stanton's fears to the contrary. We are definitely pro-Holladay and pro-Overland."

Inwardly, Marlin relaxed, the anxiety going out

of him. "Then we can count on your support, sir, in case of an emergency?"

"If it involves the Overland, yes," Young replied. "Ben should know that."

"He'll be very glad to hear it again."

The Mormon smiled dryly. "It's not all just friendship, Mr. Marlin. Utah needs the Overland. Not just the stage and mail line, but the freighters as well. They're both necessary to our survival. Naturally, we will protect our own interests. If, in the process, we can also help the Overland, well and good. You understand?"

Here was a pragmatic idealist, Marlin thought. A man who realized that he could not successfully separate the interests of his own people from those of the nation. A man who could be counted on because he needed Ben Holladay, the Overland, and the Union as much as they needed him.

"How large a force, sir, can we count on from you in a critical situation?"

Young ran his fingers through his beard. "A company of a hundred," he said. "Fully armed, mounted, equipped and provisioned for thirty days."

"That's the best news yet," Marlin said and stood up. "We need every show of loyalty and every bit of help we can get."

Young rose, grasped his hand strongly and saw him to the door. "If I don't see you again before you leave, Mr. Marlin, God go with you!"

"Thank you, sir."

Back at the Overland office, Marlin found Bob Ridley waiting for him. The jehu was in a bad humor; he had already talked to Webber.

"Goddammit, Joe's got no right to send us back without more rest!" Ridley fumed. "Eight hundred miles of that kind of driving will kill a man—if Indians don't get him first!"

"Save your breath," Marlin said. "Go out and have a good meal and a few drinks and then get to bed early. We'll be leaving by starlight."

Reinforced by a new escort, Marlin pulled out early the following morning, only hours ahead of a Canadian-spawned blizzard that chased them all the way.

Four days later, he brought his battered stages to a triumphant halt before the Overland office in Julesburg. For the first time in weeks, the Julesburg–Salt Lake route had been opened in both directions. It was a small victory, perhaps, but a victory, nevertheless.

Standing in the kitchen doorway, Marlin said quietly, "Is the coffee hot, Emma?"

Busy forking venison steaks upon a huge platter, Emma Ashley looked up, startled. "Lord God Amighty!" she cried. "I didn't hear the post horn."

She wiped her hands on her apron and poured him a big steaming mug of coffee. "Sit down! Sit down!" She carried his cup to a small utility table and took a chair opposite him. "I'll have you know I spent more time on my knees praying for you than I did on my feet working! How was it out there?"

"Bad." Wearily, Marlin sipped his coffee, then went on. "We brought back twenty thousand pieces of mail piled up at Salt Lake. Ed's going to have to separate the local stuff right away. Joe Holladay wants a stage going east today."

He looked around the kitchen. "Where's Susan?"

"Probably at home waiting for you to hunt her up." Emma Ashley's eyes twinkled; but then suddenly her mood changed and she spoke with a marked seriousness.

"Susan's a hard girl to understand, Kurt. Most women are like mountain streams, fast and shallow. Susan's like a river, deep and quiet. Maybe that's why men are attracted to her. She could have married a dozen times. But she's never shown the slightest interest in a man until you came along." Emma Ashley's eyes met Marlin's steadily.

"I don't mean to pry, Kurt; but is there anything between you and Virginia Slade? I've my reasons for asking. You see, Susan overheard what Virginia said to you in the dining room the morning you left for Salt Lake. And, well, she's got the idea that there's something going on between you two."

Behind Emma Ashley's words, Marlin sensed a half-frightened appeal. Touched, he laid his hand on her arm. "Emma, Virginia Slade is an attractive woman; and I would be less than honest if I told you that I did not like her as a person. But I haven't the faintest interest in her as a *woman.*

"As for Susan"—the lines of his face softened—"she keeps growing on me every day. I've never felt so close to anyone in my life. But until this uprising is over, I've no right to even think about her. Besides, I'm not sure that she would even want me to."

"Are you really that blind?" Emma smiled, shaking her head in amusement. "If you are, then I'm afraid you'll just have to find out for yourself." She jumped up, remembering. "Good Lord, here I am babbling while you starve!"

She had just served Marlin when Ed Ashley came in, stomping the snow from his boots. "Man, but it's cold out there!" Ashley said, warming his hands at the big wood range. "Must be near zero."

"How's the mail sorting coming along?" Marlin asked, attacking his food. "Can you get the eastern stuff on its way today?"

"Not a chance." Ashley sat down at the table. "Emma, can I have something to eat? I'm starved. Meanwhile, Kurt, how about a quick run down of your trip?"

"Why don't we wait until Slade's present,"

Marlin suggested. "It will save me making the same report twice."

Ashley's face clouded. "Slade's out running down a bunch of horse thieves. We lost thirty head of racers last night. One of the stock tenders was killed and another wounded. The wounded man swears the whole gang was white and that he's seen them around town before. Jack thinks Jules Reni is involved. I tell you, those two are heading for a showdown. Anyway, there's no telling when he'll be back. So you'd better give me your report."

"Here—" Emma placed a platter of food before her husband. "Eat while you're listening."

When Marlin had finished his report, Ed Ashley sat silent a moment, his face grave, thoughtful. Finally, he said, "Do you think we can keep the division route open?"

"We can probably push through two out of three stages with luck," Marlin assured him. "But we'll lose men and we'll have to rebuild and restock stations as fast as the Indians burn them out. And we can count on virtually no passenger traffic. The mail contract will be our principal source of revenue."

"Well, unless we produce, the Overland's going to lose that mail contract when it comes up for renewal," Ashley predicted. "Wells-Fargo and Butterfield are both eager to snap it up."

Loss of that mail contract, Marlin thought,

seemed to haunt everyone from Ben Holladay, Jack Slade, and Joe Holladay right on down through the ranks to Bob Ridley. It was like a jugular artery constantly in danger of being cut.

"All I can tell you," he answered truthfully, "is that I think we can get most of the first-class stuff through this division. That is *if* we can find out who's helping to strengthen this uprising."

A little of the worry lifted from Ashley's face. "No one can say you're not doing your part. Holladay will be well pleased when he arrives."

They had finished their meal and were lingering over their coffee. Marlin, eager to have a chance to observe Ben Holladay at close range, said, "When is he due?"

"Any day now," Ashley answered. "And, with this thing between Slade and Reni building up, the sooner the better."

Emma Ashley sighed. "I just wish to God he wouldn't bring Notley Ann with him. The last time she was here—"

"Emma!" Ashley shook his head.

"I don't care!" Emma Ashley said stubbornly. "Her an' her high-falutin' ways! As if the Carvers were the only ones to come over on the Mayflower!"

"Emma, why don't you be quiet!"

"Why should I?" Emma Ashley's round, pleasant face mirrored her indignation. "She don't care for Ben, only for what he can give her. Mansions with crystal chandeliers and Persian carpets in Washington and San Francisco and Portland, Oregon—and livered servants and fine carriages and fancy dresses from Paris! And the more she gets, the more she wants. I don't like her and I don't mind saying so to her face!"

"Emma!" Ashley said sharply. "For the last time . . ."

She looked at her husband, and the indignation slipped from her face and her mouth softened. "Oh, all right!"

Ashley rose, kissed her on the mouth and went out. After a moment, Marlin followed. In the doorway, he turned. "Did you say Susan was at home?"

"And waiting for you," Emma Ashley said, smiling.

A light glowed warmly in the living room of the Ashley home as Marlin stepped upon the snow-covered porch. He knocked on the door and waited, wondering at the quickening beat of his heart. That had to stop. At least until his mission was completed and the war ended. Perhaps then . . .

Light splashed across his face as Susan Ashley opened the door. "Hello, Susan," he said. "Your mother said you were here. May I come in?"

Wordless, Susan took his hand and drew him

inside. Closing the door, she smiled up at him, her face shining with pleasure.

"Oh, Kurt, I'm so happy you're back!" she cried. "I heard the post horn; but I knew you'd be tied up at the office for a while. So I came on home.

"Come on!" Leading him into the parlor, she motioned toward the sofa. "Make yourself comfortable. Would you like some coffee?"

"No, thanks." Marlin settled himself on the sofa. "I just had breakfast while I gave your father a report."

"Was it a bad journey?"

He did not lie to her. "It was bad," he said frankly. "We lost a couple of men. But the important thing is that we got through for the first time in weeks."

"Two of you didn't." Sitting down beside Marlin, Susan observed him with grave, quiet eyes. Then with a little sigh, she murmured, "Now I'm beginning to understand what Mother went through when Dad was driving stages through Indian- and bandit-infested country. Sitting at home worrying and wondering whether he'd been robbed or scalped or caught in a blizzard and frozen to death or . . . Oh, Kurt—" Impulsively, she reached out and laid her hand over Marlin's. "I worried myself sick about you while you were gone!"

Stretching his feet out toward the hearth, Marlin

turned a curious face toward her. "Why should you worry about me?"

"Why?" Susan asked. "Why because there's a jillion Indians out there on the Plains, killing and scalping and just waiting to attack Overland stages and . . . well, it's natural to worry about those we . . . we care for. Everybody was worried about you. Mother, Dad, Hank, Bob, and"—she could not keep the resentment from her voice— "Virginia Slade."

"Virginia!" Marlin laughed, but warmly. "Virginia worries about everyone who rides out of here. She loves people."

"She loves you," Susan replied quietly. "And don't pretend you don't know what I'm talking about."

Drawing in his legs, Marlin sat up, no longer smiling. "You're getting a little out of line, Susan," he said. "Virginia is a married woman."

"That's never bothered her before," Susan retorted, suddenly bitter. "You're not the first man she's gone after."

"Well, I'd say that's her business, wouldn't you? After all, she's no child."

"She's anything but that!" Susan flared. "And you've no right to sit there and defend her!"

"What in the world's gotten into you?" Marlin exclaimed. "I thought you and Virginia were friends. You've no right to talk about her that way."

"Oh, I haven't?" Susan Ashley tossed her head, her normally calm eyes indignant. "Do you know the whole town's gossiping about you two? They're saying Virginia ran half a mile to give you a kiss and her own gun the morning you left for Salt Lake! And that it isn't exactly a platonic relationship! They are saying . . ." Her voice died away, and he could read the hurt in her eyes and could not be angry with her, only deeply concerned about what was happening to them.

"Susan," he said patiently, "people always gossip about women like Virginia Slade, women who aren't afraid to be human, to show their emotions. Now Virginia's a friend of mine; I like her. You don't expect me to turn against her just because of vicious gossip, do you?"

"You would if you cared anything about me!" Susan's voice sharpened with a mounting resentment. "Do you realize how humiliating it is for me, knowing what people are saying? Can't you understand? You're blowing my dreams away like leaves in the wind!"

Placing his hands on her shoulders, Marlin turned her toward him, then sat for a moment, studying her flushed, angry face. He had come here expecting a quiet, pleasant visit; instead, things had somehow gotten out of hand—and he still didn't know how or why.

"Susan," he said gently, "I care a great deal for you. Perhaps more than I'm willing to admit even to myself. But right now, anyway, neither of us can afford to get too deeply involved. We're at war, and no one can predict the future. Besides, I think we both need time to think about how we really do feel toward each other. Remember—I told you that if I ever found the right woman, you'd be the first to know.

"As for Virginia Slade, your heart should tell you that she means nothing to me as a woman. You can't stop people from talking, but you don't have to believe everything they say."

If he had hoped to reassure Susan Ashley, he failed completely. "If Virginia means nothing to you," Susan said stubbornly, "then why won't you stop seeing her?"

"Because she's my friend." A trace of irritation slipped into Marlin's voice. "And she's done nothing to deserve being treated that way."

"Then you won't stop seeing her? Even for me."

"No."

With a little cry, Susan jumped to her feet and fled upstairs, and Marlin knew she would not return. Slipping into his coat, he quietly let himself out into the street.

Disturbed, Marlin walked slowly back to the Overland office, not quite understanding what had happened to the warm intimacy between himself and Susan Ashley. It was their first quarrel and, somehow, he had handled it badly. He should have been more patient, more tolerant of her attitude; but her incredible candor had taken him off guard and he had reacted defensively. In a few days, he would call on her and apologize. Meanwhile, he could not have his mind clouded with personal conflicts at this stage.

A crowd was gathered outside the Overland office when he arrived. Inside, he found the place jammed. A harried mail clerk moved back and forth behind the counter. Another doggedly attacked a huge pile of mail in the rear. Seeing there was nothing he could do, Marlin went back outside.

A hundred feet down the street, he ran into Virginia Slade, looking as flamboyantly attractive as ever.

"I've been hunting all over for you." Her bold, smoky eyes ran over him in critical appraisal. "I hear you had a rough trip. But you don't show much signs of wear and tear. How come?"

"All on the inside, I guess," Marlin said. "Just wait until I let down. I'll probably climb the walls." He turned serious. "Ed Ashley says Jack is out running down a bunch of horse thieves. You have any idea when he'll be back?"

"No more than Ed does," Virginia replied. "But I'm not worried about horse thieves. It's this thing between Jack and Jules Reni that bothers me. Jack thinks that Reni pulled this job just to humiliate him. You know—as a kind of 'What are you going to do about it?' gesture. It's gotten to him. He was in one of his black, crazy moods when he left." Virginia Slade hesitated, her lovely face troubled.

"Please, Kurt, when he returns, no matter what he does or says, just ignore it. Jack likes you; you know that. But—well, he heard about me running half a mile in zero-degree weather to see you off the morning you left for Salt Lake. He's been acting strangely ever since. I think he's jealous of you."

Marlin stared at her. "You can't be serious!" he exclaimed. "Jack has no reason to be jealous of me." And yet, he recalled, Susan Ashley had believed the same thing.

"Hasn't he?" Virginia Slade's eyes veiled. "You're a *man,* Kurt. You know better than that."

Meeting her bold, challenging eyes, Marlin could not mistake her meaning, nor even pretend to do so. She was a willful, headstrong woman, governed solely by her emotions. Frustrated, she could be as dangerously unpredictable as her husband.

Completely uninhibited, she was openly suggesting that Slade's jealousy might not be unfounded. She was not only available; she obviously believed that he, Marlin, was interested in an affair.

Marlin hesitated. It was a delicate situation. He could not risk antagonizing Slade. Yet to reject Virginia Slade might bring about the same result as to become involved in an affair with her . . . a head-on clash with one of the most dangerous men in the West.

"Perhaps you're right," he said carefully. "I'll watch my step from now on."

Virginia Slade's mouth curved. "So will I." She moved away with the sensuous grace of an animal, her red hair glinting in the sun.

Marlin stared after her with a thoughtful expression. She was a bomb which, if lighted, could blow him and his mission to hell. A bomb with a dangerously short fuse.

An hour before sunset, Jack Slade rode into town leading three body-draped horses and driving the captured thoroughbred racers ahead of him. Turning the racers over to a couple of stock tenders, he continued down the street, his face black with a three-day beard and blacker still from the frustrated rage burning inside him.

Joe Baker, a storekeeper, rushed into the Overland office with the news. "Slade's bringing in those horse thieves, dead!" he cried excitedly. "And he's in one of them moods of his! You'd best get out there fast!"

He fled, slamming the door behind him.

Looking at Ed Ashley, Marlin asked dryly, "Do they all run like that when Slade goes on a rampage?"

"The ones with any sense do." Ed Ashley's tone

was grim. "Here—" He took Marlin's heavy coat from the rack and handed it to him. "It's close to zero outside." Slipping into his own jacket, he opened the door. "Come on."

"What do you intend to do?" Marlin asked, following and closing the door behind him.

"Reason with Jack if I can," Ashley said. "Meanwhile, I'll expect you to back me up. Now I want you to put your gun in your coat pocket and keep your hand on it. But no matter what he does or says, don't do anything to antagonize him. Shoot only as a last resort. But if it comes to that, *remember that teamster and shoot to kill.*"

By now, a crowd had gathered, saloons, stores, and restaurants emptying as the word spread. To Marlin, there was something unreal about the whole thing. The rutted, frozen street, the snow-covered buildings, the clustered little groups of people—and him and Ed Ashley standing alone in front of the office with everybody waiting to see what the man riding toward them was going to do.

Silently, Marlin watched Slade dismount ten feet away. For a moment, the big man just stood there, shoulders hunched, feet widespread, swinging his head from side to side like an enraged buffalo and glaring at the crowd, but not really seeing them. Suddenly, all the pent-up violence within him erupted.

"They wouldn't talk!" he shouted. "The goddamned bastards wouldn't talk! They hung by their heels, with their heads a couple of inches above the coals until their brains cooked and their skulls popped open, *and they never talked!*"

Grabbing a terrified bystander by the coat, Slade dragged him over to the body-draped horses.

"Take a look!" he said savagely. "Would you fry your brains to protect a yellow-bellied Frenchman? Answer me! No, by God, you wouldn't! No man with any sense would. But these fools did!"

He sent the frightened man spinning back into the crowd and looked around for someone else to vent his rage upon.

Watching him, Marlin thought: *All we need now is for Jules Reni to turn up. That would set Slade off like a Roman candle.*

Marlin looked questioningly at Ashley, and Ashley nodded and walked toward Slade; and Marlin felt the butt of the Navy Colt in his pocket cold and hard against his hand and knew that, if he had to, he would kill Jack Slade. He wouldn't want to, but he would do it.

"Come on, Jack . . ." Ashley took Slade by the arm. "You're worn out. Get some sleep and tomorrow you'll feel a lot better."

"God damn you, Ed!" Slade jerked his arm violently free. "Don't you tell me what to do! Don't you *ever* tell me what to do!" He stepped back, almost stumbling over his own feet, his hand close to but not touching the gun at his hip.

"Jack!" Marlin said—quiet, commanding, finger curled firmly around the trigger of the gun in his pocket.

Slade's big shaggy head swung slowly in his direction and, just for an instant, Marlin saw the kill-lust glowing in the pale gray eyes. And then, inexplicably, the madness went out of them and Slade was shaking his head as though he were coming out of a too-deep sleep.

"Marlin!" he exclaimed in a normal voice. "When did you get back?"

Thank God, Marlin thought, it was over and without a killing. His finger eased off the trigger. *Whatever you do remember that teamster.* Finger quick-curled around the trigger again. Eyes and mind alert, ready for treachery.

"Yesterday afternoon," he said. "The westbound stage is well on its way to California by now. And the twenty thousand pieces of mail we brought back from Salt Lake and all points west pulled out for Atchinson a few hours later. Perhaps the best news comes from Brigham Young. I'll tell you about that later in private."

The effect upon Slade was dramatic, incredible. He straightened, throwing off his exhaustion. His eyes cleared. A smile replaced the black, murderous expression of only a few moments before.

Involuntarily, Marlin shivered. Now he had seen both sides of Jack Slade's dual personality. And, having seen, he understood why Slade was both respected and feared throughout the West. More than ever—as he took his hand out of his pocket—he understood and appreciated the warning Ed Ashley had given him. *Remember that teamster.*

"Well, by God, that *is* good news!" Slade exclaimed. "Ed, you're right. I am worn down to the bone. What I need is a bath and twenty-four hours sleep." He waved a hand toward the dead men. "Bury the bastards. And have someone take care of my horse. I'm going home and have Ginny fix me the damnedest breakfast she can stir up. And then me and her are going to bed and I'm going to stir *her* up!" He roared with laughter; and then as quickly as it came, it was gone. "I'm goddamn tired," he said. "Damn, I'm tired!"

Big, dangerous, lonely, he walked down the rutted street while men watched in silence—and Marlin thought with mixed emotions, *What the hell makes you tick, Slade?* And knew, even as he thought it, that no one, probably not even Jack Slade himself, would ever know the answer.

The following morning, Marlin coded a message to the President informing him of Adam Burgess's death and of his own progress to date. When he rode out to Camp Rankin later, he would have the fort's telegrapher wire it to Henderson, his "contact" in Atchinson. Henderson, a top intelligence agent, would relay it to the President's military aide in Washington, who would then personally hand-deliver it to the President. Although only Marlin and the President knew the code, Marlin intended to take no chances of the message being intercepted.

A long, carefully worded statement, it took him more than an hour to write and code. When he finished, he reread his original copy to make certain that he had omitted nothing of importance.

I am obliged to inform you, Mister President, that Mr. Ben Holladay's charges of a Confederate conspiracy have been tentatively confirmed, but that, unfortunately, leadership and scope of that conspiracy have not yet been determined.

Regarding those charges made against the Overland Mail and Stage Line by Senator Conness of California, I regret to inform you, Mister President, that I have personally observed mishandling of the U.S. mails by Overland personnel; but there is no evidence to support the Senator's charges that Mr. Holladay is in any way involved in the current Indian uprising.

I feel compelled to point out, Sir, that whatever the South's role may be in this tragic situation, the climate for its increasing savagery was created by Colonel Chivington's brutal, senseless massacre at Sand Creek.

Word of the treachery and murder committed by the Colorado soldiers under his command has spread throughout the winter camps of the Central Plains.

It has enraged the Cheyennes in their villages at the head of Smoky Hill. They have sent runners bearing war pipes to the Southern Sioux and Northern Arapahos on the Solomon and Republican Rivers. Nearly all the chiefs have smoked the peace pipes. The mood of their people has left them no choice. By smoking the peace pipes, the chiefs have formally declared war against us, committing their full tribes to hostilities.

According to scouts, traders, and Major Stephen Beauchamp, commanding officer of Camp Rankin, a great village is now assembled on Cherry Creek, one of the main streams of the Republican River. Numbering eight or nine hundred lodges, it boasts more than fifteen hundred warriors and their families. Denver is currently under a state of virtual siege.

Besides the Cheyennes, now under Leg-in-the-Water and Little Robe, Tall Bull's Cheyenne Dog Soldiers, the Southern Oglalas of Bad Wound and Pawnee Killer, the Northern Brules of Little Thunder and Spotted Tail and the Northern Arapahos are all there. Although I have not been able to confirm it, it is my belief that Crazy Horse, Red Cloud, the medicine man, Sitting Bull and others may also be involved.

Having traversed the route from Atchinson to Denver to Salt Lake, I can assure you, Mister President, that this Indian uprising is a bloody reality. Beyond Fort Laramie, the route is a shambles, with Overland way stations, settlers' cabins and small villages being attacked and the people tortured and murdered. Passenger traffic is at a standstill, as well as most freighting. Schedules cannot be maintained because of heavy snows and Sioux attacks; but mail service is gradually being restored. I believe that Mr. Holladay is doing everything possible to keep the route open and the stages running. He is due to arrive here within the week to assume personal command of the operation.

Meanwhile, Mister President, I strongly recommend that you institute a security check of all military and civilian personnel directly attached to your staff. Also those serving on the staffs of Secretary of War Stanton and Postmaster-General Montgomery Blair. There is reason to suspect an enemy agent may be operating within one of these departments.

Satisfied, he slipped the message into his pocket and walked down to the Overland office. Two stages were drawn up in front. A score of men milled around in the bitter cold, stomping their feet to keep warm.

As he entered, Jules Reni looked up from his desk, his small eyes hot-black and vindictive, but said nothing. The Frenchman had not introduced himself nor once spoken to him during the past three weeks.

Bob Ridley, sitting hunched over on a waiting bench, slanted Marlin an odd, quizzical glance.

"Morning, Bob." Marlin walked over to where Ed Ashley was checking way bills for the departing east-bound stages. "Where's Slade?"

"Catching up on his sleep." Without pausing in his work, Ashley spoke quietly. "That was a close thing yesterday, Kurt. If Reni had been there, Jack would have killed him. And once started, he'd have gone berserk and shot up the whole town."

"Yet Holladay still keeps him on the payroll," Marlin said. "It just doesn't make sense."

Ashley shrugged. "Like I told you, it takes a Slade to tame a town like Julesburg."

They went out into the street together. Tossing a dispatch pouch up to the driver of the lead stage, Ashley called briskly, "Okay, Jeb, get going! And good luck!"

As the stages wheeled out of town, the team's hoofs clattering over the frozen ground, Marlin turned, frowning, to Ashley. "What are their chances, Ed?"

Ashley shook his head. "I wouldn't want to be riding with them." He moved back toward the office, but stopped and turned as Marlin said quietly, "We've got company."

An eight-man cavalry detail, headed by a sergeant, was coming down the street at a brisk trot.

"I wonder where they're heading," Ashley said.

"I don't know," Marlin replied, watching the horsemen approach. As the squad reined up alongside, he recognized the sergeant, a hard-faced, blue-eyed blond named Reynolds. He had seen Reynolds at the fort the day before when he had ridden out to see Captain Bowers, the medical officer.

"Morning, Sergeant," he said. "Scouting party?"

Reynolds gave him a cool glance. "Escort duty, Colonel. And the Major's compliments. He'd like to see you as soon as possible."

"Thank you, Sergeant," Marlin said. "Now if you want to catch up with those stages, you'd better get started."

With a curt nod, Reynolds wheeled his horse and led the detail out of town at the gallop.

Shaking his head, Ashley turned back to the office. "That's the first escort Beauchamp's given us in weeks," he said. "I wonder what made him change his mind?"

"Who knows?" Marlin followed Ashley inside. "Maybe that's what he wants to talk to me about.

I think I'll ride out to the fort and find out."

Ashley slipped out of his coat, hung it on the rack, and settled himself behind his desk. "Sorry, Kurt, but that will have to wait. Slade left orders for you to ride over to Crow Junction. It seems they've got troubles. The station was hit yesterday and they lost some of their people."

"Dammit, Ed . . ." Quick anger caught at Marlin. "I've just returned from an eight-hundred-mile nightmare! I need some rest!"

"I don't give the orders," Ashley came back mildly. "I just pass them on. And Slade said that you were to leave right away."

"Sorry, Ed," Marlin said. "I'll see Beauchamp when I get back."

Half an hour later, he mounted up and rode out of town.

At Crow Junction, he found the entire station on an around-the-clock alert. The day before, a band of fifty Oglalas had swooped down on a hay train a mile out and had killed and scalped the three men working there. They had then attacked the station, killed a stock tender, wounded a marooned driver, and made off with the stock in the corral.

The wounded man swore that Pawnee Killer, a Southern Oglala chief, had led the raid; but a civilian scout, Grey, who had ridden in just before the trouble started, disagreed.

"Hell, ain't no war bonnet chief like Pawnee Killer goin' to waste time on a hayin' crew," Grey snorted. "Him an' Bad Wound are with them Cheyennes and Arapahos on Cherry Crick."

Taking the scout with him, Marlin worked a ten-mile circle around the station, but spotted no hostiles. He did cut sign of a sizable band riding unshod ponies and moving rapidly southward. There were no marks of travois poles, which meant no squaws, children, or old people.

"Crotch-cloth party," Grey said. "Young bucks out countin' their first coups. They won't be back."

On the return trip, a solitary horseman topped a ridge a quarter of a mile away and rode toward them. When the rider was fifty yards distant, Marlin turned to Grey. "Recognize him?"

"Yep," the scout replied. "Name's Hamlin Weatherby. Major Beauchamp's father-in-law. Artist. Paints Injuns, cavalry, scouts, Walk-a-Heaps, stagecoaches, buffler. Onct I seen him crawl 'thin a hundred feet of a war party an' then, by God, lay there flat on his belly an' draw the whole kit an' caboodle of 'em as real as life. I allus figgered them painters to be half squaw. He ain't. He's cold as froze trout an' dangerous as a grizzly sow with cubs. He'll lose his h'ar one of these days sure as hell."

"Hamlin Weatherby!" Marlin couldn't believe it. "You mean *he's* Major Beauchamp's father-in-law?"

The scout regarded Marlin curiously. "Sound surprised. Know him?"

"No." Marlin shook his head. "But I've heard of him, and I've met his daughter. I thought he would be more like . . . well, like her."

"Uh-uh." A crooked grin spread the scout's thin-lipped mouth. "That one's all class, but don't let her fool you. Underneath, she's like a buffler heifer in heat. Th' fire's deep as she is, an' ain't no man goin' to put it out. Leastways, not the Major. I've never been able to figure out why she married him; but she sure must a had a powerful reason.

"Weatherby's a different breed. Fire'n ice mixed together. Th' fire melts th' ice an' th' ice freezes th' fire an' ain't no way you kin tell which is goin' to do what when! I tell you, he ain't no man to fool around with."

Watching Weatherby approach, Marlin found it difficult to imagine a man like Stephen Beauchamp tolerating an artist father-in-law around. But as Hamlin Weatherby reined up alongside, it was obvious that the Major had had no choice in the matter. For this handsome man with the thin, aesthetic face and the cool, impersonal eyes that observed the world as though it were a gigantic guinea pig—this man, Marlin sensed immediately, was not tolerated. *He tolerated.*

Crossing his hands on his saddle horn, Weatherby said calmly, "You're wasting your time. They're long gone." He shifted his weight in his stirrups. "You're Colonel Marlin, aren't you? I've heard a lot about you." He extended a gloved hand. "I'm Hamlin Weatherby."

The strength of his handclasp surprised Marlin; and some of that surprise must have shown, for Weatherby smiled.

"Frontier artists are not weaklings, Colonel," he said. "We have to be Jack-of-all-trades. Artist, historian, scout, hunter, linguist, and peace-pipe smoker all rolled into one—with a good bit of luck thrown in if we are to survive."

"Grey here doesn't think your luck will hold forever," Marlin told him. "He thinks you'll lose your hair sooner or later."

Weatherby shrugged philosophically. "If a man's going to paint the West as it really is, he has to know it. And to know, he has to live it."

He was unlike anyone Marlin had every known—quiet, impersonal, obviously intelligent and with a controlled inner ruthlessness which he carefully masked behind a pleasant smile. A refined version, Marlin thought, of Jack Slade. And then quickly rejected the comparison. Hamlin Weatherby was as different from Slade as Machiavelli from a peasant.

"It's clear that you've lived what you paint," Marlin said. "Someday, I'd like to see your work."

"Any time," Weatherby replied agreeably. "Currently, I'm doing a series on the Overland for

Harper's Magazine. I think you might appreciate it." Settling himself in his saddle, he reined away.

"We're both wasting valuable time. There's a spot near the river I want to sketch before dark. You can tell Sam Haines at Crow Junction to relax. Those Oglalas won't bother him again this time."

As Weatherby rode away, Marlin remarked thoughtfully to Grey, "I wouldn't want that man for an enemy."

The scout spat. "Like I said, he ain't quite human."

Abruptly, Marlin swung the bay around. "We'd better head back for the station." There, he relayed Weatherby's information to Sam Haines, ate, and hit the blankets.

The following day, Marlin returned to Julesburg, arriving almost simultaneously with Ben Holladay.

Leaning forward in his seat, Ben Holladay stared impatiently at the country rolling past his window. Although the team of matched gray racers was clipping off a brisk six or seven miles an hour, it seemed to him as though he hung suspended in Time. But then it always seemed thus. No matter how fast he moved, Time was always one step ahead of him. Or perhaps it was only an illusion created by an ambition that was forever conscious of the finiteness of life.

At forty-one, his empire spread from the Missouri to California, up the coast to the Pacific Northwest and across the Pacific to the Orient. Banks, railroads, freighting companies, steamship lines. Distilleries, packing plants, stores, and warehouses. And, queen of them all, the *Overland.*

He did not merely control this vast empire; he owned it . . . lock, stock, and barrel. Furthermore, he ran it. The wheels of his own specially built Concord seldom stopped rolling save when he exchanged them for the great steel drivers of an Eastern passenger train.

At one time, he might have stopped. Now, he thought, his eyes on the rolling Platte hills, it was too late. The savage, no-quarter-asked, none-given world in which he moved had firm hold of him. Even had he wished, he could not have pulled out. He had too many enemies driving him on. Besides, he did not want to stop. It was a good life. A damned exciting life.

King of Wheels, men called him. And, by God, king he was! Fighting desperately in this year of 1864 to keep his tremendous empire from collapsing under the combined attacks of white enemies in Washington and red enemies here on this blazing frontier.

He sighed, knowing a faint regret for the days of his youth when life had not been quite so complicated. For instance, the excitement of that first time in the Plaza in Sante Fe, feeling the lively black eyes of the *senoritas* upon him and the sudden heat rising in his loins and . . .

"For God sakes, Ben!" Notley Ann's high, petulant voice set his teeth on edge. "How much further is it? Why couldn't you have handled things by telegraph from Washington? Can't you ever do anything the sensible way?"

Turning from the window, Holladay stared thoughtfully at his wife—prim, auburn-haired, sharp-featured, her mouth tight with a chronic dissatisfaction. He knew how she hated these trips, preferring instead the gay, glittering parties at their Washington, New York, and San Francisco mansions, as well as the fabled Ophir estate in Portland, Oregon.

This time, however, she had made only a token protest. Shrewd, greedy, ambitious, she had been quick to recognize in the mounting hostility toward the Overland a threat to her way of life. If it meant spending a month or two in this Godforsaken land, she was prepared to make the sacrifice; but she would hate every single moment of it. A fact which Holladay knew she would communicate to him with a stinging sarcasm. Already she had begun to do so.

Meeting her cold eyes, he flinched inwardly, knowing that whatever feeling she might once have had for him had long since died. He no longer harbored any illusions about that—or about her. He knew her now, down to the very core of her shallow, selfish nature. She had no desire, no real goal other than social status and recognition. And he, Ben Holladay, served no other purpose save to buy that status with the power which his wealth gave him. For every rung he climbed, she demanded yet another, and still another.

Sometimes he wondered if being forced to feed that insatiable appetite had not become the driving force behind his success. And, on occasion, he wondered with mixed emotions just what would happen if he could no longer satisfy that ever-increasing hunger.

She would leave him, of course.

To escape from her coldness and contempt for him, he had plunged into the jungle of big business which he knew so well. There, he was in his native element. To Notley Ann, he might be nothing. But in that jungle, he was a lion, and men trembled when he moved among them.

"Ben!" Notley Ann's voice shrilled. "Answer me! Or didn't anyone ever teach you manners? Why in the name of God, I ever married you I'll never know! As Father said, the Carvers are aristocratic . . ."

"Damn 'Father,' " Holladay said calmly. "Damn the Carvers. Damn the aristocracy. And damn you, too, Notley Ann!" Then while she sat tongue-tied with outraged indignation, he removed the cigar from his mouth and regarded her as though she were a Virginia City dance-hall girl.

"You know why you married me, all right. So does every man and woman who eats caviar and drinks champagne at your fancy parties that my money pays for. Why? Because no fancy Dan, blue-blooded aristocrat could afford to keep you one year in the style I've kept you in for twenty.

"And *don't*"—noting her fiery expression—"start winding up for one of your tongue-lashing tantrums. I've got enough troubles without fighting with you."

He had never before spoken to her in such a manner. Now he derived a certain satisfaction from her wide-eyed, openmouthed reaction.

"Why, you insufferable clod! You loud-mouthed, gambling, wenching excuse for a man! You and your stinking buckskins and your greasy squaws!" Her face was livid with disgust. "You think I haven't known about them?"

He had hoped, for her sake, she hadn't. Now he was mildly surprised to discover he didn't care. She had hurt him too much, too long.

"At least, they *are* women," he retorted. "And, to them, I'm a *man,* not a gold mine. And if I stink sometimes of sweat and horses, they don't mind; they're used to it."

He opened the door and swung out onto the iron steps. "I'm going to get a bit of fresh air." The door swung shut behind him.

Hank Monk and Bill Pederson, the messenger, made room for him on the seat. He muscled between them, wiped his forehead with the back of his sleeve and grinned.

"Gettin' kind of hot down there."

Monk spat wickedly. "Sounded like it."

"Blast you, Hank! One of these days I'm going to marry you off to the worst floozie that flips her hips at you! Then, by God, we'll see who laughs last!"

Relaxed, his quarrel with Notley Ann forgotten, he watched the shifting contours of the land with a growing eagerness. Within an hour, they'd be in Julesburg. Then he could begin to clean up this mess. Something he would have done weeks ago if his enemies had stopped ripping at him. That damned Conness from California, for instance, getting up on the Senate floor and charging that the Indian raids were "Holladay fabrications to cover up the Overland's inefficient handling of the U.S. mails!" And accusing him, Ben Holladay, of having his own Overland people "rifle gold shipments!"

Unconsciously, he flexed his big, powerful shoulders, forcing Hank Monk and the messenger to yield him more room. Anger against Conness, a suspicious Congress, and yellow-rag newspapers in Washington, Denver, and San Francisco, who were crucifying him, began to build up, wiping out his momentary good humor.

The sons of bitches! With inexperienced Volunteer troops replacing Army Regulars withdrawn from the frontier for fighting in the East, his Overland racers were bursting their hearts outrunning bandits, guerrillas, and inflamed war parties across the Kansas prairies through the Platte regions and clear to the Rockies—trying to keep the route open to California.

A sudden gust of wind almost whipped his hat from his head. He jammed it savagely down upon his ears, his sense of anger and frustration mounting to the boiling point. He was losing a fortune because the President had said that, regardless of the cost, the West must be held to the Union—and the Overland was the sole connecting link between the two. And what kind of thanks was he getting for it? Even the man in the street was beginning to believe that he was some sort of murdering master criminal.

If people were out here where they could actually see what was going on, they'd damn well change their minds in a hurry! Along the Platte, way stations and home stations going up in flames, the men who ran them killed and scalped. Huge stores of feed, piles of mail, shops, ware-houses, and extra stages put to the torch by Indians who then outran pursuing cavalry on captured Overland racers. Instead of accusing him of robbing his own stage line, Congress ought to be providing him with more troop protection and putting a stop to this damn Reb conspiracy!

Hell—he glared at the off-wheeler's bouncing rump—you couldn't blame Mitchell for his failure to put down the uprising. The General was no Indian fighter. Even if he had been, he couldn't protect twelve hundred miles of stagecoach roads in Nebraska, Colorado, Utah, Idaho, and elsewhere with a force of only six hundred and eighty men. The Sioux were running him ragged, drawing him to the scene of one massacre and then wiping out a way station or a settler's place a hundred miles distant. It was enough to take the starch out of any man. But that was Mitchell's problem. He, Ben Holladay, had his own. And, by God, he'd solve his! He'd show those bastards in Washington who was King of Wheels!

By the time Holladay reached Julesburg, he had climbed back into the coach and made his peace with Notley Ann. It was not difficult. Deep, lasting hurt was impossible between them. They could not even drift further apart. They could only go their separate ways, strangers bound together by mutual convenience and the Law.

Flying the famous blue and white *BH* pennant, the brilliant red-and-yellow Concord, surrounded by a twenty-man escort, thundered past Marlin five miles out of Julesburg—sun splashing over the gold-plated door handles and the matched white team's harness. A shower of wet, dirty slush, thrown up by the racers' drumming hoofs, spattered him from boots to face; and then the little calvacade was gone at a full gallop.

By the time Marlin reined up before the hotel, a trim, black-haired maid was directing the unloading of two baggage coaches . . . trunks, valises, feather beds, cases of special foods and imported wines . . . while a curious crowd gathered around the fabulous Holladay "Special."

"Hey, Hank!" a teamster standing near Marlin yelled at the stage driver. "I heard you c'n eat off a mahogany table, do paperwork, write a letter, read a newspaper at night, get drunk from a fancy bar, an' make love on a feather bed 'thout ever havin' to stop them wheels from rollin'. That true?"

Dressed in a fancy corduroy uniform with black lapels and a black, wide-brimmed hat and shiny boots, the jehu nodded. "Yep," he said. "Only one of its kind in the world that you can—"

"Snow-drench a horseman twenty feet away when it's traveling at full speed!" Marlin kneed the bay alongside the stage. "Or do you take credit for that?"

Unabashed, the jehu grinned at Marlin good-naturedly. "Kind of caught you square an' center, didn't I? Must have hit a chug hole just as we passed you. Wait'll I finish here an' I'll buy you a drink." His good nature wiped out Marlin's irritation.

"Thanks," Marlin said, dismounting. "I'm Kurt Marlin, division trouble-shooter."

"Heard about you on the way out." The jehu climbed down from his seat. "I'm Hank Monk."

"Not *the* Hank Monk," Marlin said, "who hauled Horace Greeley to Placerville?"

Monk grinned self-consciously. "That's me," he admitted. "How'd you know about that ride?"

"Why, as publisher-editor of the New York *Tribune*, Mr. Greeley wrote an article about it for his newspaper," Marlin replied, fighting to keep a straight face. "He swore that it was the most hair-raising experience he had ever had. I understand he's now crusading for better roads and saner drivers."

"To tell you the truth," Monk said slyly, "there was times when I thought he was a mite upset over the way I drove. Especially around them hairpin curves with a thousand-foot drop off on one side. But, hell, I had a tight schedule to keep."

"How about your trip this time?" Marlin asked. "Any trouble?"

"Trouble!" The jehu grimaced. "More damn Injuns than raindrops in a clodburst. But no horses living, not even Overland stock, can outrun Ben Holladay's personal racers. An' no crotch-cloth party roamin' them plains out there can outride, outshoot, or outfight that escort of his." He spat, brown-streaming the snow with tobacco juice. "You want the whole story, you'd best talk to Wes Bender, the scout who came with us. He just went over to the Wagon Wheel Saloon."

"Thanks." Marlin swung back into the saddle. "I'll have that drink with you later."

"Marlin."

"Yes?"

"Wes Bender is a half-breed," Monk said. "Sioux. He's damned sensitive about it."

Marlin nodded and rode down the street.

He found Wes Bender standing alone at the far end of the Wagon Wheel's bar. There was no mistaking the man. His Sioux heritage showed in the dark skin, the lank, shoulder-length hair and the proud, bold features. He wore gray woolen trousers tucked into knee-high scout moccasins. A Mexican silver necklace gleamed against the dark blue Union cavalry tunic with its yellow sergeant's chevrons. A Colt hung at his hip and a new Spencer seven-shot, rapid-fire rifle leaned against the bar. There was a half-empty whiskey glass in his hand.

Moving along the line of men jammed shoulder to shoulder at the front end of the bar, Marlin paused next to the scout. "Bender?"

The half-breed turned. Rejection had thinned the wide mouth into a knifelike slash and burned a bitter resentment into the pale gray eyes flashing from the copper face.

"What do you want?"

"I'm Kurt Marlin, Overland trouble-shooter. Hank Monk said you could tell me about your trip out."

The wide mouth thinned. "Why didn't he tell you?"

"He said you could do a better job."

For a moment, Bender hesitated. Then he nodded. "Let's go over to a table where we can talk."

Marlin motioned to the bartender. "Cochran, bring us a bottle of Bourbon."

Cochran, a sullen-faced man with mean eyes and a bald head, followed them over to the table. He set down a bottle and a couple of glasses, collected his money, and went back to the bar.

Pouring the drinks, Marlin pushed a glass toward the scout and then leaning back, waited.

Bender drank his whiskey, not gulping it down, Indian fashion, but slowly, as a man who likes the taste of it, not the effect. Yet it did not relax him, for Marlin could sense the bitterness, the resentment just below the surface.

"So you want to know what it's like to the east?" Abruptly, Bender put down his glass. "I'll tell you what it's like. It's a bloody nightmare. The same as everywhere else on the Plains since that goddamned preacher-turned-soldier, Chivington, loosed his mad dogs at Sand Springs last month!

"Now I'll tell you something else." He hunched

forward, his acquiline features taking on a bold, harsh cast. "Everybody's scared that the chiefs in that big village on Cherry Creek are going to raid Denver. They're wrong. Denver is not the place to turn back emigrants or run out settlers. So they'll—"

"So," Marlin interrupted, "they'll hit Julesburg. Right?"

"Where else?" Bender poured himself another drink. "It's at the junction of the Fort Laramie Road and the Denver-Colorado gold fields cut-off of the Overland Trail. It's a principal emigrant supply town, with replacement facilities for rolling equipment; and its stores are jam-packed with food and general supplies. Loot and burn Julesburg and it will shut down all traffic on the Overland Trail. That will mean an end to settlement in the valley. I figure that's exactly what Chewing Black Bone intends to do."

"Chewing Black Bone?" Marlin frowned. "I've never heard of him."

"You should have." Bender regarded him curiously. "This country is the home of Chewing Black Bone's Broken Cooking Pot tribe—Brule Sioux. He's been restless for a long time because too many whites have been settling in his territory."

Bender sipped his whiskey like brandy, swishing it around in his mouth, then swallowing it a little at a time. The Mexican silver necklace gleamed dully as it caught the pale winter sunshine slanting in through the window behind him.

"Chewing Black Bone is bold, smart, and a first-class fighter. It's my belief that he plans to use the Sand Creek survivors, Cheyenne and Arapaho—plus the Sioux and Arapahos who've been raising hell in the Kansas and Smoky Hill valleys—to help him drive the whites completely out of the South Platte valley. In exchange for their help, he'll probably offer his allies a share of the loot and the right to stay in the valley if they want."

Listening, Marlin wondered, for the first time, if this was not, after all, simply an all-out Indian uprising growing out of the Sand Creek massacre—with no Confederate involvement. It seemed logical, and yet the very situation itself invited a conspiracy—an alliance between the Confederacy and a smart, aggressive Sioux war chief, with white and Indian both seeking to use each other to their own advantage.

"How many of the chiefs camped on Cherry Creek will follow Chewing Black Bone if he does go through with such a plan?" Marlin asked. "Because if what you've told me is true, then the danger to Julesburg is not only real, but imminent."

Bender pursed his lips, frowning. "I'd say that depends upon how well armed they are," he replied. "Last year, Chewing Black Bone ambushed an ordnance train commanded by Lieutenant Hutchins and got enough rifles to outfit his people. If all the tribes on Cherry Creek had rifles—"

"Massacre," Marlin finished for him. "Is there a chance they might somehow get hold of that many guns?"

"A damn good chance," Bender said. "An Army ordnance outfit, guarded by a couple of squads of cavalry and headed for Fort Laramie, left Atchinson the same day we did. It's carrying a thousand rifles and a hundred thousand rounds of ammunition. It's due to pass through here en route. My guess is that Chewing Black Bone will attack it somewhere between here and Fort Laramie. If he gets those rifles . . . good-bye Julesburg and maybe Denver, too."

The news surprised and alarmed Marlin. "Have you mentioned any of this to Holladay?" he asked. "Or gone to Major Beauchamp about the matter?"

Bender shrugged indifferently. "I figure Holladay knows as much as I do. As far as that damned Major's concerned, no one can tell him anything. I served under him until General Mitchell ordered me detached from regular duty to serve as a personal scout for Holladay. If you wonder why . . . I have a reputation as one of the best scouts on the Plains. Anyway, the Major's bound to know that ordnance wagon train will be passing through here." He rose abruptly and picked up his rifle. "Thanks for the drink."

Silently, Marlin watched him pad across the

room, his moccasined toes pointed inward like an Indian's—and wondered which Bender hated the most, white or red; both had rejected him. Finishing his own drink, Marlin followed moments later.

Back at the Overland office, the Holladay "Special" had disappeared, along with the two baggage coaches and the English maid. A half-dozen hard-faced buckskin-clad men—part of the escort—rode past Marlin at a brisk trot.

As he turned into the office, he almost collided with Ed Ashley, who was just emerging. Ashley's expression was relaxed for the first time in days.

"I was just on my way to get you," Ashley said. "Hank Monk told me you'd gone over to the Wagon Wheel to see Bender. Holladay's here. He wants to see you right away."

"It can wait a couple of minutes," Marlin replied. "Before I go in there, tell me . . . just what kind of a man *is* Ben Holladay? The newspapers claim he's a murdering, thieving bandit-tycoon. I'd like to hear from someone who really knows."

"That's a tough question," Ashley frowned. "Boil it all down, I guess you can say—silk hat an' tails or buckskins an' moccasins—Ben's a shrewd, ruthless, sometimes unscrupulous man with a driving ambition. His friends swear by him; his enemies fear and hate him. Get in his way and he'll smash you like glass. But if he likes you, there's nothing in the world he won't—"

"Dammit, Ed," a heavy voice shouted from inside, "if that's Marlin, bring him in here! I haven't got all day to fool around!"

"One more thing." Ashley smiled faintly. "Hollering just comes naturally to him." He led the way inside and into his own private office at the rear.

Still wearing the broadcloth suit with the grosgrain lapels that he had arrived in, Ben Holladay sat solidly entrenched behind the massive oak desk, a dollar Havana cigar in one hand.

In that first instant of confrontation, he reminded Marlin of Brigham Young. Big, powerful, wide of shoulder and deep of chest, with a strong, heavy-jawed face and a well-groomed beard, he radiated the same dynamic energy, the same compulsive inner drive of the natural leader. Plus something else . . . a suggestion of violence and ruthlessness in the set of the mouth and in the shrewd, watchful eyes.

A man, Marlin thought, who trusted few people, if any, and was perhaps not to be trusted himself.

Marlin stood waiting, aware that he, in turn, was being sized up by the mind behind those shrewd eyes. Then Ben Holladay rose and extended his hand.

"So you're Marlin," he said. "Jack here tells me

that you're an ex-colonel, a cavalry officer. Frankly, I've got no use for the Army, and even less for the cavalry. But I'll not hold that against you." He motioned to a chair. "Sit down. You, too, Ed. We've got problems to discuss." Settling back behind his desk, he swept his little circle of listeners—Slade, Ashley, Marlin.

"That's the god-damndest nightmare out there on the Plains I've ever run into," he said. "And it's getting worse. As I told the President just before I left Washington, the way we're going, our losses will run into a million and a half dollars by the end of the year. We can't take that kind of beating and survive.

"If Mr. Lincoln hadn't promised me that Congress would recognize my claim at the end of the war, I'd shut down until this uprising is over. But the President insists that it's vital to keep the route open to the coast. So we're going to do our best and hope it's enough." He turned to Marlin.

"Slade tells me you've been looking into this Indian trouble. You found out anything yet? I think that that damned butcher, Chivington, started it . . . or at least fanned the flames higher. Now I think the Confederacy has joined up with the tribes to run us right off the Plains. What do you think?"

For a moment, Marlin hesitated, wondering just how much he should tell Holladay. After all, the Overland owner was still an unknown factor.

Cautiously, he committed himself to a guarded answer.

"I think you're right about Chivington," he said. "It's a known fact that the Sioux, Cheyennes, and Arapahos have smoked the pipe and vowed to avenge what happened at Sand Creek. Personally, I think that there probably *is* a conspiracy—with a Confederate spy sitting in at war councils, and Confederate soldiers or outlaw mercenaries operating under his orders. Stagecoach raids, horse stealing, things like that."

"By God, I wish that damned Conness could hear you!" Holladay banged his fist down on the desk. "He's got everybody in Washington stirred up against me, from the newspapers to the man in the street." He leaned forward impatiently. "Tell me; do you have any idea who this Reb spy is? Could it be Jules Reni?"

Marlin shook his head. "I don't think so. He hasn't got the brains. But he may be heading up some of the outlaw gangs. It's almost certain he's robbing you blind, inside and outside the company."

"Jack"—Holladay turned a scowling face toward Slade—"I want that son of a bitch fired and out of town by the end of the week. You understand?"

"All right," Slade, who had remained silent until now, said. "But I'll have to kill him. He'll not leave voluntarily."

"Then kill him, by God!" Holladay flared. "And be done with it!" He swung toward Ashley. "Ed, you'll take over as chief agent here." With an abrupt change of mood, he hauled out a fine Havana, clipped it, and lit up with professional care.

"Now, Marlin, tell me about your trip to Salt Lake. How's my brother, Ben? What came from your meeting with Brigham Young? How much hostile action did you run into? Where was it worst? I've had Slade's report, but I want to hear the details from you."

Marlin told him in short, terse language. When he had finished, Holladay nodded approval. "You did a good job. Especially with Brigham Young. We may need his help before the winter's out." Shoving back his chair, he rose.

"I've got to get over to Ed's place and change. Notley Ann will raise hell if I don't take a bath. Damndest woman for cleanliness I ever saw. Come to think of it . . . damndest woman, period.

"By the way"—he paused in the doorway—"she's throwing a party tonight. Time's seven-thirty. And you'd better come properly dressed or she'll send you home to change!"

Arriving late, Marlin was admitted by Susan Ashley, lovely in a pale blue formal gown that brought out her quiet, dark-haired beauty. It was the first time he had seen her since they had quarreled the day he had returned from Salt Lake.

"Hello, Kurt." Susan's smile was forced, her manner distant. "We had all but given you up."

"I'm sorry." He stood looking at her a moment, troubled by the schism between them. "I had a lot of things on my mind. I simply forgot."

"What you really mean"—quick tears filled her eyes—"is that you didn't want to come because of me."

"That's not true." Upset by her tears, Marlin threw up a defensive shield. "What's happening between us, Susan? First, it was Virginia Slade. Now what is it this time? I don't understand you!"

He saw the deep hurt spring into Susan Ashley's eyes and spread across her face. Without a word, she led him into the parlor, already crowded with a dozen guests, most of whom he knew. Yet looking around him, he found it difficult to believe that this was Julesburg, Colorado Territory . . . and not the drawing room of a town house in Boston.

Holladay, handsome in formal attire, a diamond stud blazing in his starched white shirt front.

Jack Slade, almost matching him in elegance. Beside her husband, Virginia Slade, her red hair falling down over her shoulders, looking wickedly beautiful in a mint-green taffeta gown.

Standing aloofly to one side, the Beauchamps. The Major, in formal dress uniform, every inch the West Point career officer. Janet Beauchamp, her honey-blond hair swept up in classic simplicity, a diamond pendant sparkling against the dramatic black evening gown.

A prominent banker and his wife, a well-to-do local merchant and his spouse, an attorney, Dr. E. C. Lindley, the town's most popular physician—with Ed and Emma Ashley, neatly dressed, adding a touch of the frontier to the gathering.

Spotting Marlin, Holladay came over, a glass of champagne in his hand. He was perspiring lightly and it was quite obvious that he would have preferred to have been elsewhere.

"I thought maybe you'd gotten scared of Notley Ann's reputation an' cut for the tall timber," he said. "Wouldn't have blamed you. God, how I hate these parties! Damned boiled shirt collar rubs my neck raw; I eat too much, drink too much, talk too much, get bored and start an argument with someone . . . and then catch hell from Notley Ann!

"Here." He handed Marlin the glass of champagne. "Fortify yourself before you meet Her Royal Highness! A man's got to be drunk to stay around her!" Half-drunken banter, but behind it Marlin sensed a deeply ingrained bitterness and knew that Ben Holladay was not a happy man.

"Thanks." Marlin raised his glass, then paused as Jack and Virginia Slade joined them. He sensed immediately that Slade had been drinking too much and was in an aggressive mood.

"Well," Slade said abruptly, "I fired Jules Reni.

Gave him until tomorrow night to get out of town."

"What did he say to that?" Marlin asked.

"Nothing," Slade retorted. "The minute he opened his mouth, I threw him out on his ass . . . excuse me, Susan . . . in the street."

"I wouldn't take him lightly if I were you," Marlin cautioned. "He's the kind who'll put a bullet in your back."

"I never take anyone lightly," Slade snapped. "If they get in my way, I kill them!"

"Oh, for God's sake!" Virginia Slade laughed. "This is a party; let's enjoy it!" She flicked Marlin a provocative glance; and he knew that she was in one of her devilish moods. "Where've you been keeping yourself? I've missed you. Don't tell me you were afraid Jack might guess the truth and—" The blood rushed from her face in swift panic. *"Jack, I was only joking! Jack, don't!"*

Switching his glance back to Slade, Marlin stiffened. Slade's eyes glowed with an unnatural brightness. Great drops of perspiration trickled down his face. His voice, when he spoke, was almost inaudible.

"Have you been fooling around with my wife, Marlin?"

"Please!" Marlin felt Susan Ashley's hand on his arm. *"Don't say anything!* He'll kill you."

As Marlin hesitated, Holladay stepped quickly between the two men. "You're drunk, Jack,"

135

Holladay said. "You don't know what you're saying. Now calm down."

Without turning his head, Slade snapped, "You stay out of this, Ben."

"By God," Holladay flared. "You're forgetting where you are and who *I* am! You start any trouble here and you and Jules Reni will both be heading out of town. You don't scare me one damn bit, Jack!"

No man living but Holladay could have spoken thus to Slade and have gotten away with it. For a moment, it appeared as though he had gone too far.

Then, slowly, Slade's eyes cleared. He shook his head, took out a handkerchief and wiped his face. But the tension still lingered, making his smile tight, humorless.

"Hell, everything's all right," he said. "I just had a little too much to drink—and Ginny had to get a little too bitchy. It's over; forget it." He turned an expressionless face to his wife. "You almost got a man killed, Ginny. I think we'd better go home before you cause more trouble."

"Now just a minute!" Holladay protested. "You walk out and it will ruin the party; and then Notley Ann will raise hell with me!"

"Does it give you pleasure, sir, to picture your wife as a shrew?"

Marlin turned and stared at the woman standing halfway up the spiral staircase. Several years

136

younger than her husband, Notley Ann Holladay was neither tall nor beautiful although, in her youth, she must have been attractive, for her figure was still well preserved. Her auburn hair, parted in the middle and brushed severely away from her face, accentuated the rather long, thin nose and the high cheekbones and gave her face a faintly shrewish look. A chronic dissatisfaction with life had thinned her mouth and filled the gray eyes with a cool calculation.

Although the fashionable burnt-orange gown tended to soften the hardness of body, and diamonds sparkling at ears, throat, and breast made one forget the sharpness of her features, Marlin knew that only her husband's wealth and power brought the famous, the brilliant, the talented to her parties and made those parties the talk of the nation.

"Well, Ben"—Notley Anne descended the stairs with a practiced poise—"aren't you going to introduce me to the gentleman?"

Glad for the diversion, Holladay led Marlin over to her. "Mr. Marlin, my wife, Notley Ann. Ann, this is Kurt Marlin, an ex-colonel in the Union cavalry. He is this division's new trouble-shooter."

"My pleasure, ma'am," Marlin said, bending over the jeweled hand and caught the faint surprise on Notley Ann's face as he straightened.

"I must say, sir," she murmured, "that I had not expected to find a gentleman in this primitive country. Let us hope that you are as efficient as you are well-bred, and that you can help resolve the problems here quickly. Frankly, I have no love for the frontier."

"I regret to hear that, ma'am," Marlin replied smoothly. "The West needs women such as you to bring it culture and beauty."

A quickening interest lit Notley Ann's cool gray eyes, and a faint smile softened the thin lips.

"If there were more men like you on the frontier, sir, it would not lack for women like me." With a not ungraceful gesture, she laid her hand on Marlin's arm. "Will you escort me to dinner, sir?"

Seated between Notley Ann and Susan Ashley, Marlin could not help but be struck by the incongruity of the situation. He had never seen a more ill-matched group, having so little in common. Crisscrossing the length of the table, he could sense the individual animosities just below the surface. Susan Ashley's hurt resentment of Virginia Slade . . .

Notley Ann was observing him with an amused smile. "You seem to have an unusual talent for attracting beautiful young women, sir. I wish that you could use your charms on the Overland's enemies. Senator Conness, for instance." Her eyes were deceptively clear and innocent. "Did you know him while you were in Washington?"

Instinctively, Marlin threw up his guard. The question was no idle one; she was fishing for information. Already she was suspicious of his presence here.

"I have never met the Senator, ma'am."

Notley Ann's eyes lost their innocence. "But you have been to Washington, Colonel?"

"I've been many places, ma'am," Marlin countered. "But then my life cannot possibly interest you. Tell me more about—"

"I'm not going to argue with you, Major!" Suddenly, Ben Holladay's voice rose angrily above the polite conversation, shutting off Marlin's words and focusing all eyes upon the Overland's owner.

Half turned in his chair in order to see past Janet Beauchamp, Holladay was glaring at Major Beauchamp with open hostility.

"My stages are entitled to cavalry escorts," he said, "and they're going to get them!"

A dull flush stained the Major's cheeks. He set down his glass and replied sharply, "Sir, both the Secretary of War and the Postmaster-General have expressed the opinion that the problem of keeping the route open is strictly up to the Overland. Frankly, I share their views."

Holladay scowled, his heavy black eyebrows drawing down until they almost met in the center. "Stanton and Blair are entitled to their opinions, Major, as are you. But the final decision on the matter rests with the President. And the President informed me just before I left Washington that he had ordered the Department of the Platte to provide the Overland with cavalry escorts."

"Then you must also know," Beauchamp retorted, "that that order allows post commanders considerable flexibility in its implementation."

The line of Holladay's heavy jaw ridged. "I'm not a highly educated man, Major. So just put all that fancy talk into plain language."

In the thin strung silence, Beauchamp's voice, edged with contempt, reached the length of the table.

"To put it bluntly, sir, I—not you—will decide if and when cavalry escorts are to be provided the Overland. May I remind you that my first responsibility is to protect Julesburg, as a major emigrant outfitting center, from Indian attack . . . and to offer sanctuary to settlers in the area should such attacks occur. My second responsibility is to support the Colorado Volunteers in the event of a mass attack upon Denver. Consideration will be given to the Overland's needs only when—"

"By God, Major," Holladay shouted him down, "you'll carry out the clear intent of the President's orders, or I'll see you court-martialed and drummed out of the service! I've had my bellyful of your arrogance!"

Instantly, Beauchamp was on his feet, his face pale. "May I remind you, sir, that, as guests, my wife and I are entitled to at least formal courtesy. Despite your hostility toward me in the past, I came here tonight to try and make you understand my position. But one cannot reason with a fool."

"Guests be damned!" Anger thickened Holladay's words. "No man can come into my house and vow to defy the President of the United States! Either you come to your senses or I'll take this matter to General Price and, if necessary, straight to the President! Now, get out! I'm sorry, Mrs. Beauchamp."

In the awkward silence, Janet Beauchamp rose and looked at the group with unruffled calm. She slanted Marlin a brief smile; and, in that moment, he could not help but admire her composure under such humiliating circumstances.

"My husband is right, sir." She spoke directly to Holladay. "From the military point of view, which is more important? Julesburg and the lives of innocent women and children—or the Overland?" Placing her hand on her husband's arm, she said, "Let's go home, Stephen."

Beside him, Marlin felt Notley Ann stiffen and her hostility reach out for the other woman. "When the cause of the Union is threatened, Mrs. Beauchamp?" Notley Ann said in her high, brittle voice. "Why, the Overland, of course!"

Janet Beauchamp paused in the dining-room doorway; and, for a moment, the two women

141

smiled at one another with the quiet hatred of natural enemies.

"You wouldn't be influenced by your personal greed, would you, Mrs. Holladay?"

"Or you," Notley Ann shot back, "by your husband's arrogant stupidity?"

If she hoped to break through Janet Beauchamp's composure, she failed. A frigid little smile touched Janet's mouth. "My husband's arrogance is a well-known fact," she replied. "So also is his brilliance. Only you and the Army seem to lack the intelli-gence to recognize it."

She turned and looked straight at Marlin and said in a quiet, pleasant voice, "I am sure, Colonel, this has been as difficult for you as for my husband and me. We had looked forward to becoming better acquainted with you. Please feel free to call upon us at any time."

"Thank you, ma'am," Marlin replied. "With the Major's approval, I'd like to."

"By all means, Colonel," Beauchamp said. "Any differences you and I may have can be dealt with in a sane, reasonable manner. Janet?"

"Take me home, Stephen." Janet Beauchamp smiled. "I've had enough for one evening."

Her exit, on the arm of her husband, was as dramatic as had been Notley Ann's entrance—and it left Notley Ann's elaborate party in a shambles. Not all her skill nor the gourmet food and imported wines could salvage it.

"Ben!" Notley Ann's voice shrilled imperiously. "I've a terrible headache. I'm going to my room. See to it that everyone gets home. Good night, Mr. Marlin." Then ignoring her other guests, she swept from the room, leaving Holladay to try and soothe ruffled feelings.

Still angry from his clash with Beauchamp and fuming at Notley Ann's arrogance, Holladay was in no mood to apologize to anyone.

"All right," he snapped, "the party's over. You can all let yourselves out. I'm going to get damn good and drunk. Marlin, you want to stay and get drunk with me? Hell, a man hadn't ought to have to drink alone. Or had you rather do your drinking with Beauchamp? Officer and gentleman and all that!" An ugly note slipped into Holladay's voice. "As long as you're on my payroll, Marlin, you stay away from that bastard! You hear me?"

"I hear you," Marlin retorted. "Now you listen to me. Who I see socially is my business—and that includes the Beauchamps. Don't try pushing me around like one of your teamsters. I won't stand for it. Good night."

He looked back as he was closing the door. Ben Holladay was standing motionless, a champagne magnum in one hand, a glass in the other, the diamond stud in his shirt front blazing under the lights and contrasting with the brooding darkness of his face.

• • •

"Hey, Mr. Marlin!"

He slowed his pace, trying to locate the speaker in the freezing predawn. At six o'clock, it was still dark, with a pale, sickled moon riding low in the sky and yellow squares of lamp light framing restaurant, saloon, and hotel windows.

"Over here!" A man's voice called from the telegraph office across the street. "It's Jake Corning!"

Quickly, Marlin angled toward the telegraph office, a small, one-room building jammed between the Overland office and a mercantile store.

Corning, a gray-haired man in his mid-fifties, stepped back to let Marlin enter. The telegrapher's eyes were red-rimmed and sleepy and his narrow shoulders slumped from fatigue. He still had another hour to go before he would be free.

"Morning, Jake," Marlin said. "What's wrong?"

"A message just came through from Vernal that I think you ought to see," Corning answered. "Actually, it's for Major Beauchamp; but since it involves the Overland, I figure you're entitled to read it. Here." He handed Marlin the quick-scrawled message sheet.

Marlin scanned it with a single glance, noting that it was signed by James Reynolds, Sgt., 7th. Iowa Volunteers. It was brief and to the point. The two east-bound stages had been attacked, robbed, and burned by a war party of two hundred Cheyennes a hundred miles out. There was no Overland survivors. The eight-man cavalry escort had managed to break through and reach Vernal after a running battle in which one trooper had been killed. The Sergeant was bringing the detail back immediately and requested that a support column be dispatched to meet him.

Sixteen men, a gold shipment, and precious mail—gone; and the success of the westward run ruined by this tragic disaster. Conness and the newspapers would really have something to scream about this time!

Grim-faced, Marlin handed the message back to Jake Corning. "Write me out a copy of this, will you?" he said. "Holladay will want to see it. And you'd better notify Beauchamp right away."

"Sure." Corning sat down at his desk and scribbled out a duplicate copy. He handed it to Marlin with a worried frown. "When's all this killing going to stop anyway? Seems to me things are getting worse instead of better."

"I wish I knew," Marlin replied, pocketing the message. "Well, if anything else comes in, I'd appreciate it if you'd let me know."

Darkness had yielded to pale gray dawn when he stepped out into the street. Shadowy figures, heads bowed against an icy wind, hurried along the narrow walks, their footsteps crunching loudly in the silence. He wondered just how many of them realized that Julesburg might well be living out its last days. That any time now, a thousand Indians might sweep down upon the town—with no organized force to oppose them save the small garrison at Camp Rankin.

About to turn into the hotel for breakfast, he changed his mind and kept going. He had lost his appetite. The prospect of breaking this latest bad news to Holladay was not a pleasant one. He would have preferred that Slade do it, but he was not one to pass the buck.

A light was burning in the Overland office. Someone was already at work. He opened the door and went inside. The outer office was empty, but a light shone from beneath the door of the inner office. He knocked.

"Come in!"

Seated behind his big desk, Ben Holladay glanced up from beneath bushy eyebrows as Marlin entered. His face was haggard, drawn with tension. Leaning back in his chair, he drummed impatiently on the desk top with blunt fingers.

"Where in the hell are Slade and Ashley?" he demanded. "We're not going to get anything done sitting on our asses."

"It's not seven o'clock," Marlin reminded him. "They'll be along."

"Well, what did you want to see me about?"

Silently, Marlin handed him the copy of the telegram. Holladay read it. For a moment, he sat perfectly still, his heavy jaw ridging, the color rising to his face. Then crumpling the message into a tight ball, he hurled it to the floor.

"Forty thousand dollars, the mail, and sixteen men lost!" He slammed his big fist savagely down on the desk top. "Goddammit, I brought three stages all the way from Atchinson through country swarming with hostiles—and me with only twenty men—and never lost a scalp! Now you tell me why sixteen heavily armed men, including a cavalry escort, can't push *two* stages through a *hundred* miles without being wiped out! That's the damned cavalry for you, Colonel!"

"For one thing," Marlin pointed out, "you *did* have three coaches; and the Sioux had no idea how many more men you might have inside. For another, you weren't carrying a gold shipment and coast-to-coast mail. And, finally, you were just plain lucky.

"As for the 'damned cavalry' . . . ," Marlin's voice sharpened. "You've been yelling for cavalry escorts for weeks. Now that Beauchamp's providing them—or some, at least—you ought to be satisfied."

"By God, I'll never be satisfied until—" Holladay broke off, his eyes narrowing. "How'd the Sioux know those stages were carrying gold and mail unless—the Reb?"

Marlin nodded. "Probably."

"Then find the son of a bitch!" Holladay cried.

"That's what I'm paying you for." He rose, took his heavy coat off the wall rack and shrugged into it.

Marlin's mouth tightened. "I'm doing the best I can," he retorted. "If that's not enough to suit you, then maybe you had better find someone else."

It was the first time they had clashed head on; and it was Holladay who backed down. "Sorry," he said. "All this pressure is beginning to get to me." As he headed for the door, Marlin called after him.

"Where will you be if anything comes up?"

Holladay swung a grim face toward him. "Those bucks that hit the Crow Junction station may still be around. They owe me sixteen scalps. I intend to try and collect. If anything comes up you can't handle, see Slade."

A half hour later, Marlin watched Holladay lead his heavily armed "war party" out of town. As they rode past, Sergeant Bender spotted Marlin in the doorway and raised a hand in unsmiling salute.

Sight of the Sergeant reminded Marlin of his need to inform Beauchamp of his plans. Having already met Beauchamp, he now felt reasonably certain of the Major's co-operation.

Not until Marlin had locked the office and was halfway to the livery stable did he realize that it was only seven-thirty. He would wait a couple of hours before riding out to Camp Rankin. Meanwhile, he might as well have breakfast.

• • •

At the hotel, a remote Susan Ashley served him in hurt silence; and he could think of nothing to say that might reassure her. The dining room was well filled; but he saw no sign of Slade, Ashley, or Jules Reni.

The Frenchman's absence worried him. He had spent several hours the previous day sampling small talk in saloons, stores, freightyards, and corrals, hoping that a carelessly dropped word might give him a clue to the Reb spy's identity. Or, at least, to Reni's activities. He had drawn a blank.

However, he had sensed a vague unrest, a hostile expectancy in the Wagon Wheel Saloon and around the freight yards—as though the town's toughs were waiting for something to happen.

Now the unease which he had felt then still troubled him. Was Jules Reni gathering a group of outlaw friends for a showdown with Slade? If so, then Slade should be warned; but then he realized that Slade sensed danger like an animal, instinctively and from afar.

Marlin ate slowly, his appetite dulled by a growing frustration. There were so many paths crossing and recrossing one another that he could not tell which might lead him to the Confederate.

For instance, how many of the raids upon stages and way stations were Indian, and how many were faked by white outlaw bands? How many of these cutthroat killers did Jules Reni control? Was the Frenchman simply a renegade outlaw—or was he a working part of a Southern conspiracy? Was it Reni who was providing the Reb spy with inside information about stagecoach schedules, gold shipments, and special mail runs?

If there was a connection, then he had to find it. So far, Jules Reni was his one likely lead to the Reb. It might be wise to keep a close check on the Frenchman's movements in the future.

"Morning, Kurt." Emma Ashley paused beside him, coffee pot in one hand. "More coffee?"

"No, thanks, Emma." He was in no mood for conversation; and he could tell from her manner that she had something on her mind. "I've got to ride out to Camp Rankin."

Emma Ashley hesitated, her round, pleasant face worried. "Kurt, maybe it's none of my business, but what's come between you and Susan? For a while, I thought that . . . Is it Virginia Slade?"

Wiping his mouth on his napkin, Marlin rose. For a moment, he looked at Emma in smiling silence. Then he said gently, "No, Emma, it isn't Virginia Slade, although Susan seems convinced it is. And when Susan makes up her mind about something, it's hard to change. But don't worry. Things will work out. It will just take a while."

He left Emma Ashley standing there, coffee pot poised in midair, her face mirroring her pleased relief.

Outside, he stood in the bitter cold air, debating whether to wait a while longer before riding out to the fort. Beauchamp would probably be tied up for at least another couple of hours. And the Major would expect a fellow West Pointer to know and respect that.

Suddenly, Marlin thought of Hamlin Weatherby. The artist must have met a lot of people, white and Indian, out there on the Plains. If he knew anything, there was no reason why he shouldn't be willing to talk. After all, he owed the Overland a favor for helping him with his stagecoach series for *Harper's Magazine.*

Buttoning up his coat, Marlin headed for the livery stable. Shortly before nine o'clock, he rode out of town with a bone-chilling wind at his back.

Nestling among a thick stand of spruce a half mile from Camp Rankin, Hamlin Weatherby's cabin was almost invisible from the road. Had Weatherby, chopping wood in the small clearing, not spotted him, Marlin would have missed it.

As he dismounted and flipped the reins over a pole hitch rack, Weatherby propped his ax against a tree and came forward to meet him.

"I was wondering when you would drop by," Weatherby said, shaking hands. "Come on inside."

In the main room, Weatherby expertly shifted the logs in the great stone fireplace. Bright flames leaped up, throwing a warm glow over the bearskin rugs, the hand-made couch with its Navajo blanket cover, the trophy-studded walls: quilled-and-beaded Sioux pad saddle, seven-foot Sioux war bonnet, Cheyenne lance, Arapaho feather-rimmed shield, Comanche woman's doeskin dress, a hooped scalp, the thick black hair flowing down the wall like dark water. And everywhere, Hamlin Weatherby's paintings of frontier life.

Near the east window, Marlin spotted an easel with a nearly finished canvas of a stagecoach under attack, with a detail of cavalry defending it in a dramatic running battle with Sioux. Walking over to the easel, he studied the painting with a critical interest. Although no expert, he knew enough to recognize that Hamlin Weatherby was a fine artist. Composition, brush stroke, color, and an amazing knowledge of subject matter all came together with dramatic, impelling force.

"Well"—Weatherby came over and handed him a drink—"what do you think of it?"

"It's powerful," Marlin said. "I don't think I've ever felt so much hate coming straight at me. That chief, for instance . . . Who is he?"

"Tashunko Witko," Weatherby replied. "Crazy Horse. Probably the greatest military strategist the Plains Indians have ever produced. The one next to him is Makpiya Luta, Red Cloud, War Chief of the Seven Tribes. And just behind and to the left of him is Napka Kesela, Iron Plume, wearing his famous seven-foot war bonnet. We call him American Horse."

Thoughtfully, Marlin continued to study the canvas. "Do the Indians really hate us that much?"

"They fear us as we fear them," Weatherby answered. "And, like us, they hate what they fear. The only way they can erase that fear is to drive the white man off the Central Plains . . . or die. And, of course, they will die. Some in battle; some like sheep on reservations. A few will adapt to the white man's ways—and live to wish they had died as warriors."

"Somehow"—an inner frustration nagged at Marlin—"it just doesn't seem right. There ought to be some other way." He was conscious of the artist's amused expression—amused and cynical.

"My friend, there's no such thing as right and wrong in the jungle," Weatherby said. "It's simply a case of kill or be killed. And the world *is* a jungle, with man the worst killer ape in it." He finished his drink, put down his glass, and returned to the fireplace.

With a last look at the canvas, Marlin followed. Resting his arm on the mantel, he swept the trophy-studded walls with appreciative eyes.

"You must have gotten to know the Sioux, Cheyenne, and Arapaho pretty well before this uprising broke out," he said. "Tell me, did you ever hear any rumors of any of them aligning themselves with the Confederacy? Or run across a trader who might have been a Confederate spy?"

Weatherby threw him a quick, sharp glance. "I knew many of the chiefs," he admitted. "Crazy Horse, Red Cloud, Iron Plume, Spotted Tail, Gall, Gray Bull, Chewing Black Bone. But I was never invited to sit at their council fires. Nor have I ever heard any rumors of the tribes joining up with the Confederacy.

"As for traders . . . There are always traders around. Some sell the tribes liquor, maybe even a few guns. But I doubt that any of them is a Confederate agent." His eyes rested on Marlin thoughtfully. "Why do you ask?"

Marlin shrugged. "I've heard rumors that the South is involved in this Indian uprising. Do you believe there's any truth to that?"

The artist straightened, and Marlin could feel the man's inner coldness surfacing. But when Weatherby answered, his voice was as impersonal as ever.

"There are many, including Holladay, General Ingalls, and perhaps even the President himself, who are convinced of it. Others, including my son-in-law, Major Beauchamp, believe that these attacks on the Overland are faked to cover up Holladay's pillaging of U.S. mail and gold shipments."

Idly rubbing his brandy glass with his hand, Marlin pressed his point. "Why would Holladay rob his own stages?"

"To cover up his losses from real Indian raids," Weatherby said. "It's a known fact that those losses are staggering. And if, on top of that, the Overland's mail contracts are canceled, he could go broke." Weatherby shrugged. "Anyway, that's Beauchamp's reasoning."

"And do you agree with the Major?" Marlin asked. "I mean that Holladay is no better than a murdering renegade?"

"No." Weatherby's expression altered subtly. "But then there are few things we do agree upon. The Major is an arrogant, headstrong man who tends to act first and reason later. He resents authority and shows it. The Army won't tolerate insubordination. That's why the War Department has forgotten him. His career is finished and he knows it."

Almost the same words, Marlin thought, as those used by Virginia Slade. And it brought up another question. "I can understand why the Major might hate top Army brass," he said. "But why does he hate the Overland. I get the idea that he'd like to see it wiped out completely."

For a moment, Weatherby hesitated, seeming to ponder the question. "Beauchamp doesn't really hate the Overland," he said. "He hates Holladay, as he hates all men who remind him of his own failures."

"Is that why the Major has refused to furnish the cavalry escorts the President has ordered for the Overland?"

A hot coal exploded on the hearth, sending a shower of sparks flying through the air. Bending, Weatherby shifted a sputtering log. "I'd say it has a good deal to do with it," he said slowly. "Stephen Beauchamp's a complex man. He hates those with power; yet he craves power himself more than anyone I've ever known.

"Take this matter of escorts for the Overland. It's tied in with Beauchamp's sense of frustration. Ben Holladay is a crude, rude, and tremendously successful man. The Major is a cultured, brilliant failure." Straightening, Weatherby regarded Marlin with a thin, humorless smile.

"Yet powerful as Holladay is, the Major, for the moment, has him over the barrel. Without cavalry escorts, the Overland could well be destroyed—and Holladay along with it. Of course, the Major knows that, sooner or later, he'll have to co-operate—or Holladay will see to it that he's relieved of his command here and court-martialed.

"But for the moment"—Weatherby laid a heavy emphasis upon the words—"Stephen Beauchamp is in the saddle, so to speak, and he's making the most of it. It's good for his ego—especially after the way Holladay humiliated him at that party. That's made him even more stubborn."

"I can understand Major Beauchamp's resentment," Marlin said. "Holladay lost his temper and acted like a teamster. But as an Army officer, the

Major is endangering not only the Overland, but the war effort itself. It's vitally important that the Union's link with the West be maintained. I'm sure he's well aware of the consequences to himself if he refuses to co-operate."

A shadow darkened Weatherby's eyes and the thin lips tightened. "Stephen Beauchamp does not think in terms of consequences," he said tersely. "It's a fault I tried to point out to my daughter when she married him in '61. But she has a mind of her own. For a while, I thought things might work out for them. But after the first year, I don't think Janet ever had any illusions.

"When Beauchamp was transferred out here, she begged me to follow. There was nothing to hold me back. I knew that even if the Confederacy survived, the South would be ruined economically. If it lost, I wanted no part of a Yankee dominated land. So in March of '62, I came out here." Weatherby leaned back, laying his arm on the mantel. His mood suddenly became introspective.

"You know, Marlin, this country shapes a man to fit it. If it can't, it rejects him. Stephen Beauchamp is an exception. The country can't shape him and, because of the Army, it can't reject him. These past three years have been hell for both him and Janet. Knowing they have nothing to look forward to except more of the same. Can you blame him for being bitter?"

"I think we all tend to create our own hells," Marlin said, not unfeelingly. "Major Beauchamp seems to be no exception. But I can understand what it must be like for such a man to be isolated out here."

Putting down his glass, he slipped into his heavy wolfskin coat. "Thanks for the drink and the chance to see your work. Frankly, I'm impressed. You are a fine artist. Tell me—what were you before you decided to turn professional?"

"Why, you might say I was a Southern gentleman," Weatherby smiled easily. "That's another way of saying I was a Mississippi planter. Until one night when them damn niggers of mine decided they weren't going to wait for Lincoln to free them and set fire to the house, the outbuildings, the stables, the fields . . . the whole plantation . . . and then scattered to hell and gone. It wiped me out completely. That's when I began painting for money instead of pleasure." His smile widened; his whole face assumed an amused, cynical expression.

"Now you're going to ask me if I don't miss the old life. The white pillared mansion, the scent of magnolias, the mint juleps, the fox hunts, cotillions, politics, gambling, beautiful women . . .

"Do you know what all that added up to? Nothing! Until I was fifty years old, I sat on my ass and let a bunch of buck niggers make a living for me while I pretended it was all my doing. Hell, if it hadn't been for them, I'd have been a whitetrash-poor 'gentleman' . . . along with every other planter in the South. I knew it and they knew it and, underneath their fear, they despised me, and I sensed it and hated them for their contempt. By the time I was thirty, I'd lost all self-respect without even realizing it. I was a wealthy, powerful parasite. And then, suddenly, I was nothing.

"Now look at me." Weatherby moved so that he stood within the warm circle of firelight. An erect figure with quick, cold eyes, radiating health and a ruthless self-confidence. "I'm fifty-three years old. I feel thirty. I haven't been sick a day in the past three years. Financially . . ." He laughed as though at some secret joke.

"Do you know that some of my work brings as high as two thousand dollars? Last year, I sold twenty-eight paintings. But it's not the money; it's the power to stir people's emotions, to shape their thinking and their actions that—" He broke off, something dark and cruel and hungry trapped behind his eyes. "You should have asked me what I am, Marlin, not what I was. It would have saved time."

In the firelight, their glances locked and held. "Yes," Marlin said slowly. "Yes, it would have." He opened the door and stepped outside. "If you learn anything, I'd appreciate it if you'd let me know."

It was late afternoon when he rode out of the clearing and headed back toward Julesburg. He was still half a mile away, when he heard the blast of a shotgun and then a fusillade of pistol shots.

Grimly, he put spurs to the bay.

Pushed along by a brisk wind, he raced into town under a leaden gray sky and along a deserted street, the bay's hoofs pounding loudly in the unnatural silence. As he swung around a Conestoga in front of the hotel, he caught sight of the crowd gathered in front of the Overland office and knew that Jules Reni had called Slade's hand.

Dismounting, he looped the reins over the hitch rack and pushed his way through the silent crowd. Ed Ashley, his face pale, his expression grim, stepped out of the office to meet him.

"Slade?" Marlin asked.

Ashley nodded.

"How did it happen?"

"Just like I was afraid it would," Ashley said. "Reni got the drop on Slade from behind and then shot him down. Buckshot and five pistol bullets. I don't know why it didn't kill him instantly."

"Then Slade's still alive?" Some of the tension eased out of Marlin.

"Barely," Ashley replied. "Doc Lindley's delivering a baby; but, thank God, Captain Bowers happened to be in town. He's doing what he can."

"Have you sent for Virginia?"

"She's in the back office with Hank Monk and Bob Ridley," Ashley informed him. "And threatening to go after Reni herself."

"I'll talk to her," Marlin said, moving toward the office, "as soon as I check on Slade."

The crowd, which had now doubled in size, parted to let him through. Followed by Ashley, he entered the outer office and then stopped, his eyes adjusting to the light.

Jack Slade lay sprawled on his back on top of the baggage counter, blood spattering the floor around him. An Army surgeon's mate stood by, watching, as Captain Bowers worked over the wounded man. Without looking up, Bowers said, "I'll be through here in a minute."

"Fine." Marlin turned to Ashley. "You'd better wire Crow Junction and see if they can't get hold of Holladay."

"I've already done that," Ashley assured him. "They will have scouts out hunting for him in an hour."

"Good." Swinging his attention back to Bowers, Marlin asked, "Well, Captain?"

Carefully, Bowers wiped his hands on a piece of clean sheeting and closed his medicine bag. "He needs surgery. If he can survive the trip to Denver, he might have a chance. I won't guarantee it though."

Marlin cast a dubious glance at Slade's bloody

figure. "Can he make it to Denver in his condition?"

"Frankly, I don't know." The Captain's shoulders lifted. "But if he stays here, he'll die. I can guarantee that."

For a moment, Marlin hesitated. "Will you make the trip with him?"

"Sorry." Bowers handed his bag to the surgeon's mate. "It's a civilian matter. But I've sent for Dr. Lindley. He's a good man. If you want to risk it, I'm sure he'll go." He stood looking at Marlin, waiting for the answer; and Marlin, feeling the weight of Slade's life bearing down upon him, could not escape the decision.

"Ed"—he turned abruptly—"I want a stage and an escort ready to move out in half an hour. Meanwhile, I'll talk to Virginia."

"Kurt, I don't know." Ed Ashley shook his head skeptically. "With a bad storm moving in and having to travel at night, a broken wheel or a downed horse and . . . But it's up to you." He pursed his lips. "We can't count on the cavalry, so I'll have to round up a volunteer escort. Give me forty-five minutes."

"Half an hour," Marlin said relentlessly, not telling Ashley that now they *could* count on the cavalry, but they could not wait that long. As Ashley hurried out, Bowers said, "You want me to stay here, Marlin, until Lindley arrives?"

"I'd appreciate that," Marlin said and stepped

around the baggage counter and entered the rear office.

"Oh, Kurt!" Virginia Slade brushed past Hank Monk and Bob Ridley and ran to him. "That son of a bitch Reni shot Jack down like a dog!" she cried. "So help me, Kurt, I'll kill that bastard! I'll kill him! I'll . . . Oh, damn!" She laid her head on Marlin's shoulder and cried quietly because tears did not come easy for her. "How is Jack?"

Marlin did not lie to her; she would have hated him for it when she found out. "We're sending him to Denver for surgery, Virginia. He may die en route; but if he makes it, he has a fighting chance."

She lifted an anguished face to Marlin. "Are you going with him?"

"No," Marlin said. "I've got to deal with the situation here. But Dr. Lindley's making the trip." He searched her face intently. "What about you? There's a storm coming in. If it catches up with you, you could all die."

Virginia Slade's chin came up and her eyes met his steadily. "Do you think I'd let him die alone? I thought you knew me better than that."

"I'm sorry." Gently, Marlin pushed her toward the door. "If you're going, you'd better hurry. You haven't got much time."

As soon as she was gone, he turned to Bob Ridley and Hank Monk. "I want fifty of the best men in that crowd out there, rifle- and pistol-

163

armed," he said. "As soon as that stage leaves, I'm going after Reni! Now move!"

The alacrity with which they obeyed sobered him. He knew why . . . the bold decision, the sharpness of voice, the quick, no-nonsense authority. . . . In moments of crisis, he was still a cavalry officer, and it came through to men.

By the time Marlin reached the street, a stage with a bedded-down interior was drawn up before the door, along with a dozen sharp-shooting scouts for the journey. Dr. Lindley, tall, handsome, gray-haired, nodded to him but did not speak.

As they placed Slade inside the stage, he opened his eyes and glared up at Marlin with fierce, pain-glazed eyes. "You tell that bastard Reni I'll have his ears for this!" he whispered. "You hear me, Marlin? *I'll have the bastard's ears!*" Then he lapsed into unconsciousness.

Closing the stage door, Marlin leaned on the open window frame and looked questioningly at Virginia Slade. Her face was very pale; her manner was composed. Yet he could sense the tension inside her.

"Are you all right, Virginia?"

Her eyes met his, held a moment, and then the tears came, running down her face like slanting rain. Still, she did not break. "I'm all right," she said. "I'll wire you when we reach Denver. Meanwhile, be careful, Kurt. Reni's a dangerous man. *Please, for me.*"

"I will," Marlin reassured her. Then stepping back, he waved to the driver. "Get going!"

The jehu laid the foot-long popper near the high leader's ears. The team surged against their collars; the big wheels began to turn. The crowd watched silently as the coach spun out of town, Denver bound.

Studying the fast-rising bank of slate-gray clouds rolling in from the northwest, Marlin sniffed the air and shook his head. "Snow," he said to Ed Ashley. "Maybe a blizzard."

"It might keep the Sioux in their tipis," Ashley replied, trying to be optimistic.

"Don't count on it." Marlin stood there in the middle of the street, thinking—not of the Sioux, but of the consequences of Jules Reni's swift, savage action. In a single, bloody moment of gunfire, the Frenchman had removed the one immediate threat to his power in Julesburg. Even if Slade lived, he would be out of action for weeks; and by the time he returned, Reni's hold on the town might be too strong to break.

That Ben Holladay, when he returned, would take swift retaliatory action was certain. But whether he could drive out a well-organized, firmly entrenched Reni-led bunch of killers and renegades without Slade's help was doubtful. Slade's own strategy had been to handle Reni on a personal, man-to-man level, confident that his gun speed would resolve the problem. His confidence had almost gotten him killed. He had thought Reni would run. The Frenchman had outwitted him. Now Reni was in a position to force Holladay's hand.

It was a bad situation, Marlin thought. For Holladay, a rough, tough, fearless man, was a leader, a man who gave orders rather than carried them out. In a stand-up, knock-down and drag-out fight, he would kill Reni; in a middle-of-the-street showdown, such as Slade had counted on, he might even outdraw the Frenchman. But Reni was no fool. Having downed one of the most dangerous men in the West, he now had the solid backing of every outlaw in Julesburg. He didn't have to confront anyone and risk losing. All he had to do was stand pat and make the Overland come to him.

Grimly, Marlin walked toward the growing crowd, sensing the tension mounting in them. The sight of Slade being loaded into the stagecoach, bloody and maybe dying, had aroused them to an ugly pitch. They needed only leadership to set them off; and he knew that they were looking to him for that leadership.

Standing in front of the crowd, Bob Ridley, Hank Monk, and some fifty or sixty heavily armed teamsters and scouts waited expectantly. Marlin stopped and looked at Ridley.

"Where's Reni holed up, Bob?"

"Down at the Wagon Wheel," Ridley said

tersely. "Him an' forty or fifty others. All hardcases."

Marlin frowned. "You think they'll stand with Reni in a showdown?"

The jehu shrugged. "I don't know," he said. "If they see that they're outnumbered and that you mean business, they might back down."

A damp, freshening wind laid against Marlin's face, reminding him of the impending storm. If it hit before the scouts from Crow Junction found Holladay, the Overland chief might not return for several days. The situation here could not wait that long; it had to be met head on, and now.

"Well, there's only one way to find out." Marlin looked at Ridley and the grim-faced men around him. "Come on. Let's go."

Fanning out across the street, the group moved forward, the crunch of snow-ice beneath their boots loud and ominous in the winter silence. At the far end of the block, a lone figure in front of the Wagon Wheel turned and ran back inside. By the time they had gone fifty yards, the street was deserted save for a score of horses standing hipshot at the Wagon Wheel's hitch rack.

Flanked by Ridley, Monk, and Ed Ashley, Marlin halted in front of the Wagon Wheel. Signaling his men to take cover, he shouted, "Reni, come out with your hands up and I'll guarantee you a fair jury trial. If you don't, I'm coming—"

Window glass shattered and a bullet whined past his head. He dived for cover as a second bullet pocked the hard frozen ground where he had stood.

"You go to hell!" Reni yelled. "I'll give you what I gave that bastard Slade!"

"Hold your fire!" Marlin shouted to his men, whose rifles were zeroed in on the Wagon Wheel. "Reni, you've got five minutes. If you're not out by then, we're going to burn you out."

No answer.

Crouched in the shelter of the commissary, Marlin waited while the minutes sand-glassed away and fine, powdery snow drifted in on the wind.

"Marlin!" A man shouted from the Wagon Wheel. "I don't want my place ruined. Suppose we turn Reni over to you. What about the rest of us?"

"Is that you, Cochran?"

"Yes."

"You can stay if you want to," Marlin called back. "The rest of you in there will have one hour to get out of town. If you're not, we'll pick you off one at a time."

"Jesus Christ!" a strange voice cried. "There's a storm moving in!"

"If you ride fast," Marlin retorted, "you can keep ahead of it."

Silence again, with the cold beginning to seep

into Marlin's body, sending shivers up and down his spine, numbing his hand around the butt of the Navy Colt.

"Okay!" Cochran shouted. "Hold your fire! We're coming out."

Yelling, cursing, a pistol shot—-and then Jules Reni came hurtling through the door, propelled by half a dozen tough-featured characters, with a dense press of figures behind them.

"You chicken-livered bastards!" Reni, big, tough, and mean even now, turned an enraged face toward his friends. "We could have taken them in a showdown! An' then we could have run this town our way, like we've been doing!"

"Sure, you could have," Cochran retorted. "Take a look around you." He jerked his head toward the riflemen stationed on rooftops, at store windows, and in the alley across the street . . . then at the angry crowd closing in from all sides. "You could have got us all killed."

Swinging his head from side to side, Reni began to back away. "Stay away from me, you sons of bitches!" he yelled, "or I'll . . ."

He struck out savagely as the Overland men came at him in a swift, silent rush. Bloody-faced and still fighting, he was hustled to the nearest tree. A rope swished over a branch. A noose dropped around his neck.

"Hoist him!" a man shouted and began to haul on the rope. Quickly, other hands took hold and

Reni rose up on his toes, screaming and cursing with fear.

"Hold it!" Marlin shoved his way through the press of bodies. "There'll be no lynching."

The men on the rope turned angry faces toward him. Most of them had suffered humiliation and abuse at Jules Reni's hands and were in no mood now to be cheated of revenge.

"Hell," a teamster protested, "the bastard has it coming to him!"

"That's for a jury to decide," Marlin snapped. "Now take off that rope."

They hesitated, sullen, defiant; then slowly they eased off on the rope, letting Reni come down flat-footed on the ground. Still, no one made a move to remove the noose from the now terrified Frenchman's neck.

In the growing silence, Marlin sensed the tension building in the crowd and knew that the situation was dangerously explosive. These were men with just, long-standing grievances. To stand between them and a back-shooting degenerate like Jules Reni . . .

The rapid pounds of hoofs upon the frozen ground shredded the silence. Turning, Marlin watched as the rocketing stagecoach bore down upon the crowd. At the last minute, the driver brought team and stage to a skidding halt. A man jumped out and walked quickly toward Marlin. He stopped, took in the situation with a single glance and then said, "I'm Ben Ficklin, route superintendent for the Overland. Who the hell are you—and what's going on here?"

"I'm the division's trouble-shooter," Marlin answered. "This man, Reni, backshot Jack Slade. The crowd wants to hang Reni."

Ficklin swore fervently. "Is Slade dead?"

"No," Marlin replied. "But he may die. I sent him to Denver with a doctor aboard about half an hour ago."

"Then what are you waiting for?" Ficklin demanded. He wheeled toward the men on the rope. "String the bastard up!"

"Wait!" Marlin protested. "Reni has a right to a fair trial."

"He has a right to nothing!" Ficklin snapped. "You ever hear of Overland Law?"

"I've heard of it." Succinctly. "I don't like it."

"It works." A hard-bitten, practical man, Ben Ficklin walked over to Jules Reni. "You damn renegade," he said softly. "I sentence you to be hanged forthwith for the attempted, if not actual, murder of Jack Slade—and for other known acts of murder, theft, and violence against the Overland and the Union during time of war."

His eyes challenged the gathering crowd of Reni sympathizers—known and suspected outlaws, cutthroats, gamblers, and horse thieves— daring them to make a move.

"All right!" Ficklin motioned to the men on the rope. "Up with him!"

As Reni was hoisted up, struggling and kicking, the outlaw crowd surged forward in a wild melee of swinging fists and clubbed guns. Breaking through the ring of Overland men, they cut the purple-faced Frenchman down.

But they had underestimated Ficklin, a stubborn, relentless man. Three times, he ordered the screaming, cursing Frenchman strung up. Three times, Jules Reni swung and twisted against the leaden sky, eyes popping, tongue protruding. And three times, the outlaws battled savagely to cut him down.

Stationed on rooftops, at store windows, and in the alleys, Marlin's men watched helplessly, unable to fire for fear of hitting friends in the struggling mass.

It ended in a Mexican standoff.

With the two factions, battered and bloody-faced, squared off ten feet apart, Ficklin called a halt.

"All right," he cried. "Let the bastard go. He's through in Julesburg."

Casting off the noose, Jules Reni stood spraddle-legged, greedily sucking air into his tortured lungs. "You didn't do it, Ficklin. Marlin had us whipped before you even drove up! But I'll remember this—and one of these days, I'll get you just like I did Slade!"

The route superintendent's lips thinned white. "You listen to me, Reni, and listen well." He brought his face within inches of the Frenchman's. "Get on your horse and ride—and keep on riding right out of the Territory. Beginning tomorrow, you're fair game for any Overland man who spots you. The rest of you, too. You've got ten minutes to clear out."

Marlin pushed his way through the crowd. "I promised them an hour, Ficklin."

Slowly, Ficklin turned, his eyes holding steady. "You interfere one more time, Marlin," he said harshly, "and you're fired. I don't like the way you were handling things when I drove up."

"And I don't like the way you've handled the situation since then," Marlin retorted. "I don't think Holladay will either when he hears how you backed down from a showdown you created. Go ahead—make your complaint."

"By God, I will!" Ficklin cried in a voice thick with anger. "But, meanwhile, I'm not going to stand around here arguing with you." Hauling out a big silver watch, he looked at it, and then at Jules Reni.

"Nine minutes," he said inflexibly. "You'd better make the most of them."

For a moment, Reni glared at Ficklin, hating him in silent frustration. Then, walking unsteadily to the hitch rack, the Frenchman mounted and reined away. Swinging aboard their horses, the outlaw faction followed. At the far end of the street, Reni turned in his saddle and shook his fist in a defiant gesture. Then the band put their horses to the gallop, with the fast-closing storm already beginning to chase them.

Ignoring Marlin, Ben Ficklin walked over to Ed Ashley. "I've got business further down the line," he said. "Tell Holladay I was here—and that I'll give him a full account of what happened when I get back."

He walked briskly to his coach, climbed inside and, a moment later, the jehu's whip cracked and the stage spun away in a spray of muddy slush.

Holstering his gun, Marlin motioned to Ed Ashley and, together, they walked back to the office through the silent crowd, feeling the dissatisfaction, the angry frustration of these men who felt that they had been cheated of justice.

And to the extent that Jules Reni had escaped scot free, Marlin agreed that their anger was justified. Unfortunately, Ben Ficklin had stubbornly refused to settle for a fair trial. He had insisted upon enforcing lynch law and, having failed, had ended up with no justice at all.

Realistically, however, Marlin thought, even if Ficklin had not intervened, he, himself, would probably have fared no better in handling the situation. True, he and Ficklin had run Jules Reni out of town; but now the Frenchman would simply hole up in the mountains and, from there,

174

openly launch raids upon Overland stages. It was like putting out a fire in one place, only to have it break out in another.

Inside, Marlin watched through the steam-dimmed window as the crowd slowly dispersed—and knew that, for the moment at least, Julesburg's confidence in him had been shaken. Perhaps not so much as in Ben Ficklin, but shaken, nonetheless.

"Colonel Marlin!"

A fist pounding heavily upon the door snapped Marlin awake. He threw back the covers and sat up on the edge of the bed. Faint star sheen outlined the window looking out upon the street.

"Colonel! Wake up!"

"Who is it?" he called. "And what do you want?"

"Sergeant Brill, sir! Cap'n Bowers wants you out at the post right away, sir. He said to tell you it's damned important."

Hastily slipping into his trousers, Marlin opened the door. "Come in." Then as Brill, a square-jawed, solidly built man in his forties, entered: "What's happened?"

The Sergeant shrugged. "All I know, sir, is that a bunch of Cheyennes ambushed those east-bound stages you sent out yesterday. And that Sergeant Reynolds and the rest of his detail have got more bullet holes in their uniforms than Swiss cheese."

Stuffing his shirt into his pants, Marlin slipped into his heavy coat and stepped out into the hall. "Let's go, Sergeant." Quickly, he led the way down the stairs, through the deserted lobby, and out into the night.

Dawn was still an hour away when he and the Sergeant rode into Camp Rankin. Lights burned in the headquarters building and in the hospital. A small group of troopers gathered before the hospital parted silently to let them through.

"Where's Sergeant Reynolds?" Brill asked.

"In a huddle with the Major," a trooper replied. "Been there ever since the detail rode in."

"Cap'n Bowers still inside?"

"Yep."

Down the narrow hall, Brill stopped and knocked on a door on his right. "Sergeant Brill, sir. I have Colonel Marlin with me."

Bowers, a *big,* broad-shouldered man of thirty-five with a magnificent red mustache and a ruddy face, opened the door. He nodded to Brill. "That will be all, Sergeant."

Brill saluted and walked away.

"Come in, Colonel," Bowers said. "Sorry to have gotten you out of bed at this ungodly hour; but there's something I think you should know." Closing the door, he motioned across the room. "That's why I sent for you."

Marlin walked over and looked down at the corpse on the examining table. *Not even old enough to grow a beard.* He turned to Bowers with an inquiring frown.

"One of the escort detail?"

The Captain nodded. "Sergeant Reynolds reported him as being killed in a running battle with Cheyennes. The Sergeant's a liar." Bowers rolled the body over. "See those powder burns? This man was murdered—shot in the back at point-blank range with a pistol."

Marlin threw him a sharp glance. "Why would Reynolds want to kill one of his own men?"

"To keep him from talking."

"About what?"

Covering the corpse, Bowers raised his eyes and looked steadily at Marlin. "About the Confederate conspiracy the President sent you here to uncover, Colonel."

"So I *did* talk when I was delirious from that Sioux wound," Marlin said quietly, trying to hide his chagrin. "Who else knows—the Ashleys, Virginia Slade?"

"I don't think so," Bowers told him. "If they did, I'm sure they'd have mentioned it. The Ashleys, anyway. Have you told the Major?"

"The day before I left for Salt Lake," Marlin said. He tilted his head toward the dead trooper. "You really believe he knew something?"

"He had to."

"Then why . . . ?"

Bowers shrugged. "Maybe he was scared.

Maybe his conscience was bothering him. Hell, I don't know. Why don't you wring the truth out of Reynolds? He's in the Major's office now, giving his report."

"Thanks," Marlin said. "Have you informed the Major of this?"

"Not yet," Bowers answered. "I thought I should talk to you first."

"I appreciate that." Marlin opened the door. "It may be the break I've been waiting for."

He went down the hall, past the troopers still waiting outside, and across the parade ground to the headquarters building. A light burned in Beauchamp's office. He knocked and then, without waiting for an answer, went inside.

Seated at his desk, Beauchamp turned a harried face toward his visitor. Obviously routed out of bed without advance notice, his uniform was only half-buttoned, his hair uncombed, and a dark stubble of beard covered his chin.

Standing "at ease" before the Major, Sergeant Reynolds threw Marlin a cold stare. His face was flushed, sullen; he had clearly been in the process of being raked over the coals.

"Good morning, Colonel." Without rising, Beauchamp nodded a weary greeting. "It appears that bad news travels fast." He dismissed Reynolds with a curt gesture. "I'll talk more with you later, Sergeant."

"If you don't mind, Major," Marlin spoke quickly. "I would like a few words with him first."

Halfway to the door, Reynolds paused, his face suddenly guarded. He looked toward Beauchamp for orders.

"You'd better stay, Sergeant."

Walking over to the fireplace, Marlin placed an arm on the mantel and laid a hard glance on Reynolds.

"I just came from the hospital, Sergeant," he said. "It seems that you and Captain Bowers disagree on how trooper Howard died."

An invisible ramrod stiffened Reynolds' back. Although he kept his voice carefully respectful, it did not completely conceal the insolence behind his words.

"Since I personally witnessed Howard's death, Colonel," he replied, "I think I'm the best authority on how it happened. No disrespect to the Captain, sir."

"Then suppose you tell me, Sergeant," Marlin said evenly. "Just how it *did* happen."

Anger burned in the NCO's eyes. He squared his shoulders, his face taking on a rigid set. He half-turned to Beauchamp, seeking support.

"Sir, I've already given you the details," he protested. "I don't see why I have to—"

"Answer the Colonel," Beauchamp ordered curtly.

"Yes, sir!" The words came out through

clenched teeth. "Those Cheyennes came at us out of nowhere. It was all over in ten minutes. With the stage crews dead, our only chance was to make a run for it. Somehow, we broke through and got the hell out of there. We'd put a couple of hundred yards between us and them hostiles when Howard got it. He yelled and grabbed his horse's mane. Trooper Barnes fell back and gave him a hand. Howard died a couple of miles out of Vernal. That's it, sir."

"Let me get this straight," Marlin said carefully. "You say that Howard was shot at a distance of two hundred yards by a Cheyenne?"

"That's right, sir."

"Then how do you explain Captain Bowers' medical report stating that Howard was shot in the back at point-blank range with a pistol?"

The Sergeant's face became a wooden mask; he spoke through stiff lips. "The Captain is mistaken, sir."

"Is that all you have to say?"

"Yes, sir."

Beauchamp, who had been listening quietly, brought the front legs of his chair down with a sharp click.

"By God, Colonel," he cried, "I resent the way this matter's being handled. Why didn't Bowers report his findings to me instead of sending for you? I *am* commander of this fort and his superior officer."

It was a quick, explosive outburst, filled with the resentments of a man who felt his authority threatened. Sensing this, Marlin sought to soothe his ruffled ego.

"Bowers had no choice, Major. He'd uncovered evidence of a conspiracy which he knew I was here to investigate. It was his duty to see that I got that information immediately."

The Major started. "Bowers knew of your mission?"

"I talked when I was delirious from that Sioux wound."

"Then Bowers should have told me."

"He should have done just what he did, Major . . . kept his mouth shut."

"I suppose so," Beauchamp conceded reluctantly. "But I still think I should have been notified of Bowers' medical report at the same time as you."

"Well, now you have been," Marlin said and turned his attention back to Reynolds. The NCO stood watching him with an air of sullen defiance. He thought of all the people dead because of this man, and his mouth thinned.

"One way or another, Sergeant," he said softly, "I'm going to put a noose around your neck. I know you and your detail have been attacking Overland stages, murdering their crews, destroying U.S. mail, and otherwise aiding this Indian uprising. I'm positive you're involved in a Confederate conspiracy to interrupt communication with the West. And I can prove that you murdered Howard because he was about to expose your activities. What I don't know—but what I intend to find out—is who is masterminding this conspiracy. Who is he, Reynolds? Who is the Reb?"

Little flecks of light danced in the Sergeant's pale blue eyes. When he answered, his voice was openly aggressive.

"I don't know what the hell you're talking about, Colonel." He swung toward Beauchamp. "Major, sir, are you going to sit there and let him hassle me this way?"

"You are not being harassed," Beauchamp said coldly. "You have been accused of being a Confederate spy and of having killed a trooper under your command to conceal that fact. Do you deny these allegations?"

"Yes, sir!"

"Very well." Rising, Beauchamp stepped to the door of his orderly's cubicle. "Smith! Find Captain Nash and tell him I want to see him right away."

The orderly left on the double, letting in a rush of icy air on his way out.

Beauchamp returned to his chair and waited silently. Marlin leaned his arm on the fireplace mantel. Reynolds stood stiff-backed and defiant, staring at the wall behind the Major's head.

The clock on the wall ticked loudly, its gears slipping now and then with a grinding sound of brass on brass. At ten minutes after five, Captain Nash came in, stomping the snow from his boots, followed by the shivering orderly.

"You wanted to see me, Major?" Nash asked.

Curtly, Beauchamp jerked his head toward the stiff-backed Reynolds. "This man is under arrest on suspicion of murder and treason. So is every member of that escort detail that rode in with him. You will post an around-the-clock squad over the prisoners, with orders to shoot to kill if they try to escape."

"Yes, sir."

As Nash moved forward to relieve Reynolds of his side arm, the Sergeant cried angrily, "My God, Major, what are you trying to do to me? I tell you, Cap'n Bowers made a mistake! I'm not—"

"Shut up!" West Point, career officer, insubordinate, but not permitting insubordination. *"Don't you ever raise your voice to me, Sergeant!* Get him out of here, Captain. If he gives you any trouble, manacle him and put him on bread and water."

"Damn you, Major!" Reynolds cried passionately. "I will not—" He gasped in pain as Nash rammed a pistol barrel against his spine and said, "Get moving!"

When they had gone, Beauchamp opened a desk

183

drawer and drew out a bottle of whiskey and a couple of glasses.

"Colonel?"

"Yes, thanks,"—even though it was almost reveille—"I think we can both use one."

Beauchamp took half his drink in a quick gulp, set the glass down on his desk with a trembling hand. His face was white, haggard.

"Maybe Holladay is right," he said heavily. "Maybe there is a conspiracy. And if Reynolds and his details have been helping to make a shambles of the Overland route, then, God help me, I'm as guilty as they are. I should have suspected the truth a long time ago." He shifted in his chair and looked straight at Marlin with tormented eyes. "Colonel, Reynolds and the entire detail are Confederate prisoners of war, paroled to fight Indians here on the frontier."

"My God!" Incredulously, Marlin thrust away from the mantel, feeling the painful pressure of his fingers vise-squeezing the whiskey glass. "You mean you've knowingly permitted Confederate prisoners to escort Overland stages carrying gold and U.S. mail? In God's name, man, *why?* Didn't it ever occur to you to wonder at their reasons for volunteering for such hazardous duty? Or to question how the same detail always managed to escape when the stage crews were massacred to a man?"

His words were harsh, abrasive, and he fully

expected Beauchamp to lash back. But Beauchamp took it, the color high in his cheeks and his lips thinned. There was nothing else he could do.

"I realize now that I should have," he admitted. "But if you will recall, I've never felt it was the cavalry's place to protect the Overland. Maybe that's why I handled the matter too routinely. When a request for an escort came through, I made the decision to either honor or reject it. I then turned it over to the Duty Officer. He, in turn, left the actual selection of the detail up to the Sergeant." He spread his hands in a defensive gesture. "I never knew who the volunteers were, or that the same detail was riding out time and again. However, even if I had . . ." His chin lifted and his eyes held steady. "Colonel, if a bunch of damn Johnny Rebs want to go out and get themselves killed . . . well, I'd rather it be them than my own men."

He finished his whiskey and stood up. "As soon as the weather clears, I'll send them to General Mitchell for courts-martial. If they're guilty, they'll hang."

"I want them kept here," Marlin said, "until I complete my investigation. I'm going to hammer away at every man in that detail until one of them cracks. *I want the Reb, Major.* When I get him, then it will be up to the President."

"Whatever you say." Beauchamp buttoned his tunic, ran his fingers through his hair, and smiled ruefully. "What do you do, Colonel, when you suddenly wake up to the fact that you're a square peg in a round hole and it's too late for you to do anything about it?" Then before Marlin could say anything, he spoke quickly. "I'd ask you to stay for breakfast, but my wife never rises until seven o'clock."

"Forget it." Hunching into his coat, Marlin stepped away from the fire and walked to the door. "I'll eat when I get back to the hotel. Meanwhile, if Reynolds or any of his men decide to talk, I'd appreciate it if you'd get word to me immediately."

"I'll do that." Beauchamp's smile was thin, wintry. "I'll have Nash train a Gatling gun on the guardhouse. If they try to escape, they'll be killed."

"Good." Stepping out into the graying light, Marlin walked briskly back to the post hospital, swung into his chilled saddle, and rode rapidly toward town. With him rode an indefinable unease, a just-below-the-surface awareness of something radically wrong.

Julesburg's main street was all but deserted as Marlin cantered down its rutted length, the bay slipping and sliding on the hard-crusted snow. Smoke curled upward from chimneys and stovepipes as merchants and townspeople fed wood to fireplaces and potbellied stoves. The predawn temperature held steady at five degrees above zero.

The Overland's waiting room was empty; but through the open door of the front office, Marlin could see the tips of Ed Ashley's boots propped on the battered desk. He went inside and said, "Morning, Ed. You're up early."

"Morning." Ashley sat up, bringing his feet to the floor. "Couldn't sleep. Ate too much and had a bellyache all night. You run into Jake Corning on your way in?"

"No, why?"

"The telegraph line between here and Denver's been repaired," Ashley said. "A message just came through from Holladay. Slade's still alive, but in critical condition. They plan to send him to St. Louis, maybe even Chicago for more surgery and medical treatment. Ginny will be going with him."

"That's good news," Marlin replied. "When did Holladay say he would be back?"

"He didn't; he's still trying to get the newspapers off his back." The agent gave Marlin an inquiring glance. "What was the trouble out at the fort? The hotel clerk said he saw you leaving with Sergeant Brill around four-thirty and that you seemed to be in a mighty big hurry."

Drawing up a chair, Marlin sat down, waited a moment, and then said quietly, "We lost those two east-bound stages and their crews, Ed.

Cheyennes. The escort escaped with one casualty."

"Damn!" Ashley swore fervently. "Just when it looked like we had the route open. That will be bad news for Ben."

"It's a lot more serious than that," Marlin added. "Sergeant Reynolds swears his trooper was killed in a running battle with the Cheyennes. Captain Bowers insists the man was shot in the back at close range—murdered."

"Murdered!" Ashley straightened, his face mirroring his surprise. "Why would Reynolds want to kill one of his own men?"

"To keep him from talking."

"About what?"

"Figure it out for yourself," Marlin told him. "In the past six weeks, we've lost eleven stages and their crews. Every one of those stages was escorted by a cavalry detail under Sergeant Reynolds. Yet, until this time, that detail has never suffered a single casualty. Do you see what the odds are against that?"

Ashley jerked his pipe out of his mouth with a startled expression. "You mean Reynolds and his detail have been responsible for all these raids on the Overland? That they're nothing but a band of renegades in uniform?"

"Not quite," Marlin said. "After every one of those massacres, I sent out rescue parties to recover the dead and what mail they could. They all backed up Reynolds' claims that the stages had been hit by hostiles. Crews' throats slashed from ear to ear—the trademark of the Oglalas—or arms hacked off by the Cut Arm people. Unshod pony tracks of large war parties. Wes Bender followed one of those war parties half way back to Cherry Creek. They were real Indians, all right."

"Then how . . ." Burning tobacco spilled from Ashley's battered briar as he almost dropped it. "My God, you mean Reynolds is the Reb?"

"I don't know," Marlin admitted. "I doubt it. But he's definitely a part of the conspiracy, working closely with the Sioux, Cheyennes, and Arapahos. The evidence is all there, including the fact that he and the entire detail are Confederate prisoners of war paroled to fight here on the frontier."

"What!" Ashley cried explosively. "You can't be serious!"

"Major Beauchamp confirmed it less than an hour ago," Marlin said. "He's arrested Reynolds and the detail on suspicion of robbery, murder, and treason. They're confined under heavy guard. Before I'm through with them, Ed, one of them is going to talk."

"I can't believe it!" Ashley sat shaking his head from side to side like a punch-drunk fighter. "Johnny Rebs in Union cavalry! Are you sure of that?"

"I'm sure," Marlin replied. Yet even to him, the Confederate's boldness was incredible. The man had gathered together a hand-picked murder detail of Confederate parolees right under Major Beauchamp's nose. And with just those eight troopers and a Sergeant, the Reb had turned the Overland route into a bloody shambles for a hundred and forty miles along the Platte, all but closing down the entire division. A link in the Overland chain was being broken. And a broken chain was no chain at all.

Pushing away from his desk, Ashley started to rise. "Then I'd better get off a wire to Ben. He'll want to come back as soon as possible."

"Ed, I'd rather handle this myself," Martin said quietly. "If Holladay races back here and demands that Beauchamp turn Reynolds over to him, there will be serious trouble. Those men are prisoners of war. Beauchamp will not surrender them to a lynch mob. If he has to, he'll order his troopers to open fire and men will die. Holladay's in enough trouble as it is; let's try and keep him out of any more."

Slowly, Ashley sank back in his chair. He rubbed his forehead with a tired gesture. "Ben will probably fire us both," he said. "But you're right. We'll wait and let him find out for himself."

Relieved, Marlin stood up and laid his hand on Ashley's shoulder. "Thanks, Ed. Now I'm going to have breakfast, and then I'm going to do a little thinking. I'll see you later."

Returning to the hotel, he had a lonely meal and then went upstairs to his room. There he wrote a coded message to the President detailing this first break in his investigation. Leaning back, he stared, frowning, at what he had written. He could not rid himself of the nagging suspicion that had plagued him ever since he had left Stephen Beauchamp's office.

There were questions which demanded answers. Answers which he sensed he would not get from the Major. Picking up his pen, he wrote with quick, decisive strokes.

It seems highly improbable, Mr. President, that the commanding officer of a post as small as Camp Rankin should be unaware of what is happening within his command. Yet the only alternative—that a Union Army career officer is involved in a Confederate intelligence operation—seems even more unacceptable. Nevertheless, I urgently request that a copy of Major Stephen J. Beauchamp's complete service dossier be forwarded to me via the fastest possible communication. Such information is highly important to my investigation. I hope Mr. President, to complete this mission very soon.

Slipping the message into his pocket, he went downstairs and along the street to the Overland telegraph office.

"Morning, Jake." He handed Corning the coded

message. "Get this off to Atchison right away, will you?"

"Sure, Colonel."

When he left, Corning's key was already transmitting. Now all he could do was wait.

On the Central Plains, the carnage continued. Stages departed, heavily armed. Most ended up, bullet-scarred and arrow-studded, their crews murdered and scalped, their fleet racers stolen. Gold was taken and mail scattered to the winds. Even the carefully screened cavalry details which Major Beauchamp, co-operating with Marlin, now sent out with each stage suffered heavy casualties. Beauchamp urgently requested reinforcements from General Mitchell. He got eighteen men, barely enough to cover his casualties and to replace the loss of Reynolds and his detail.

Six days after their arrest, Reynolds and his men somehow managed to break out of the guardhouse. They made a desperate run for the stables. The Gatling cut them down before they had gone fifty yards. There were no survivors.

For Marlin, it was a crushing setback. He had, he felt, been very close to cracking one of the detail, a boy from Georgia, only the day before the tragic escape attempt. Now he had to start all over again.

Finding the Confederate became an obsession with him. Grimly, he widened his investigation, concentrating on the higher levels—bankers, lawyers, and merchants. Listening, asking innocuous questions, watching men's faces for some unguarded reaction. He even flattered wives, encouraging them to talk about their husbands when obviously they would have preferred more exciting subjects. He learned nothing.

He saw Susan Ashley only briefly at mealtimes. She had grown more and more remote until now she seemed part of another world. But although he missed the warmth that had once been between them, he was too concerned with his mission to try to reopen closed doors.

Once, he had dinner with the Beauchamps, with both the Major and his wife, Janet, hungrily absorbing news of life in the East. The Major's interest was in the progress of the war, his wife's in the cultural life. It was difficult for Marlin to associate the "at home" Beauchamp with the "arrogant, insubordinate" officer which the Army held him to be. He should have been, Marlin mused, a scientist, a lawyer, a writer, an artist, fields where a brilliant mind and a rebellious spirit were not destroyed by blind authority.

Loss of his Confederate prisoners seemed to weigh heavily upon Beauchamp. His failure to suspect them when he should have, and now their deaths in an attempted escape, he viewed as the end of any hopes of ever making colonel.

"Major," Marlin said, standing on the porch,

"every man makes mistakes. It would have been much worse if they had escaped."

In the dim light, Beauchamp's mouth twisted into a thin, crooked smile. "Sir, the Army doesn't look that far ahead and you know it. I made a mistake, period. It will go on my record in indelible ink." He shrugged indifferently. "It really doesn't matter anymore, Colonel. I buried my dreams a long time ago. And the Army will still let me finish out my service, if not here, then somewhere else."

Walking back to the hotel through the still, clear night, Marlin could not help but feel compassion for this man who wanted so desperately to stand in the sun, but who was crippled by the dark shadow of his own nature.

Yet chilling that compassion was the persistent suspicion that Beauchamp should have known what was going on during Reynolds' bloody forays against Overland stages. He wished that the President would come through quickly with Stephen Beauchamp's complete Army dossier. He had a feeling that it would tell him something, one way or the other.

Several times he rode out to see Hamlin Weatherby, hoping for some new bit of information. But the artist was off on another of his "sketching" trips.

Acting on his own initiative, Sergeant Wes Bender disappeared on a solitary scouting trip.

Cochran, the Wagon Wheel owner, hinted darkly that "the damn breed is probably powwowing with his Sioux brothers!" But Marlin knew better. Bender was hunting the Confederate.

Instead, the Confederate found him.

"Colonel!"

Marlin came instantly awake, the faint rap on the door dying in the silence. Moonlight slanting in through the window laid quietly upon the opposite wall.

Carefully, he reached for the Colt in the holster draped over the bedside chair. He waited, finger curled around the trigger.

"Colonel!" A man's voice came urgently through the door. "This is Sergeant Bender. Are you awake?"

Laying aside the Colt, Marlin sat up on the edge of the bed, struck a match and lit the lamp. "Come in."

Bender slipped inside, closed the door and said in a tight voice, "Help me out my coat. I've been shot."

Stripped to the waist, he straddled a chair and sat stolidly while Marlin examined the wound. The bullet had passed cleanly through the fleshy part of his side, just above the belt line.

"You'd better have Dr. Lindley take care of that," Marlin advised. "It could get infected."

"Just wash it out with a little whiskey and

bandage it with something," Bender said. "I've got news for you."

He grunted only once as Marlin flushed out the wound with whiskey and then bandaged it with strips from a pillow case. "Who did it?" Marlin asked.

Bender shook his head. "Too far away to see. He fired from about five hundred yards out and then took off."

"Which way did he head?"

"I think he circled and came back to town."

"Then we'll find him."

The Sergeant rose, slipped into his shirt, and turned his startling gray eyes upon Marlin. "I doubt it, Colonel. He knows every move you make. He even knew I was hunting him."

"You must have been getting close to something," Marlin said. "You think it was the Reb?"

The eyes in the dark face narrowed. "Him—or one of his men." Bender moved to the door. "I aim to find out."

"Where are you going now?"

Without answering, Bender was gone.

Blowing out the lamp, Marlin sat for a long time, staring at the moonlight-framed window. His relentless ferreting and Bender's dogged scouting obviously had the Confederate worried. First the trooper. Now the attempt on Bender's life. Logically, the next move would be to try and kill him, Marlin. It was becoming more and more difficult to tell just who was the hunter and who was the hunted.

Suddenly, he thought of Hamlin Weatherby. The artist just might have been in the area where Bender was attacked, and could have perhaps seen something. Tomorrow, he would ride out and talk to Hamlin Weatherby.

Smoke spiraled upward from the chimney of Hamlin Weatherby's cabin as Marlin dismounted and tied the bay's reins to a small sapling. There was no sign of Weatherby, but a light rig was drawn up in front. He knocked.

Janet Beauchamp opened the door, her green eyes lighting with pleasured surprise. "Why, Colonel Marlin!" she exclaimed. "How nice to see you! Come in. My father isn't here, but I'm expecting him back shortly."

Marlin hesitated, feeling that perhaps he should leave, yet sensing that this was an excellent opportunity to fish for information as to the Major's movements the past few weeks.

A pink flush rose from Janet Beauchamp's throat to the smooth cheeks, and her eyes met Marlin's with a faint trace of amusement.

"I assure you, Colonel, it's quite all right. My father is a very understanding man."

"And the Major?"

The green eyes veiled and something flickered in their depths. "The Major and I lead separate lives, Colonel. I'm surprised that you have not already sensed that."

"No," Marlin said. "I'd thought you to be a very happy couple."

She started to say something, caught herself with a little laugh, and drew him inside. "Do sit down, Colonel." She motioned him to the gayly covered couch. "I seem to have forgotten my manners." Dropping down beside him, she half turned to face him and said cooly, "Just what is happiness, Colonel? An escape from reality? A dream? A beautiful illusion? Once I thought I knew. Now . . . I admire my husband's brilliance, sir; I do not admire the manner in which he has wasted it. And that which I cannot respect, I cannot love. Does my frankness shock you?"

"No," Marlin replied. "But it does help me to understand what a scout named Grey meant in speaking of you."

"And just what did Mr. Grey say about me?"

"Grey's a crude man, ma'am, who uses crude language."

Janet Beauchamp smiled, showing small, white teeth. "I've lived on the frontier three years, Colonel. Crude language is not new to me. Nor am I a silly prude."

"He said, quote, 'That one's like a buffler heifer in heat. Th' fire's deep as she is, an' ain't no one man goin' to put it out. Leastways, not the Major. I can't figure out why she married him, but it sure had to be somethin' besides love.' End quote."

Her expression altered subtly, her small pink mouth becoming suddenly sensuous and the green eyes deepening, darkening. "And what else did this . . . this Mr. Grey have to say about me?"

It came as something of a surprise to Marlin that, in a sophisticated way, she was much like Virginia Slade, except that she lacked Virginia's basic integrity. For whereas Virginia plunged boldly, openly into life, Janet Beauchamp approached it with a calculated deviousness. Why now, he wondered, did she choose to reveal herself?

"Well . . ." He shrugged. "Grey questioned why you ever married the Major to begin with, and decided it had to be for a very important reason."

"And now you're wondering just what that reason may have been?" Janet Beauchamp prompted cooly.

"It has puzzled me," he admitted, "why a beautiful, intelligent woman such as you would marry a cavalry officer with no future, no wealth and follow him all the way to a small frontier fort."

"What's so unusual about that, sir?" Janet Beauchamp challenged, smiling. "Many women do it."

"Generals' wives, perhaps," Marlin conceded. "Sergeants' wives, yes. But not cultured, well-bred women who can take their pick of the best."

She tilted her head, still smiling, but with an unconscious sharpening of the fine, cameolike features. "Why are you so curious as to why I married Stephen? Aren't you being just a little presumptuous?"

"I have not meant to be," he said quietly. "If I have been, then I apologize."

Immediately, her manner softened. She laid her head back against the couch with a little sigh. "Forgive *me,* Colonel. It is I who have been rude. Your question upset me because I've asked myself the same thing many times—and I still don't know why.

"At the moment, it seemed perfectly right. But no one was thinking clearly then. With men marching off to war, it was all raw emotion, and Stephen and I were caught up in the middle of it. Stephen, with his brilliant mind and his West Point polish and his handsome uniform with his Major's epaulets, about to, so I thought, join the troops at the front, maybe to die for . . ." A bitter, disillusioned expression darkened her face.

"And then, after we were married, and he was sent here instead of to the combat area, I had to face up to the truth. That Stephen and I would live out our lives in one grubby frontier post after another, with no hope of escape."

Starting on a low key, her voice suddenly began to mount; and Marlin could feel the intensity of her emotions passing through to him from the couch. She raised her head, her eyes a dark, glowing jade and looked at him with a "symbolic" resentment.

"Why did Lincoln have to interfere with something that was none of his business? Why couldn't he have left the South alone, him and the whole damn nigger-loving North! Why did they have to . . ." Her voice died away, and she sat silent with flushed cheeks and tight lips.

Now, Marlin thought, he knew at least a part of what Major Stephen Beauchamp's service dossier would reveal.

"So that's why you married him!"

Janet Beauchamp brought her head up in a proud, defiant gesture. "That's why I married him. But I failed; I couldn't win him over. He's plagued by a distorted sense of honor."

A new bitterness entered her voice as she studied Marlin's face. "I know what you're thinking—what you've thought ever since you found out Sergeant Reynolds and his men were Confederate parolees. You believe that Stephen and me . . . Stephen, at least, are involved some way in this Indian uprising. We're not! But if I had my way, we would be!"

Suddenly, her composure completely shattered. "Damn those kinky-headed niggers! And damn nigger-loving Yankee bastards like you! You'd destroy the South, a way of life, for a bunch of black apes! Oh, damn you! Damn you!"

Staring at the lovely, rage-marred face, Marlin thought of the young trooper, Howard, stretched out on the table in Captain Bowers' surgery with a bullet hole in his back, of the scalped bodies of men, women, and children he had seen out there on the plains.

"I would destroy anything that robs another human being of his dignity and his right to live and die a free man."

He gave Janet Beauchamp a long, final look and then went outside. Without a backward glance, he mounted up and rode away.

Marlin received the President's coded telegram the afternoon of December 21, 1864, the same day that Ben Holladay returned from Denver. Immediately, he went to work decoding. A westering sun slanted in through the window by the time he finished. He sat staring at the message, digesting the facts.

Stephen J. Beauchamp, Major, US Cavalry. Born 1827, Vicksburg, Mississippi, son of William S. Beauchamp, wealthy plantation owner. West point, '48, second in class. Brilliant, ambitious, but insubordinate conduct limits career. Requested assignment to cavalry. Resigned commission outbreak of hostilities, but withdrew request before it could be acted upon. No known association with pro-southern groups, but wife, Janet, an ardent Confederate sympathizer. For this reason subject officer has not been assigned to critical combat areas nor given important commands. Known to be dissatisfied with current status.

These facts, plus those you communicated to me, make this officer strongly suspect your investigation. If proof of guilt positively established, act promptly in accordance with "terminate" instructions. Advise greatest caution. Observe absolute secrecy this matter.

Crumpling the message, Marlin dropped it into the potbellied stove. He had the suspects; there was no longer any doubt of it. Still, he had no positive proof. And that he *must* have before . . .

"Kurt!" He swung around as Ed Ashley stuck his head inside. "Ben's down at the hotel. He wants to see you right away. He's got a burr under his tail about something."

"Probably about Reni," Marlin said, getting to his feet. "I figured Ficklin would lodge a complaint against me. I'll see you later."

By the time he entered the hotel dining room, Holladay had ordered for the two of them. Nodding curtly, the Overland's owner motioned him to a seat.

"Now I'm not going to waste time beating around the bush," Holladay said. "I ran into

Ficklin at Oak Springs. He was mad as hell. He claimed you refused to back him up when he tried to hang that bastard, Jules Reni. Frankly, I'm not happy about the way either one of you handled the situation. Ficklin should have killed the first outlaw to lay a hand on that rope. He had the authority, and you had fifty armed men to back him up. Instead, the two of you let the son of a bitch off scot free. I want to know why."

Slowly, Marlin put down his coffee cup. "If Ficklin had stayed out of things to begin with, I might have jailed Reni. But once Ficklin stepped in, the situation got out of hand. If we hadn't stopped it, there would have been a hell of a shoot-out. Reni wasn't worth it."

"Men get killed every day upholding the law," Holladay retorted. He leaned back, his heavy face flushed, the great white tiger's claw hung on the gold watch chain across his vest gleaming in the lamplight.

"Maybe I made a mistake about you, Marlin," he said coldly. "Maybe you're just not the man for the job. I'll admit you've cleaned up the town, got at least some stages to rolling, and made sure of Brigham Young's help in case we need it. *But I don't like the way you handled this matter. And you still haven't found that damn Reb!*"

"I think maybe I have," Marlin replied calmly. "But I'm not going to make a move until I have more proof."

"Proof be damned!" Holladay slammed his fist down on the table, rattling dishes, and slopping coffee on the tablecloth. "By God, if you know something, tell me! It's my stage line that's being wiped out!"

"No," Marlin said firmly, pushing back his plate. "If I did, you'd organize a lynch party and hang a man who just might be innocent. Then we'd never trap the real Reb." He gave Holladay a critical, unsmiling scrutiny.

"You're too hotheaded for your own good. When I'm positive I have the right man, I'll let you know; but not until then."

A reluctant admiration flickered in Holladay's eyes, cooling his quick, explosive anger. He studied Marlin shrewdly a moment, then shrugged. "All right, handle things your way. But I want results, and I want them fast."

Rising, Marlin picked up his coat. "Don't push me," he said evenly. "I don't like it. You can't put a timetable on trapping a man like the Confederate. Now, I've got things to do."

"Oh, I almost forgot." Lighting up a cheroot, Holladay spoke through a cloud of blue-gray smoke. "Slade's on his way to St. Louis for more treatment. Ginny went with him. She said to tell you good-bye and that a coat cut from the same cloth wears longer than one made of wolf and sable . . . whatever the hell that means. She said you'd understand."

With a faint smile, Marlin nodded. He would miss her bold, vivacious personality; yet he could not help but feel relieved. With her gone, perhaps Susan's bitterness would fade.

As he turned to leave, Holladay called after him. "I'm counting on you, Marlin! Get that damn Reb!"

He did not bother to reply.

"Kurt!" Susan Ashley caught up with him in the lobby. He turned, not speaking. Light from the kerosene lamps overhead shadowed her oval face and the candid gray eyes. It was the first time that he had seen her alone since the night of Notley Ann's party; and only now did he realize just how much he had missed her.

"Kurt . . ." Susan blinked rapidly, her eyes misting. "Would it do any good for me to apologize for the way I've acted? I know how you must feel about me, and I can't blame you. But I just couldn't stand the thought of you and Virginia . . ." Her voice broke and she just stood there looking at him, the tears rolling down her face in little crystal streams.

Touched by her humility, Marlin said quietly, "It was never the way you thought, Susan."

Her face tilted up to him, her mouth quivering. "I realize that now," she admitted. "But it took time. You see, from the first day I met you, you were something special to me. Something more than just another man. You were a symbol of all the things I've searched for but never found in anyone else. And having found you, I couldn't bear the thought of losing you to another woman." The quiet, grave smile of old lighted her face.

"I know it sounds foolish and unreasonable; but then, in some ways, all women are foolish and unreasonable—especially when they're in love." Sweetly. "Will you forgive me, please?"

In that moment, the wall which had separated them for so long dissolved; and all the love which had been damned up behind it flowed forth, free and uninhibited, carrying away the last of Marlin's defenses.

Only the desk clerk, dozing in his chair, was in the lobby. Drawing Susan to him, Marlin searched her face intently. Then he said in a low voice, "Forgive you for what? For being yourself? I'm the one who was at fault. I should have been more understanding, more tolerant. Will you forgive me, Susan?"

"Yes! Oh, yes!" With a little cry of gladness, Susan Ashley turned and fled back to the dining room, the tears spilling down her face.

Marlin fought down the urge to follow her, to tell her what he now knew himself—that he loved her and that he had not admitted it before because of the danger of his mission. But now was neither the time nor the place. Soon, however, he would tell her. Very soon.

Soberly, he left the hotel and made his way through the gathering dusk to the telegraph office. There he wired Brigham Young, requesting the Mormon company and furnishing guarded particulars. At this stage, he trusted no one fully.

Returning to the main office, he found Ed Ashley just entering. "Well, what did Ben have to say?" Ashley asked, giving him a curious glance.

Marlin's mouth twisted in a faint smile. "You can sum it up in one sentence," he replied. *"Find that damn Reb or else!"*

"Did you tell him about Reynolds and that detail being 'galvanized Yankees'?" Ashley asked. "And about what happened to them?"

"No," Marlin said. "And I'd rather you didn't. Holladay's a willful, headstrong man. At this stage, he could wreck everything."

Ashley drew thoughtfully on his battered pipe. "You think you can get the job done alone?"

"If I can't, I'll ask Holladay for help," Marlin told him. Then, abruptly switching the subject. "Have you seen Sergeant Bender?"

Ashley frowned. "Not in a couple of days. Why?"

Worry furrowed Marlin's forehead. "Somebody shot him the last time he was on a scout."

"You didn't tell me that," Ashley said sharply.

"Ed," Marlin explained, "there are lots of things I don't tell you. They're not a part of your job. But that doesn't mean I don't trust you. Sometimes, I have to. For instance, if Bender doesn't turn up by dawn, I'm going out looking for him. If I don't come back, then you'd better send someone out to look for us both. Now, I'm going out for a drink. You want to come along?"

"No, thanks," Ashley said with a trace of irritation. "I've still got some work to do. But watch your step. You could end up dead."

Nodding silently, Marlin stepped out into the night and made his way along the snow-packed walk. A growing unease nagged at his subconscious. He could not rid himself of the feeling that something had happened to Wes Bender. Nor did a couple of drinks at the Canary House ease his tension. It was still there when he returned to the hotel and called it a night.

Awakening at six o'clock, he dressed, went downstairs, and had breakfast. There was no sign of Wes Bender. He finished his meal and leaving the hotel walked the short distance to the livery stable.

By the time he rode out of town, Julesburg had begun to come to life. Here and there, lights bloomed out of the darkness, and the sound of voices mingled with the clomp of boots. Heads turtle-necked deep in their collars, men slogged along the snow-crusted streets, heading for stables, stores, or the hotel for breakfast.

Cochran came out of the Wagon Wheel, a cigar glowing redly between his teeth. He looked at

Marlin, tossed away the cigar, and went back inside.

A mile out of town, Marlin reined up, studying the white hills all the way to the paling skyline. No snow had fallen for four days; but there was the "smell" of a storm in the air that disturbed him. He knew the killing cold of Plains blizzards; and only the thought of Bender somewhere out there, perhaps badly wounded, kept him from turning back to town.

For just a moment, he hesitated. Then he swung the bay's head toward the northeast and put Julesburg behind him.

He found Bender late in the afternoon, lying on his back outside a trader's tent, his dark face turned toward the lowering sky—and, ten feet away, the body of the trader. They had shot it out at point-blank range.

In the tent, Marlin found a saddle, a couple of dirty blankets, and a jug of whiskey. The packs outside yielded thirty rifles, a thousand rounds of ammunition, and twenty gallons of cheap trade whiskey.

Oblivious to the wind gusting out of the north, bringing with it the first bite of the blizzard, Marlin stood staring down at the dead trader. The man, he was certain, had been a part of the conspiracy. Bender must have accused the trader and perhaps have tried to bring him in. A shootout had followed, and now both were dead.

How many others like him, Marlin wondered, were operating in the Julesburg area? And from where and how were they getting their contraband? Was Jules Reni, after all, involved? Was the Frenchman raiding Overland stations and Army ordnance trains to supply the Reb's organization? If Beau—

The bullet killed a pack mule directly behind Marlin and threw the other animals on the picket line into a panic. Falling sideways, Marlin rolled for cover as bullets tattooed the snow around him. Sheltered by the packs on one side, a big spruce on the other, a boulder at his back and with the dead mule providing a frontal barricade, he waited for the quick winter night to fall. In half an hour, he stood a good chance of escaping under cover of darkness.

The enemy was no fool. Anticipating such a move, he killed every animal on the picket line, one by one. Only Marlin's bay, snapping its reins, escaped into the timber.

Cautiously, Marlin shifted position, sending one of the packs rolling. A bullet slammed into it. The man up there on the slope, five hundred yards away, was an incredible marksman. Crouched down behind the dead mule, Marlin considered his position. Afoot somewhere between Julesburg and Crow Junction, and with a blizzard making up, he couldn't stay where he was. He would have to move out soon. Wind slammed against his improvised fort. Grimly, he waited out the waning light, the marksman silent now.

Darkness, when it came, was absolute. No moon, no stars, no horizon. Earth and sky and man were encapsulated in a black cocoon in which one was indistinguishable from the other.

Breaking out a rifle, Marlin stuffed a dozen rounds of ammunition in his pocket and slipped into the timber. Half an hour, and the ground began to slope downward. Since he had been climbing when he stumbled into the camp, he must be retracing his route.

The wind dropped off into a muttering whisper; he quickened his pace, blundering into trees, stumbling over rocks, cursing the ambusher with a dull anger. Had there been two traders, and had the second one been returning from a parley with the Sioux when he'd spotted Marlin? No, it had clearly been a one-man camp.

If not a trader, then someone had followed him from Julesburg with the clear intent to kill him. But who? Only Ed Ashley had known of his plan to scout the area for Bender if the scout did not—

Good God, was Ashley in it, too? Who was better qualified? Shrewd, quick, intelligent and with access to the most confidential information, Ashley would be the perfect "inside" man . . . except for one thing. Like Ben Holladay, Ed Ashley simply did not fit the role.

Who then?

The wind out of the north hit Marlin savagely. Cold. Colder than the hubs of hell with the axles frozen. Bone-marrow cold seeping through the heavy wolfskin coat. Eyebrows ice-tipped from breathing.

By the minute, the wind built up, buffeting, whipping. Within an hour, it was belching out of the mouth of a vomiting gale, its noise now the only sound in the world. Numbed by the ferocious cold, Marlin felt his nostrils driven together and sealed. He opened his mouth, gasping to let in air. Inhalation struck his lungs, frost-cold. After a few deep breaths, his chest ached so that he could scarcely draw the next. Within half a mile, his hands were icicles to the wrists, his feet wooden clumps.

Thirty degrees below. Hoarfrost and caked snow encrusted his entire body. The storm a howling banshee now. Hands numbed within fur gloves. Feet—did he still have feet?

Forty degrees below. Body and mind frozen senseless. Only the spirit driving him on.

Suddenly, the wind which had been screaming for an eternity fell to a ghost's whisper. The snow fell straight down. He walked blindly into the bay, moving almost parallel to him. On the third attempt, he made the saddle. Man and horse one.

An hour's reprieve.

Then the freezing black darkness and again the

wind. Always the incessant bawling of the wind, screaming at him, slashing, buffering, hammering, pushing, twisting until his brain reeled from the sheer noise of it.

Sheeting snow. His feet clumps of ice in his boots. No identity. No world outside this yammering black void which was driving the life force out of him.

And then, like a bright star, a light gleaming from the darkness ahead of him, and the furious barking of a dog and a man's voice shouting, "God Amighty, Liz, somebody's out there in that hell! Stir up the fire an' heat the coffee!"

He could see the man now—a tall, spare figure outlined in the doorway with lamplight from inside carving a small white island in the darkness. He reined the bay to a halt, half swung himself from the saddle—and then his stiffened fingers lost their grip on the saddle horn and he fell heavily upon his back in the snow.

He was on his knees, trying to get up, when strong hands pulled him to his feet. "Liz, give me a hand!" the rancher called. "Nate, you take care of his horse! All right, mister, we're going to get you inside. You give us all the help you can."

Somehow, he made it inside where, for an hour, the rancher and his wife took turns massaging his numbed hands and feet until circulation was normal. Afterward, he wolfed down hot food and a second stiff shot of whiskey. In a spare bedroom, he fell across the bed and was instantly asleep.

Once, the yapping of the dog half-roused him, but then he drifted off again, thinking he must have been dreaming.

He found Hamlin Weatherby seated at the table eating steak and eggs when he entered the kitchen the next morning. The artist looked up, smiled, and motioned to a chair.

"Clay Dennison told me you were here. He said you rode in, half-frozen, last night. You were lucky you didn't die out there."

Marlin dropped into a chair. "When did you get in?"

"About an hour after you," Weatherby replied. "The Dennisons are friends of mine. When that blizzard started building up, I headed for here."

"You've been out a lot recently," Marlin observed. "Every time I've dropped by, you were gone. Sketching?"

"Trying to," Weatherby said, "but it's getting dangerous on the Plains, even for me. I think . . ."

Liz Dennison, a good-looking woman in her early thirties, placed a plate of steak, eggs, and hot biscuits in front of Marlin.

"How do you feel?" she asked. "You was sure done in when you rode up last night. Hadn't been for the dog, we might not have found you."

"I know," Marlin said, smiling, "and if that dog could understand, I'd thank him." He grew

215

serious. "I appreciate what you and your husband did."

"Hamlin wasn't in much better shape when he turned up," Liz Dennison said. "But he should have known better'n to get caught in a blizzard. After all, he's lived in this country for almost three years."

"Stop heckling me, Liz," Weatherby retorted good-naturedly. "Where's Clay? I haven't seen him around this morning."

"He's out checking the cattle." Liz Dennison's pretty face pinched, grew suddenly much older. "It must have hit fifty below last night. We're bound to have lost quite a few head. Well, if you want anything more, jus holler. I've got things to do." She disappeared into another room, leaving the two men sitting alone in a small silence.

Weatherby lighted a cheroot, looked at Marlin and asked curiously, "What were you doing so far from Julesburg in such weather? With that Confederate detail dead, I thought you would relax for a while."

"The raids haven't stopped," Marlin replied grimly. "Either the Reb's got more Confederate parolees at Fort Sedgewick, or as civilians at swing stations along the route."

"Or Reynolds and his detail were innocent and there is no conspiracy." Weatherby spoke calmly around his cheroot. "Did it ever occur to you that he might have been telling the truth?"

"Then why did he lie about that trooper's death?" Marlin countered. "He told Captain Bowers and the Major that Howard had been shot by Sioux at approximately two hundred yards. Bowers showed me the wound, with black powder blown into the skin around it. Howard was shot in the back at point-blank range—*murdered*."

A flicker of contempt showed in Weatherby's eyes. Holding the cheroot between thumb and forefinger, he twirled it slowly, watching the smoke curl upward in a lazy spiral.

"Colonel, I figured you understood human nature better than that," he said. "Look, you had eight Confederate prisoners of war accepting parole and frontier duty fighting Indians—not because they wanted to, but because they thought their chances of survival here were better than in a Union stockade. *Eight Rebs in the middle of a hundred and twenty Yankees who hated them.*" He leaned back, his eyes narrowing.

"You know what it must have been like, living pretty much to themselves and under constant tension. Friction, dislikes, even hatred were bound to develop. Suppose there was bad blood between Howard and one of the other escort troopers? And suppose during that running battle with the Sioux, the man dropped back half a length and put a bullet in Howard's back. It would have been easy to do. No one would have suspected it wasn't the Sioux."

"We're dealing with facts, not suppositions," Marlin said tersely. "The fact is that Reynolds, if he didn't kill the man himself, knew it was murder the minute I told him about those powder bums. Yet he denied it. Why?"

"All right," Weatherby conceded. "So Reynolds did know. Did you expect him to turn one of his own men—a fellow Confederate—over to Yankees to be hung for murder?"

He drew gently on his cheroot and expertly blew a series of perfect smoke rings toward the ceiling. "No more, Colonel, than he would have turned another white man, who'd raped a black wench, over to a bunch of niggers to be lynched."

Abruptly, Marlin laid down knife and fork and thrust his plate aside. "Are you suggesting that Reynolds was simply trying to cover up a grudge killing among his men?" he snapped. "And that he and his detail were not part of a Confederate conspiracy to disrupt communications with the West?"

Unperturbed, Weatherby leaned back and observed Marlin with impersonal eyes. "I'm simply suggesting that eight men may have been accused of something of which they were innocent," he said cooly, "and murdered when they tried to escape. Oh, I don't doubt but that there's a conspiracy here on the Plains, but I don't think it involves the Confederacy."

Slowly, he removed the cheroot from his mouth,

his lips spreading in a thin, unpleasant line.

"You're either a fool or a very clever man, Colonel," he said. "I don't think you're a fool. I think you're exactly what you appear to be—an intelligent, ex-Army officer hired by Holladay to drag a red herring across his path."

"I'm not one to talk in riddles," Marlin retorted. "Nor to interpret them."

"All right." Weatherby shrugged. "I'll speak frankly. Since last spring, Senator Conness has been accusing Holladay of faking Indian attacks upon the Overland. Personally, I've been inclined to give Holladay the benefit of the doubt. Now, I'm not so sure. He may have convinced the President and the Army that the Confederacy is guilty when, in fact, he's actually engineering the attacks himself."

"You can't be serious!" Marlin exclaimed. "Why would Holladay furnish the tribes with arms and ammunition to destroy his own stage line?"

"Money." Weatherby's smile was openly cynical. "Ninety per cent of these raids have been *real* Indian attacks. The Overland's losses this year will pass the million-dollar mark. Although I understand President Lincoln has promised that the government will honor his claims after the war, Holladay knows how unpredictable Congress can be. So he's covering his bets. If Congress does vote him compensation, fine. If not, he has no intention of ending up a loser."

"Are you saying that—"

"I'm saying that Holladay's found himself a Sioux subchief named Crooked Jaw for the job," Weatherby interrupted. "Crooked Jaw attacks only those stages which Holladay informs him are carrying gold and mail. The horses and crews' guns, he keeps. The gold he trades back to Holladay for more guns, ammunition, and whiskey. Gold means nothing to him; guns to kill Walk-a-Heaps and Pony Soldiers mean survival. For fifty rifles worth maybe a thousand dollars, Holladay pockets up to seventy-five thousand dollars in 'stolen' gold. Twenty or thirty raids and he's made back his million dollars. Simple and all but foolproof—if he can shut Conness' mouth."

Carefully, Weatherby tapped the pale gray ash from his cheroot onto his plate and then smiled thinly at Marlin.

"Holladay's using you to try and do just that. You've been hired to hunt down a nonexistent Confederate agent directing a nonexistent Southern conspiracy against the Union. When Holladay releases the news that the Overland's cavalry escorts were Confederate parolees, many newspapers are going to believe that there *is* a Confederate conspiracy to wreck the Overland. That could discredit Conness completely—and leave Holladay free to continue his raids."

"Where is your proof of all this?" Marlin asked. "Or is it pure speculation?"

"The proof is in a renegade trader's camp five miles from here," Weatherby said. "*Solid proof.* Thirty Spencer repeating rifles, a hundred rounds of ammunition per gun, twenty gallons of trade whiskey—and two dead men." He paused, watching Marlin closely for some reaction, but Marlin hid his shock behind impassive features.

How had Weatherby found out about Bender so quickly?

"So you stumbled onto a renegade trader's camp with a few arms and some whiskey and a couple of dead men," he replied with feigned casualness. "How does that prove that Holladay, and not the Confederacy, is responsible for these raids?"

"I didn't stumble onto the camp," Weatherby corrected. "I heard about it from Crooked Jaw, with whom I'm still friendly, a couple of hours after it happened."

"After what happened?"

"After Sergeant Bender and Jeff Hicks killed one another over the gold," Weatherby informed him. "You see, Wes Bender was Holladay's go-between with the Indians. He passed on information about stages carrying gold and mail, and then, after the raids, acted as Holladay's agent in selling them arms, ammunition, and whiskey for the 'stolen' gold."

"I don't believe it," Marlin said flatly. "Bender's been tracking the Reb for weeks. If he was killed in Hicks's camp, it was because he'd stumbled onto it and had to be silenced before he could talk."

Weatherby's expression was openly cynical. "Colonel, Bender was exchanging guns and whiskey for gold to Crooked Jaw and twenty of his braves yesterday morning."

"How do you know that?" Marlin demanded.

"When I ran into Crooked Jaw around noon yesterday, he and his men had new Spencers and plenty of whiskey. He told me he had traded Bender and Hicks gold for the stuff; and that Bender had then opened up a free jug and they had sat passing it around until they all got pretty drunk. Then Bender and Hicks started to argue over the gold. Suddenly, Hicks drew his gun and shot Bender in the chest. Bender let out a yell and 'went home,' as the Sioux call it. He emptied his pistol into Hicks and then went to work on him with his knife.

"Now Indians don't fool around with a crazy man. They jumped on their horses and took off. By the time I ran into them, they'd sobered up a bit and were heading back for the rest of the rifles."

That had been around noon, Marlin thought. Yet the rifles and ammunition had still been there when he had reached the camp late in the afternoon. And had it been Crooked Jaw's people who had surprised him there, there would have been a lot more gunfire. Nor would they have waited for dark. They'd have charged the camp and over-run him.

He studied Weatherby narrowly. "Did you go back to the camp with them?"

"You don't go anywhere with a drunken Indian if you can help it. Crooked Jaw calls me friend, but if the thought *'kill'* flashed through his mind, he'd have killed me instantly."

"Then you have no proof of anything except the word of a drunken Indian who hates whites," Marlin retorted. "He may even have killed Bender and Flicks himself, but I doubt it. I think Reynolds was a part of a Confederate conspiracy; I think he was responsible for the attacks upon the stages his detail escorted. I think Bender was killed because he'd stumbled on to something—and I *know* there is a Southern conspiracy still operating on the Plains."

"Can you prove that?" Weatherby asked.

"Given a little time, I think maybe I can," Marlin said. "As a matter of fact, I know I can."

Weatherby shook his head with frank skepticism. "Let's hope you have that time, Colonel. It's getting more dangerous out there every day."

Draining his coffee cup, Marlin rose and picked up his coat. "We suddenly seem to have different views as to what is actually going on," he said in a pleasant but challenging voice. "If you still think you have solid proof that Holladay's behind these raids upon the Overland, why not go to Major Beauchamp with it?"

Weatherby's eyes met his through the swirling gray smoke. "You've got the Major so mixed up he doesn't know what he's doing. He's thinking 'West Point' again, hoping it's not too late to save his career despite the way he bungled the Reynolds matter. And since Holladay still wields a lot of influence in Washington, Stephen is not going to do anything more to antagonize him now."

"Tell me . . . ," Marlin asked curiously, "why do you feel so strongly about this whole situation?"

"Why?" The artist shrugged. "The war is lost, Colonel; I've accepted that. But I resent the Confederacy being accused of a bloody nightmare, and Confederate prisoners being imprisoned and killed for something they didn't do."

"They weren't innocent," Marlin said. "And they weren't shot for something they didn't do. They were killed because, as Confederate prisoners of war, they tried to escape from a military stockade." He shrugged into his coat and moved toward the door. "Are you riding into town?"

"Later," Weatherby answered curtly. "If I were you, I'd keep an eye out for raiding parties."

"Thanks."

Outside, he paused, breathing deeply of the bracing air. The storm had passed, leaving behind it clear skies, subzero temperatures and window-high snowdrifts. Slogging his way to the stable, he saddled the bay and headed for town.

On the open prairie, the wind had flattened the drifts, and traveling was easier. Marlin pushed the bay steadily, constantly scanning the empty land for signs of hostiles. But around him, the smooth, untrampled snow stretched out to the horizon in a . . .

He reined up, a chill, coming from deep inside him, spreading through his body and settling in his mind.

If Crooked Jaw had been in the camp, trading and drinking, as Hamlin Weatherby claimed, the campsite should have been covered with moccasin prints and churned up by the hoofs of a score of restless ponies.

But when he, Marlin, had reached the camp, the area—save where Bender and Hicks had shot it out—had been as smooth and untrampled as the land before him now. Yet there had been no new snow to wipe out tracks in four days.

Crooked Jaw had not been in the camp when Bender had been killed; therefore, he could not have told Weatherby of Bender's death. How then had Weatherby known, unless . . .

Good God, of course!

Weatherby had trailed him from town, had tried to kill him when he had stumbled onto the camp and, after he had escaped, had ridden down and found the bodies of Bender and Hicks. By inventing the Crooked Jaw story, Weatherby had hoped to make it appear that Holladay, not the Confederacy, was guilty of a conspiracy with the Indians.

The pieces began to fit together now, sharp and clear, and Marlin wondered how he could have failed to relate them to one another long ago. Perhaps because he had been thinking "present" when the conspiracy had had its beginnings shortly after hostilities began, three and a half years before. It was frustrating to realize that while he had been desperately seeking clues, they had been available all the time.

Janet Beauchamp, deliberately marrying a brilliant, dissatisfied Union cavalry officer with Southern roots . . . Hamlin Weatherby, following the Beauchamps to Julesburg and, as a talented frontier artist, making friends with Sioux, Cheyenne, and Arapaho chiefs . . . Arranging, through Beauchamp, the transfer of Confederate prisoners of war to the frontier as cavalry parolees . . . Providing the chiefs with departure dates, secured by Beauchamp, of gold- and mail-laden Overland stages . . . Using the parolee detail under Sergeant Reynolds to murder unsuspecting stagecoach crews or to lead them into Indian traps . . .

Falling rapidly into place now, smaller bits and pieces to add to complete the picture.

The painting, "Attack On An Overland Stage," on the easel in Weatherby's cabin, depicting the savage, unrelenting hatred of the Sioux chief for the blue-clad cavalrymen . . . Weatherby's admitted loss of his plantation and a way of life which, despite his denial, he had cherished . . . his pretense of not being bitter while, in truth, his hatred for the Union was as merciless as that which he had painted into Red Cloud's face . . . his long "sketching" trips which aroused no suspicion and permitted him to run his organization of renegade gun and whiskey traders, Reynolds' "escort" and to help the chiefs set traps for stagecoaches the Confederate detail could not accompany . . . the murder, by mistake, of Adam Burgess . . . Bender's death . . . the attempt to kill him, Marlin . . .

A carefully planned, beautifully executed conspiracy, with Hamlin Weatherby the Reb agent, and the Major and Janet Beauchamp his accomplices. But for two mistakes, they might have played it out to the war's end.

Reynolds should have covered up the trooper Howard's murder by leaving the body to the wolves, instead of bringing it in. It was a blunder that had not only cost the entire detail their lives, but had forced Beauchamp to admit he had known they were Confederate parolees.

And Weatherby, a master strategist, should never have admitted to any knowledge of Bender's death. It had been an unwise attempt to try and convince him, Marlin, that the conspiracy was Holladay, not Southern, led. It was hard to believe that Weatherby, an experienced frontiersman, could have overlooked the absence of tracks around the camp; but many enemy agents had lost their lives over just such little oversights.

Drawing his rifle from its boot, Marlin turned in his saddle and swept the silent, empty land with narrowed eyes. It was not the Sioux or the Arapaho or the Cheyennes who threatened him now; but the man sitting back there at Liz Dennison's kitchen table, calmly sipping coffee and smoking his cheroot. The man who, as an artist, painted into the face of an attacking Sioux war chief his own unrelenting hatred for Union cavalry—for all damn Yankees.

Uneasily, Marlin gave the bay its head and opened the distance between himself and the Dennison ranch. It had now become a game of fox and hound, with each chasing the other in a rapidly tightening circle. If one got careless and slowed down, or the other grew daring and moved too quickly—who then would know who had been the hunter and who the hunted? It wouldn't matter. One of them would be dead.

He would be glad when the ordnance train and the Mormon battalion arrived. It was time to spring the trap, and the sooner the better.

It was midmorning when Marlin turned the tired bay over to a red-haired hostler at Meecham's

Livery. From there, he went straight to the Overland office where he was greeted by a relieved Ed Ashley.

"What happened to you?" Ashley demanded, trying to hide his feelings. "You've given the family a bad night. Susan, especially. She was worried you'd been caught out in that blizzard and . . ."

"I was lucky," Marlin said. "I managed to make it to the Dennison ranch."

"Did you run into any sign of Bender?"

"Bender's dead. I found him in a renegade gun trader's camp twenty miles from here. He and the trader had killed one another." He hesitated, then decided against telling Ashley about Weatherby at the moment. "I would have brought Bender's body in, but I wouldn't have had a chance in that storm. You can send a party out after it later—if the wolves haven't already gotten to him."

"I'm sorry," Ashley said sincerely. "He was a fine scout, and Ben trusted him. Do you think the trader was working for the Reb?"

"I'm sure of it," Marlin replied. "There were thirty new Spencers, plenty of ammunition, and a lot of whiskey in the camp."

Ashley puffed thoughtfully on his battered pipe. "Just what do you intend to do?"

"Wait for the ordnance train and the Mormon company to arrive," Marlin said. "Then I'm going to lay a trap for the Reb. He and the chiefs will hit the train between here and Fort Laramie. We'll be ready for them."

The Mormon company, under the command of Captain Joseph Pike, reached the Julesburg area on December 26, one day after the arrival of the ordnance train bound for Fort Laramie. Bivouacking in a small canyon five miles from town, Pike issued a "small fires for cooking only" order, and then slipped into Julesburg after dark.

Dismounting before the Overland office, he tied his horse to the hitching rack and went inside. The waiting room was empty, but from the office beyond he could hear the sound of men's voices. He walked behind the ticket counter and stopped in the doorway of the lighted office.

In conference with Holladay and Ed Ashley, Marlin was unaware of the Mormon's presence until Pike cleared his throat to draw their attention.

Looking up, Marlin nodded to the lean, sandy-haired man standing on the threshold with an air of quiet confidence. "Yes, sir? Can I help you?"

"I'm Captain Joseph Pike, commander of the Mormon company."

Quickly, Marlin rose and extended his hand. "Welcome, Captain. I'm Kurt Marlin, the division's trouble-shooter. We hadn't expected you for at least another day."

"There was no reason to dawdle, sir."

"Where is your company, Captain?"

"Bivouacked in a canyon five miles northwest of here," Pike replied. "My orders were to stay out of sight until I contacted you."

"Good." Marlin nodded. "Captain, this is Ben Holladay, owner of the Overland—and Ed Ashley, the stationmaster for Julesburg."

"Gentlemen." Pike offered his hand to each. Then, addressing himself to Holladay, he said, "Sir, President Young instructed me to convey to you his warmest regards and to place myself and my company at your service."

"I'm glad to meet you, Captain," Holladay replied. "And I'm very grateful to Brigham Young both for his friendship and for his help." He motioned to a chair. "Sit down, and tell us about your trip. Did you have any serious trouble with hostiles?"

Pike settled himself comfortably and then shook his head. "No, sir. We did see some small war parties on the skyline, but none of them attacked us. I hear there's a big village, eight or nine hundred lodges, camped on Cherry Creek. Are they up to something?"

"The village is there," Marlin spoke up. "But I'm not sure that the chiefs and their warriors are. We'll know in a few days."

There was a moment's silence, and Holladay swiveled his chair into line with Marlin. "I think you should have told me you were sending for the

Mormon company," he said coldly. "After all, it was my decision to make, not yours."

"Perhaps I should have," Marlin admitted. "But national security was involved and, frankly, your interference could have endangered my mission. I had no choice but to keep you in the dark." He looked toward Pike and Ed Ashley and then back to Holladay.

"Gentlemen, I am a Presidential agent assigned to seek out and destroy a Confederate conspiracy with the Indians to disrupt our communications link with the West. My orders were to maintain the greatest secrecy, identifying myself only to the military commander of Camp Rankin. But now I need your help, not Major Beauchamp's."

Holladay sat frozen, only the smoke curling upward from his cigar indicating that he still breathed. Then, abruptly, he exploded.

"Well, by God and be damned!" he cried. "So, for all that bastard Conness' yelling, the President believed me, instead of him!" The building anger in his face faded and he favored Marlin with a crooked smile.

"Colonel, I ought to be mad as hell, but I'm not. If you'll just turn up that damned Reb, I'll make you a vice-president of the Overland. Or think about it, anyway."

"You don't have to go that far," Marlin assured him. "All I ask is your co-operation. Now here, briefly, is the situation.

"Chewing Black Bone, chief of the Broken Cooking Pot tribe, has promised the survivors of the Sand Creek massacre a home here and a part of the loot if they will help him drive the settlers from the valley of the Platte. He's even offered to share with them the rifles he took in a raid last March on Lieutenant B. F. Johnson's ordnance train out of Fort Kearney. But that still won't be enough to go around.

"To get the rest, he plans to hit the ordnance caravan leaving here for Fort Laramie—and then, with the captured guns and ammunition, to raid Julesburg. All the chiefs—Red Cloud, Crazy Horse, Iron Plume, Gray Bull, Spotted Tail, Little Wolf, Dull Knife—are ready to ride with him. The Reb's fanned their hate and talked them into it. He'll be with Chewing Black Bone in the attack on the caravan."

"The son of a bitch!" Holladay slammed his fist down on the desk. "If they burn Julesburg to the ground, he can shut down passenger and freighting commerce for months! No, by God, I'll let no damned Johnny Reb stop the Overland! I'll build back division headquarters, home and way stations and replace horses and equipment as fast as he destroys it!"

Pike, who had remained silent until now, pursed his lips with a faint frown. "What is your counterplan, Colonel?"

"Your company will be part of a larger force,"

Marlin explained. "When the ordnance caravan leaves here, it will be accompanied by fifteen high-sided freighters apparently bound for Deseret with supplies. Actually, those wagons will be rolling 'forts' filled with heavily armed men, including your people. Only the Regular cavalry escort will ride in the open."

"Sir," Pike protested, "my men are a mounted group!"

"I know that, Captain. But we can't risk arousing suspicion. We've got to draw the Reb out, make him attack, and then kill him. That may not stop the Indian raids, but it will destroy the conspiracy and stop the South from taking advantage of them."

"What will be the size of our total force?" Pike asked.

"Counting drivers, ordnance escort, Overland volunteers, and your company, around two hundred men."

Frowning, Holladay fingered the tiger's claw suspended from the heavy gold chain looped across his vest. "Suppose the Reb smells a trap?"

"I'm gambling he'll still go for the bait."

Holladay's heavy eyebrows shot up. "What bait?"

"I've leaked word that a stagecoach carrying fifty thousand dollars in gold for a Deseret bank will be traveling with the caravan. The Reb will go for it. He has to."

"Why?"

Marlin smiled thinly. "The war's lost and he knows it. How long do you think he'd live if his part in these Indian atrocities became known? Sooner or later, some man who'd lost a loved one in a raid would hunt him down and kill him. Or he'd be captured by Union troops and hanged for treason.

"But with fifty thousand in gold, he could head for Mexico, book passage for some country where a man with money is always welcome and his past is not questioned. He'll take the bait, all right. And we'll be waiting for him."

"When do we leave?" Pike asked.

"Are you amply provisioned?"

"We have our own supply wagons."

"Can you move out at dawn tomorrow?"

"I suppose so, although it won't give us much rest."

"You can rest when this is over," Marlin told him. "I'll notify the ordnance escort." He swung toward Ashley. "Ed, You'll have to handle things here. Just in case it should go bad for us, you'd better have people alerted to make a run for the fort. The town wouldn't have a chance against a strong attack."

"When will you be back?"

"If all goes well, I'd say five or six days. It depends on how soon the Reb strikes. But in any case, we'll send a rider back with the news." He looked toward Pike and Holladay. "Any questions?"

"One." Ash from his cigar spilled upon Holladay's dark vest like silver powder. "Who is the Reb? I give you my word I won't interfere. But I want to know who he is and, until I do, we don't go anywhere."

Thoughtfully, Marlin studied the big man, wondering whether he could trust Holladay, and then decided he had no choice.

"All right," he said. "But I warn you, I'm going to hold you to your promise. And I don't want you interrupting me while I'm talking."

"You have my word." Holladay leaned forward expectantly, and Marlin could sense the biting edge of the man's impatience. Having lost a million dollars and been viciously harassed for the Confederate's crimes, Ben Holladay wanted blood—and could not be blamed for it.

"Well?" Holladay demanded. "Come on! Tell me—who is the Reb?"

"Hamlin Weatherby," Marlin said quietly. "With Major Beauchamp and his wife, Janet, as accomplices."

"Weatherby!" Snatching the cigar from his mouth, Holladay stabbed it at Marlin like a pistol. "You mean to tell me that that damned artist is— By God, Colonel, I'm in no mood for jokes! The Reb's a military strategist. Beauchamp, yes. I've suspected him for a long time. But Weatherby . . . !"

236

"Hamlin Weatherby's the most dangerous man you'll ever meet. He's the mastermind, the one to whom the chiefs listen with respect. Major Beauchamp provides the cover for the operation, furnishes the escorts, and gives tactical assistance to the chiefs. Janet Beauchamp's role is to keep the Major in line when his conscience begins to bother him. It all runs like clockwork."

"Weatherby!" Holladay glared at his ruined cigar, then threw it angrily to the floor. "Hell, he's done nothing but ride around drawing Indians and stagecoaches for the past three years!"

"Not quite," Marlin replied grimly. "He was planted here by the Confederacy to try and ally the tribes, as nations, with the South. He failed. No Indian nation has gone over to either the North or South, although some individual tribes have done so.

"But after the Sand Creek massacre last month, he's played upon the Sioux', Cheyennes', and Arapahos' hatred of Union cavalry and the Overland, to turn the stage route through the Platte valley into a bloody nightmare.

"Through the Major, he acquired a detail of Confederate prisoners of war, paroled here to fight the Indians. Instead, acting as escorts, they've been murdering unsuspecting stagecoach crews, burning the stages, giving the horses to the Indians, and using the gold to buy arms, ammunition for Weatherby's renegade traders to distribute to the tribes.

"Last week, I charged Sergeant Reynolds and the entire detail with being a part of the conspiracy. Major Beauchamp had no choice but to throw them in the guardhouse pending further investigation. An investigation which he knew he could not afford. He had them killed when they attempted an escape which he had arranged."

"You didn't tell me about Reynolds," Holladay flared. "As a matter of fact, you didn't tell me a damn thing."

"I'm telling you now," Marlin replied patiently. "So listen. Hamlin Weatherby was a plantation owner, a wealthy, powerful one. He lost it all, the wealth, the power, the gracious life. He pretends he doesn't mind, that he's built a better life. But he does mind. He and his daughter, Janet, have a fiery, relentless hatred for the Union and 'damn Yankees.'

"Somehow, Weatherby knew of my mission even before I reached Denver. Adam Burgess, a U.S. postal inspector, was mistaken for me and murdered in the Planter's Hotel. Last week, Sergeant Bender was shot and wounded when he was out scouting for the Reb. Several days ago, Bender was killed in a shootout with one of the renegade traders. That same day, Weatherby tried to kill me from a ridge above the camp. He's no longer fighting for a cause he knows is already lost. He's carrying on a personal vendetta against the Union. He'll not stop until he's killed."

"Then why in hell fool around with a trap?" Holladay demanded, still smarting from being left in the dark. "Why don't we just pick up those two bastards and string them from the nearest tree? That's what the government will do anyway."

"Because all we've got is circumstantial evidence," Marlin retorted. "And the President wants them caught red-handed. Also, we still have to protect that ordnance caravan."

He waited tensely, wondering if Holladay was going to break his word and what he, Marlin, would do if it happened. For what must have been two or three minutes, Holladay sat hunched forward, his arms widespread, his hands palms down on the desk, glaring at Marlin with belligerent eyes. Then, slowly, the anger ebbed from his face and he leaned back with a disgruntled sigh.

"All right," he said reluctantly. "But if your trap doesn't work, I'm going after him, with or without you." He shoved back his chair and rose. "Gentlemen, I've got some of the finest whiskey this side of hell. If we're going out and maybe get ourselves killed tomorrow, I propose we do it justice!"

"You'll excuse me, sir," Pike said quietly. "I do not drink spirits. If you don't mind, I'll take my leave and see you at dawn."

When the Mormon had gone, Holladay opened a

desk drawer and drew out a bottle of eight-year-old Scotch.

The three of them—Holladay, Marlin, and Ed Ashley—drank straight from the bottle, and, in that moment, Marlin wondered if the three of them would live to share another such experience.

The thought still haunted him when at dawn, seated beside Bob Ridley atop the "baited" stage, he led the ordnance caravan, accompanied by fifteen high-sided freighters, out of Julesburg.

Five miles out, they rendezvoused with Captain Pike and the Mormon company. An hour later, with the freighters now rolling "forts," the caravan got under way again—leaving three men and a hay wagon behind to take care of the horses until they returned.

Soberly, Marlin cradled his rifle in his arms and stared out over the heads of the trotting horses, barely visible in the predawn light. Somewhere among those rolling hills, Hamlin Weatherby and the greatest Indian chiefs on the Plains were waiting for them.

Marlin shivered, for the first time assailed by doubt. Had he been too confident? Instead of laying a trap, was he perhaps leading two hundred men into a deathtrap?

He didn't know.

Vapor, jetting from the team's nostrils, rose like tiny white clouds against the slate-gray sky.

Seated beside Bob Ridley, Marlin swept the snow-covered hills with field glasses. On the roof behind them, Ben Holladay braced his feet against the boot and covered their rear with a new Spencer.

Flanking the Concord, the cavalry escort slouched easily in their saddles while, inside, the heavily armed "passengers" kept their eyes on the troopers and their hands on their guns.

A thousand yards out, Jerimah Henshaw, chief scout, and two Mormon volunteers probed draws and ravines for fresh signs of hostiles. Marlin's nagging sense of unease persisted. He had the strong feeling that they were being watched; but, so far, Henshaw had not cut any trail, and Henshaw was one of the best scouts this side of the Rockies.

With a frown, he swung the glasses on the trail behind them. Half a mile back, the ordnance train forged slowly ahead, the ten-man special detail under Sergeant Brill, riding with their rifles thigh-butted for instant action.

Inside the high-sided freighters, Marlin knew that the Overland volunteers and the men of the Mormon company would be crouched at their gun slots, fingering their arsenal of weapons.

The famous Maynards, smooth-bore, muzzle loaders, firing a charge of sixteen pellets and an ounce ball, especially designed for Indian fighting. At close range, they were as murderous as small cannon firing grapeshot . . . Hall .44 caliber, fifteen-shot repeaters . . . Sharp .52s . . . a few of the new Spencer 50-caliber, seven-shot, rapid-firing carbines . . . the standard Army single-shot, muzzle-loading Springfields . . . the Navy Colt . . .

A little of Marlin's concern disappeared. With a string of "rolling forts," an "army" almost twice as large as the force at Camp Rankin and with a killing power three times as great, the caravan would be tough to overrun.

Shifting the glasses, he spotted Captain Pike cantering up and down the line, pausing here and there to say something to a teamster. The Mormon could be depended upon not to be caught off guard.

"Well?" Holladay swiveled around on his buttocks. "See anything?"

"Nothing." A worried note sharpened Marlin's voice. "But they're out there. I can feel them." He lowered the field glasses. "But where is Weatherby? We're far enough ahead of the caravan to draw him out."

"Maybe he's smelled trouble and decided to stay out of it," Holladay said. "Instead of laying a trap, we just may be walking into one. Hell, wouldn't that be something!"

"Somebody's out there," Marlin replied. "Chewing Black Bone wants those rifles. I figure that most of the chiefs are with him."

Raising the glasses, he resumed his scan of the empty landscape. He had been certain that Weatherby would hit the stage for the faked gold shipment. If the Reb leader did not take the bait, then his, Marlin's, mission would end in failure. For Weatherby, realizing his identity was now known, would return with the Sioux to their camp and carry on his raids from there. He would never surrender. He would, somehow, recruit more Confederates and fight to the bitter end.

Suddenly, up ahead, Marlin saw Jerimah Henshaw wheel his horse and come racing back toward them, the two Mormon volunteers close behind. Smoke bloomed from the scout's rifle as he fired a warning shot into the air. An instant later, a dark wave of horsemen erupted from the ravine and cut diagonally across the flats to intercept them.

"*Hiii-yiii-haaaa!*"

As the dreaded Sioux war cry carried high and thin across the silent land, Marlin dropped the field glasses and grabbed his rifle.

"Swing them, Bob!" he cried. "That's Weatherby! He'll try and cut us off!"

Ridley brought the team around in a tight circle, the skidding wheels throwing up a heavy spray of snow and mud. "Hi-ya! Hi-yah!" Lengthening stride, the racers pounded back along the trail.

A quarter of a mile ahead, Marlin saw Sergeant Brill wheel his detail and race back to the train and, a moment later, Captain Pike spurring up and down the column. Like a coiling snake, the train curled in upon itself. Bullwhip crackers exploded like pistol shots over the high leaders' heads, sending them lunging against their collars, their hoofs throwing dirty slush into the faces of the cursing teamsters.

With the team running beautifully, manes and tails streaming in the wind, Marlin risked a glance over his shoulder at the dark mass of riders fanned out across the skyline.

"Still too far away for a good shot," Holladay said, lowering his rifle. "But it looks like—" He grabbed for the handrail as Ridley brought the stage rocketing through the last gap in the circle of wagons. The Concord's wheels were still turning when the last freighter moved in and closed the gap.

From the shelter of one of the big wagons, Marlin watched the enemy close the distance, fanning out as they came, lances and rifles held high, screaming, yelling, some already singing their death songs. The thud of thousands of hoofs rattled the freighter's floorboards and vibrated up through the ground to his feet and throughout his entire body.

"*Hiii-yiii-haaaa!*"

Wild, savage, challenging, reaching out ahead to chill men's hearts and fear-numb their brains.

"Jesus Christ!" a teamster cried. "There must be a million of them bastards!"

"Don't let 'em scare you!" Holladay shouted. "Nine times out of ten an Indian will break his charge at the barricade if you keep pouring the fire into him an' getting him down!"

Five hundred yards.

Still at the gallop, the leading Sioux opened fire. A few bullets thudded harmlessly into the thick plank sides of the wagons, but most fell short. The range was still too great.

"Single shots, mostly," Holladay told Marlin. "An' damn poor powder. When they're right on top of us, they'll use their bows. That's when you want to watch out. They can quill you like a porcupine. I've seen a Cheyenne loose seven arrows in seven seconds. That's about as fast as you can fire that Spencer of yours."

Captain Pike, riding a big-boned sorrel, reined up alongside the wagon. "They're coming within range, Colonel. You want us to open fire?"

"Not yet," Marlin replied. "Wait until they're within a hundred yards. Then let them have it."

Wheeling his mount, Pike spurred around the circle. "Hold your fire!" he shouted. "Hold your fire!"

From inside their "forts," Marlin heard the scuff of boots and the *thunk* of rifle butts against the plank siding as men stood to their gun ports. And then there was only the chilling "*Hiii-yiii-haaaa!*"

of Sioux, Cheyenne, and Arapaho, and the mounting thrum of hoofs and the thud of his own heart hammering in his chest.

He looked around him.

In the center of the circle, Sergeant Brill had his troopers, as well as the escort, down behind their horses, ready to pick off any Indian who tried to put his pony over the wagon tongues or who, dismounted, crawled under the wagons.

A few feet away, Captain Pike stood alone, pistol in hand, as cool as though he were on the parade ground.

Spaced among the freighters, the dozen Overland stage guards rested their deadly Maynards on wheel spokes, their fingers caressing the triggers.

Methodically, Marlin checked Spencer and Colt, surprised at the unfamiliar trembling of his hands. He had killed men before and had seen friends die all around him, but, somehow, this was different.

Two hundred yards.

On they came across the frozen meadow, a thousand strong, men and horses daubed, decked, and smeared with vermillion, ocher, cobalt, eagle feathers, heron plumes, dyed hair tassels, scalp locks, buffalo horns, bear claws, beads, quills, copper and silver ornaments, pennoned lances and gaudy blankets: the full, wild treatment of the Sioux war dress.

A hundred and fifty yards.

Close enough now to recognize the chiefs leading them, if you knew them. Marlin didn't; but he knew they were all there, the cream of the warrior societies—Sioux, Cheyenne, Arapaho —their minds inflamed by the memory of the massacre at Sand Creek.

Tashunko Witko, Crazy Horse, War Chief of the Seven Tribes, a pony's length out in front . . . Makpiya Luta, Red Cloud, sitting his paint stud with an arrogant ease . . . Gray Bull, astride a plunging bay . . . Napka Kesela, Iron Plume, trailing his famed seven-foot war bonnet . . . Elk Nation, his moccasined heels dug into the flanks of a fleet steel gray . . . Chewing Black Bone, his dark face alive with passion, racing thigh to thigh with Young Two Moons . . . Dull Knife, very straight on his Appaloosa . . . Little Wolf, a footlong argent around his neck, urging on a spirited roan . . . White Bull, bent low over the ears of his sockfoot sorrel . . . Black Shield, savagely lashing a red-and-white pinto.

And behind these, others less well known, but no less brave. High Hump-Back . . . Red Arm . . . Black Horse . . . He Dog . . . Bob-Tail Horse . . . Black Buffalo . . .

One hundred yards.

Marlin laid the butt of his rifle hard against his shoulder, feeling the coldness of the stock upon his cheek. Still at the gallop, the leading riders opened fire. Bullets thudded harmlessly against the freighters' heavy sides. Marlin gently squeezed the trigger, his shot knocking a rider from his pad saddle.

Behind him, he heard Pike shout, "Give it to them!" and then flame spurted from the gun ports and black smoke billowed up from the wagons and a roaring wave of sound pounded against his ears.

The entire Sioux-Cheyenne-Arapaho front seemed suddenly caught up by a violent wind and then hurled to the ground in a tangled mass of screaming men and horses. But those behind closed the gaps and kept coming, lashing their wall-eyed ponies toward the barricade. Everywhere, they surged against the big freighters, firing through the rifle ports, sweeping in and loosing arrows through the spaces between the wagons.

From their "forts," the men of the Mormon company poured a murderous fire into the close-packed ranks, killing and wounding men and horses by the score. Black clouds of powder smoke hung over the train, half-blinding defender and attacker alike.

A chief, wearing a buffalo-horn headdress and a bear-claw necklace, charged the barrier, bow arced, arrow full-drawn to ear. Dropping his empty rifle, Marlin drew his Colt and planted a bullet just below the black, curving horns. The slim, feathered shaft whispered past his ear, and then the shaggy head disappeared in a bloody spray and was replaced by another with a single eagle's feather; and, beside him, he heard the sharp crack of Bob Ridley's rifle and the flatter bark of Ben Holladay's pistol and Holladay yelling, "Get 'em down! *Goddammit, get 'em down!*"

And then the Maynards cut loose, breaking the charge, rolling the screaming mass of men and horses back like a bloody carpet. Behind them, piled against the wagons and sprawled, dark-blotted, upon the snow, the Indians left a fifth of their number dead and wounded.

Abruptly, the firing ceased. In the ear-shattering silence, Marlin heard the groans and low curses of wounded men rising from the big freighters.

Beside him, Holladay reloaded rifle and pistol. "That was *mighty* close, Colonel. I thought for a minute they might overrun us."

Staring out across the empty meadow, Marlin asked, "You think they'll come at us again?"

"Hell, yes!" Holladay retorted. "You can count on it! These are 'feather' Indians, not Diggers! They'll keep mounting charges until they're convinced they can't break through."

Propped against a wagon wheel, Bob Ridley nodded a vigorous agreement. "And then one more after that."

Across the circle, a man began screaming, his voice mounting higher and higher until it lost its masculinity and took on the thin, hysterical quality of a frightened woman.

Holladay cursed softly. "Gut shot or thigh bone's shattered," he said. "Either case, he'll die."

"For God's sake," Marlin demanded, "where's Dr. E.C.? Why doesn't he give him something?"

"Doc's got his hands full," Ridley cut in. "Besides, nothing he could do for the poor bastard . . . except give him a bottle of whiskey an' let him die."

Looking around for Captain Pike, Marlin found the Mormon standing at his elbow. Blood ran down Pike's neck from a bullet-creased jaw.

"How many did we lose, Captain?" Marlin asked, dreading the answer.

"Five dead, sir," Pike replied, and Marlin breathed easier. "A Regular trooper, an Overland guard, and three of my men. Sergeant Brill has a bullet through his leg, but the bone is untouched. A dozen others wounded, one—the poor devil that's screaming—mortally, I'm afraid."

"How is your men's morale?"

The Mormon looked at him steadily. "We are men of faith, Colonel. Our morale is always good."

"Of course," Marlin nodded. Then: "Open the range to a hundred and fifty yards the next time, Captain. Maybe that will keep so many Indians from reaching the wagons."

Pike turned and walked away. "Sergeant

250

Jenkins!" A Mormon climbed out of one of the wagons and dropped to the ground. "Yes, Cap'n?"

"Open the range to a hundred and fifty yards," Pike ordered. "No random firing. Pick a target and bring it down."

"Yes, sir!" The Sergeant hurried away, and a moment later, Marlin heard him shouting, "Begin firing at a hundred and fifty yards next time. An' don't waste bullets!"

Checking rifle and ammunition, Marlin took a last look around him. Pike stood in the center of the compound, close to Sergeant Brill and his troopers. Marlin raised his hand in a silent gesture of good luck, but if Pike saw it, he made no move.

Across the circle, the wounded man kept screaming tirelessly, fighting to live even as he prayed to die. A brief pause, as though he had stopped to take a deep breath, and then it was torn from him—one last agonized protest against this horror that had happened to him, mounting higher and higher until men heard it only with their minds, and then, mercifully, did not hear it at all.

"My God!" Marlin whispered, and even the whisper was like a roaring wind in the silence. A silence that spread until it covered the entire train and held until Ben Holladay yelled, "*Here they come! You better get set. This will be the big one!*"

Marlin swung around, rifle at the ready.

They burst out of the timber flanking the

meadow and came charging across the frozen ground, waving their pennoned lances and rifles and screaming in high, ululating voices, with Tashunko Witko, Makpiya Luta, and Napka Kesela leading them, supremely confident of Tatanka Yotanka's medicine.

Once more, the thrumming hoofs, the pounding of his own heart, the groans of the wounded as Dr. Lindley, bare-handed despite the intense cold, moved calmly among them, patching and bandaging while bullets droned past his head and the able-bodied men stood quietly to their gun ports, waiting, as the range closed.

Carefully, Marlin drew a bead on a gaudily bedecked chief astride a black stallion and squeezed the trigger. The Cheyenne's arms flew up as though in sudden prayer, and the next instant, every gun in the train went into action, opening up huge gaps in the front ranks, but not stopping the charge.

Now the firing quickened as the Spencer repeaters began to take their toll. The Sioux-Cheyenne-Arapaho ranks started to melt away; yet still they came on, lashing their wall-eyed ponies, ignoring the slaughter around them until they, too, were killed.

Black Horse fell, He Dog, Little Elk. Blood ran down Dull Knife's thigh, but he stayed his pad saddle.

Crazy Horse, Red Cloud, Iron Plume, and

Chewing Black Bone, wrapped in the magic of Tatanka Yotanka's medicine, led the charge right up to the wagons, shouting, "*Hopo*! *Hokahay*! Come on! Let's go! Many coups, *tahunsas*!"

Around Marlin, men began to die now. A bullet punched through a rifle port, killing a man. A trooper took a bullet through the head and died instantly. From behind his dead horse, Sergeant Brill kept up a cool, steady fire, while a few feet away, Captain Joseph Pike planted bullets wherever the danger was greatest.

Charging right up to the barrier, Red Cloud shouted above the din, "Ho, *Eagle Chief! Hehaha akicita tela opewinge wance*!", and fired point-blank at Marlin. Delivered from a plunging horse, the bullet struck the iron-tired wagon wheel and ricocheted off into space. Before Marlin could snap off a shot, the chief was lost in a swirling mass of riders.

"That was Red Cloud," Holladay called out. "He said that the medicine man had promised them a hundred dead soldiers, and that he hoped one of them was you!"

Suddenly, for a split second, Hamlin Weatherby's face glared at Marlin from the melee of charging warriors, then it was gone so quickly that he wondered if he had seen it at all.

At twenty yards, the Maynards broke loose, shredding the Indian's ranks. They were so close that Marlin could see the blood spurt from faces, chests, and bodies. Horses reared, screaming, their entrails spilling in great pink coils from their ripped-open bellies.

At the last instant, the Sioux-Cheyenne-Arapaho charge broke. Wheeling, they raced back to the timber, scooping up their dead and wounded as they fled. Less than fifty warriors, led by Hamlin Weatherby and a Sioux chief in a bright red blanket, hit the wagons.

"*Hopo, sunke wakan! Hokahey! Owanyeke waste! Hun-hunhe! H'g'un! H'g'un!*"

The Sioux chief drew back his arm and hurled his pennoned lance in a beautiful arc that curved into the compound and killed Captain Joseph Pike.

"*Hiii-yiii-haaaa!*" The Sioux's mouth was still open as Marlin's bullet knocked him from his pony.

Riding close behind, Hamlin Weatherby veered and came on, firing on the run. As he brought the gallant little pony up and over the wagon tongue, Marlin shot him in the chest, killing him instantly. Yet, magnificent horseman that he was, he kept his saddle another twenty yards before falling near the body of Captain Joseph Pike.

"My God," Holladay swore, coming up on the run. "He damn near got you! *The son of a bitch!*"

As Marlin started to move away, he saw Captain Pike, lying on his back, the pennoned lance through his heart. He paused, struck by the serenity on the Mormon's face. A quiet peace, as though in that last instant of his life, Joseph Pike had found what all men sought . . . the key to his own identity. It was something Marlin was never to forget.

"Oh, hell," he said. "This will be bad news for Brigham Young." He looked at Holladay. "Will they come at us again?"

"No," Holladay replied. "They've had enough. Now they'll go back to camp and lick their wounds."

A troubled note crept into Marlin's voice. "I wish I were as certain of that as you are. I—"

"Excuse me, Colonel." Nathan Boggs, a young lieutenant who had now taken over command of the Mormon company, paused beside them. "We've got eleven dead and nineteen wounded. Dr. Lindley says some of the wounded may die. He insists that we return to Julesburg as soon as possible."

"All right." Marlin nodded. "Have him get the wounded ready to travel. And use a special wagon for the dead. We'll move out in half an hour."

After the Lieutenant had gone, he stood staring uneasily toward the timber. Chewing Black Bone was not a chief to abandon his plans so easily, and his Broken Cooking Pot warriors had suffered heavy losses. Their blood lust was bound to be up. Suppose the wily Brule chief decided to . . .

Suddenly, five hundred warriors burst from the

timber and, veering well away from the train, headed southeast at a fast clip. The rest rode slowly back toward Frenchman's Creek.

"My God," Marlin cried. "Chewing Black Bone's heading for Julesburg!"

It was the thing he had feared, the nightmare which he had warned Ed Ashley might occur. He thought of Susan and Emma and Notley Ann; and then he was shouting for Bob Ridley and Jerimah Henshaw to mount up twenty-five Overland guards on the ordnance escort's horses and the stagecoach racers and have them ready to move out in half an hour.

"Issue every rider forty rounds of ammunition for both pistol and rifle," he told the ordnance sergeant. "And, Bob, enough bacon, hardtack, and coffee for two days. We'll be traveling light and fast."

Thirty minutes later, he transferred command of the caravan to Lieutenant Boggs of the Mormon company, with orders to return to Julesburg as rapidly as possible. With so many wounded, it would not be feasible to continue the journey to Fort Laramie.

By the time Marlin led his group out, Chewing Black Bone's warriors had a four- or five-mile lead.

Settling down to a steady pace, Marlin followed the churned-up trail, knowing that with only twenty-five men he could do nothing but hang back until they neared Julesburg. Then he would make a break for it and try to outrun Chewing Black Bone to the fort.

Major Beauchamp would have no choice but to fight. He could expect no mercy from the enraged Brules, who now blamed him and the dead Weatherby for having led them into a trap. With a hundred and twenty well-armed troopers, he could probably hold the fort; but if he attempted to aid the town he would endanger his entire command. Whether he would choose to sit behind the walls of the fort and protect his own scalp, or decide to defend Julesburg out of some belated sense of guilt, would not be answered until the guns began to speak.

Uneasily, Marlin shifted in his saddle, feeling the cold begin to seep through his heavy coat and knowing that with nightfall the temperature would drop even more. Night travel depended upon the threatening weather. If the moon broke through the cloud cover, they would keep moving, pausing only to rest the horses and warm their stomachs with coffee brewed over a tiny "sock drying" fire built with small sticks carried in their saddle-bags. But if the darkness held, they would have no choice but to make camp until dawn. In the pitch blackness, twenty-five men would end up scattered all over the prairie.

Luck rode with them—for a while. They covered fifteen miles by sunset; and then a three-quarters moon, breaking through the thin cloud cover, lighted up the prairie and they kept going. Then their luck played out.

Around nine o'clock, the light overcast thickened and, within half an hour, the moon was gone and a light snow blew wetly against their faces. They rode without speaking, only the squeak of saddle leather and the snort of horses breaking the silence. The big flakes fell faster now, building up on their clothing, weighing them down, and causing the horses to stumble as it deepened on the rolling hills and in the small ravines.

By midnight, visibility was limited to horses' heads. Riders kept running into one another, spooking the animals, and gradually drifting apart. When they finally blundered into an oak grove beside a frozen stream, Marlin ordered a halt.

"We'll camp here until dawn," he told Henshaw. "Picket-line the horses farther back in the timber and set up a guard."

Sheltered by the big oaks, they started a fire with the dry wood from their saddlebags, made coffee and used it to wash down hardtack and bacon. Then building up the fire with dead branches, they crawled under their blankets and slept.

Lying just beyond the circle of firelight, Marlin stared up at the shadowy outlines of the trees, thinking. Now and then an overloaded branch sagged, dumping its clump of snow with a soft *plop.* He wondered if Chewing Black Bone had also been forced to make camp—or whether the wily Brule had taken advantage of the snow and the fact that this was well-known Brule country to open up a hopeless lead over the Overland riders.

The snow thickened, drifting down through the branches to settle wetly on his face. He tilted his hat over his eyes, pulled the blanket higher on his shoulders, and fell asleep.

He came awake, throwing the blanket aside with one hand and reaching for his rifle with the other. In the early dawn light, the fire flickered pale-yellow, and around him men slept, white-covered mounds, beneath the trees. It had stopped snowing. Through the branches, he saw a few stars shimmering faintly in the lightening sky.

For a moment, he lay unmoving, listening for whatever sound it was that had awakened him. Something was wrong; he had a strong premonition of immediate danger. He crawled over to Jerimah Henshaw and, without touching him, said in a low voice, "Jerimah!"

The scout came instantly awake, pistol in hand. "What's wrong?"

"Something's out there," Marlin whispered.

"You see anything, hear anything?"

"No; but something's wrong."

"Where are the guards?"

"I don't know. I thought it best not to call out."

"A damn good idea. We may just—"

On the other side of the grove, an owl hooted softly. Henshaw rolled to his knees, thumbing back the hammer of his single-action pistol. "That ain't no owl, Colonel," he said tersely. "That's—"

A rifle cracked once, twice, and a man yelled from somewhere among the trees, "Injuns! They're after the horses!" and then arrows whispered among the trees, snipping twigs from branches and *thunking* into the trunks; and the shrill, yipping cries of the Sioux rolled men out of their blankets in half-awake alarm.

"Keep down!" Marlin shouted. "And stay under cover!"

The rifle cracked twice more, then Buck Morris, a stocky, blond-haired man, came running toward them, blood streaming down his face, half-blinding him. He kept banging into trees and bouncing off them like a drunken teamster.

"Injuns!" he yelled. "They killed Drew an' now they're killin' the horses!"

Marlin grabbed his knees and pulled him to the ground. Flat-bellied behind fallen logs, the Overland men, too experienced to waste ammunition without a target, held their fire.

"Take it easy, Morris!" Marlin shook the wounded man roughly, trying to calm him. "How did it happen?"

"We never had a chance," Morris groaned. "We was settin' with our backs to a tree watchin' the horses—an' them damned Injuns burrowed in the snow right up to thirty feet of us an' put an arrer into Drew an' almost split my skull with a throwin' hatchet—an' then they started shootin' the horses full of arrers. My God, you ever see—"

"Dammit." Ben Holladay, who had crawled over beside them, demanded roughly, "Why in hell didn't you put up a fight? At least give us more warning!"

"Hell, I did!" Morris protested. "But it all happened so fast. Maybe twenty seconds from the time I was hit till I started firin'. Doggone it, Ben, you lose half your scalp an' see if you c'n do any better!"

"You did fine," Holladay replied. "I just had to shoot off my mouth. Jerimah"—to the scout—"see if you can find an extra shirt or drawers in somebody's saddlebags for bandages. An' maybe a little whiskey to douse on his head."

"Listen to me, Morris!" Marlin said. "How many of them are there? How many did you actually see?"

"They was ten, fifteen," Morris answered more calmly. "They're gone now. They took off the minute I started shootin'. Had their horses hidden on th' other side of the grove."

Henshaw returned with a clean shirt and a half-filled bottle of whiskey.

"Bob," Marlin called to Ridley, "fix Morris up,

will you? Pour half that whiskey on his scalp and give him the rest to drink." He turned toward Ben Holladay. "You take charge here. Jerimah and I are going to check on the horses."

With Henshaw padding quietly along beside him, Marlin moved out of the clearing and worked his way deeper into the timber where he had ordered the horses picketed for greater safety. It had been a fatal mistake. The Sioux had simply slipped in from the other side of the grove.

He moved softly, taking no chances that the warriors might still be around. Dawn, full-lighted, spread among the trees ringing the open space where they had picketed the horses.

Abruptly, he halted with Jerimah Henshaw at his shoulder. Just ahead and to the right, Drew sat with his back against a tree, pinned there by the arrow that had killed him.

In the clearing, half a dozen horses were down on the snow. Four or five more stood passively, heads down, their necks, bellies, and rumps pin-cushioned with feathered shafts.

"Damn!" Henshaw swore softly and, raising his rifle, ended their suffering while the remainder of the herd lunged against the picket line. Then lowering the rifle, he regarded Marlin with a bitter, frustrated expression.

"Thet damn Chewin' Black Bone's one smart Injun. I figgered he'd maybe drop back fifty, sixty braves to carry on a rearguard holdin' action. He plumb fooled me. He's put us practically afoot with a handful of warriors. Ain't no way, double-mounted, we kin keep up with him, much less outrun him." Henshaw's eyes met Marlin's, cool, challenging.

"I figure, Colonel, you ain't the kind of man to lose your head an' go ridin' hell-bent-fer-leather back to Julesburg alone. Why, half th' men here got more ties 'an you have. Wives an' children, an' they're jest as worried about 'em as you are about Susan Ashley."

"Shut your mouth!" Marlin said angrily. "Susan Ashley has nothing to do with it. Somebody's got to warn the town."

"Ah, hell, Colonel," Jerimah Henshaw spat in disgust, "there's men in Julesburg know more about fightin' Injuns 'an you'll ever know. An' it's how you fight 'em when you do see 'em thet counts. But go ahead, send some poor bastard ahead to git his-self kilt—'cause he sure as hell ain't got no chance of gittin' past them Injuns. An' like I said, you got no more right'n anybody else to go tearin' back to town out of plumb damn foolishness."

Without a word, Marlin put his back to Henshaw and returned to the camp. The men were standing ready, blankets rolled, beside their saddles. Holladay took one look at Marlin's grim face and scowled.

"How many did we lose?"

"Eleven."

"Goddamn!" Holladay exploded. "That finishes us!"

"Not quite," Marlin replied, "but we'll have to double up. That rules out any chance of reaching Julesburg ahead of Chewing Black Bone. All we can do is hope that Ed Ashley has the people alerted and that Beauchamp makes a fight of it."

An angry protest burst from the Overland men, then gradually died away. They stood silent, looking at him—waiting for his next move. Like him, Marlin thought, they were concerned not for their own safety, but for the safety of their friends and loved ones in Julesburg.

"Those of you with horses will mount up a lighter man behind you," he ordered. "Or if you're light, then a heavier man. That way, we'll distribute the weight evenly. Every three hours, one of you will dismount and walk an hour. Every five hours, both of you will dismount and walk an hour. Stow your extra ammunition in your saddle bags. You may need every round of it." He swept the silent circle a moment, then dismissed them with a curt nod.

"All right, saddle up the horses," he said, "and let's get going."

"What about Drew, sir?" Morris, his head wrapped in an already bloody bandage. "He was my friend."

Marlin hesitated, conscious of the silence, of the

challenge in the men's eyes. It was a difficult decision; he made it.

"Tie him across your saddle," he said. "We'll take him with us. But if one of the horses goes down . . . You understand?"

"Yes, sir," Morris acknowledged. "And thank you, Colonel."

When the group had disappeared into the timber, Marlin turned to Ben Holladay with a grave expression—and saw reflected in the other's face some of the hidden fear that haunted him. Whatever Notley Ann might be, Ben Holladay loved her in his own way.

"Well," Holladay said bluntly, "what do you think of their chances?"

Marlin looked him straight in the eyes. "I don't know. I just don't know."

They were standing there, when Henshaw and Bob Ridley brought them their horses. Mounting up, they rode shoulder to shoulder away from the oak grove, following the trail of the small Sioux raiding party.

A warming wind out of the south brought them the smell of charred timber and, as they drew closer, they could see a cloud of grayish-white smoke drifting over Julesburg.

Reining up, Marlin studied the town through his binoculars. Only the business section seemed to have been damaged; and apparently the flames had now been brought under control. At least a hundred soldiers, mounted and dismounted, moved up and down the street.

A mile to the east, the gates of Camp Rankin were closed, and the flag still whipped in the breeze above the fort. There were no signs of Indians anywhere. With almost a full day's lead, they had probably already crossed to the other side of the river.

"Looks like they hit only the business section," Marlin said, lowering the glasses. "There's soldiers down there in the street."

"You mean that bastard Beauchamp came out from behind his log walls and made a fight of it?" Holladay exclaimed. "I don't believe it!"

Marlin shrugged. "We'll find out soon enough." He raised his arm, waved it forward, cavalry-fashion, and led his group down the hill at a fast trot.

As they entered the main street, Marlin slowed the pace to a walk. His mouth set grimly. From a distance, the damage had appeared minimal. Now, at close range, he saw just how destructive Chewing Black Bone's attack had been. Buildings burned to the ground, others with their roofs gone and their interiors gutted—and a few merely smoke blackened, with smashed doors and broken windows.

Carelessly dropped loot littered boardwalk and street. Sacks of flour, sugar, and beans split open and their contents spilled onto the snow . . . an odd boot, a lady's plumed hat, trampled into a sodden mess . . . a much-prized butcher knife, accidentally dropped . . . a bolt of equally prized bright red cloth, unwound across the snow like fresh-spilled blood . . .

The Wagon Wheel Saloon still stood, its windows shattered, its door ripped off, broken whiskey bottles and splintered chairs half buried in the snow. Cochran stood on the boardwalk, a dead cigar clenched between his teeth, and watched them pass with quietly hating eyes.

Not until they reached the Overland office—or rather the charred, blackened spot where it had stood—did Ben Holladay react. He reined up, surveying the destruction with tightly compressed lips.

"We'll build it back," he said in a hoarse voice. "By God, we'll build it back!"

They rode on in slump-shouldered silence, weary, hungry, frustrated men. They had fought eight hundred Indians out there on the Plains and defeated them . . . many of their friends had died . . . they had kept a thousand rifles from falling into Indian hands. And yet, despite this, Chewing Black Bone had raided and looted the town.

Only Marlin realized that the real battle had been won by the Union, not by the Sioux, Cheyennes, and Arapahos. For the true enemy had not been Tashunka Witko, Makpiya Luta, Napka Kesela, Chewing Black Bone, and other chiefs fighting for their homelands; the true enemy had been Hamlin Weatherby and Stephen Beauchamp and the conspiracy which they had directed.

Now Weatherby was dead; Beauchamp, if not already so, was as good as dead, and the conspiracy was broken. The West would not be won over to the South. The war would not be senselessly prolonged. That was what mattered.

Julesburg might be attacked again, perhaps even burned to the ground; but it would be rebuilt again and again. Ben Holladay would see to that.

Straightening in his saddle, Marlin felt some of the weariness slip from him. He had done his job—or would have as soon as he finished with Beauchamp.

A mud-splashed cavalry officer stood in the middle of the desolate street before the hotel, watching their approach. Captain Nash and a sergeant, whom Marlin had never seen before, lounged a few feet away. Scores of soldiers moved among the burned buildings, making certain no new fires sprang up and salvaging anything of value.

Reining up, Marlin crossed his hands on his saddle horn and nodded to the mud-spattered officer. "Where can I find Major Beauchamp?"

"The Major's dead." A definite German accent. "Are you Colonel Marlin?"

"That's right."

The officer saluted smartly. "Captain Jake Kremmling, sir."

"Fort Sedgewick?"

"Yes, sir. A drummer spotted the smoke and brought us word of the attack. We mounted up a hundred and ten men, but by the time we arrived it was all over."

"Where is Chewing Black Bone now?"

"He escaped across the river near Ash Hollow," Kremmling responded, "taking his loot with him."

With the Indians gone and troops in the streets, Marlin saw no need to keep his battle-weary, trail-weary men around. He dismissed them with a wave of his hand.

"Get some food in your bellies and catch up on your sleep," he ordered. "Then report to me here in the morning."

Still double-mounted, they walked their tired horses toward the livery stable, and people watched them go with uneasy eyes. But not until Marlin and Holladay dismounted and stood stomping their feet to restore circulation did anyone speak. It was Captain Nash who voiced the concern in every man's mind.

"What about the ordnance train, Colonel?"

"Crazy Horse, Red Cloud, and Chewing Black Bone hit us two days out with eight hundred, maybe a thousand warriors," Marlin replied. "We gave them a bad mauling, a hundred, a hundred fifty dead. Afterward, they split up. Some headed for Frenchman's Creek, some for Julesburg. The Broken Cooking Pot Brules wanted revenge. We tried to get here ahead of Chewing Black Bone but lost half our horses yesterday."

"But the ordnance train, the caravan, sir," Nash persisted. "Where are they?"

"On their way in," Marlin reassured him. "They should arrive some time tomorrow."

Nash regarded him with a bitter expression. "You maul Chewing Black Bone," he retorted, "and, in turn, he loots Julesburg. Do you call that a fair trade?"

"What happened here, Captain, involves matters of national security," Marlin said evenly, "and was a calculated risk for which I accept full responsibility."

"And the Major's death," Nash shot back. "Do you also accept responsibility for that? He was a brave man. He put up a good fight."

"He was a damned fool," Kremmling snapped. "He let himself get tricked into the open and almost lost his entire command. A corporal would have shown better judgment."

"Captain," Nash protested, "the Major's dead!"

"And because of his incompetence," Kremmling retorted, "so are fourteen troopers and four civilians."

Drawn by the sound of angry voices, troopers and townsmen began to converge on the scene. Quickly, Marlin stepped between the two captains.

"Gentlemen, we're all tired," he said. "Suppose we go inside where we can relax. Or did they gut the hotel, too?"

"They tried." Kremmling indicated the splintered log walls and the arrows shafted in the door and around the broken windows. "But Ashley, the Overland station agent, holed up inside with his family and about twenty men and put up a hell of a fight. The Indians never got through the door."

In those first moments following their arrival, Marlin had been occupied with the immediate situation. Subconsciously, he had taken it for granted that Susan Ashley was safe. Now suddenly he realized that there *had* been casualties, and that Susan could have been one of them. The thought scared him.

"Was anyone in the hotel hurt?" he asked quickly. "I mean—were any of the women hurt?"

"There were casualties, yes," Kremmling replied. "But no women. Mrs. Ashley and her daughter, Susan, and"—he nodded to Holladay—"your wife, sir, are unharmed. They've turned the hotel's second floor into a hospital for the wounded. I believe you'll find them up there now."

"Well, that's a relief!" Holladay said, and only

Marlin knew just how afraid the big man had been for Notley Ann. "Come on. Let's warm our gullets."

In the hotel lobby, Marlin halted, staring at the bullet-sieved walls, the charred circles made by fire arrows shot through the windows, and at the throwing hatchet embedded in the wall behind the counter. Empty cartridge cases littered the floor, and the acrid smell of black powder stung his nostrils.

"By God," Holladay exclaimed. "Ed did put up a fight! Where is he?"

"I think he's checking the residential part of town," Captain Nash volunteered. "I don't think it was touched. The Indians seemed bent on looting the business section."

Leading the way into the dining room—with Holladay, Nash, and Kremmling following—Marlin chose a table near the fireplace. Here, nothing had been damaged. A big log burned brightly on the racks, and a couple of smoke-blackened soldiers sat drinking coffee several tables away. At sight of Nash and Kremmling, they got up and left.

There was a moment's silence, then Marlin laid his hands on the table and nodded to Nash.

"All right, Captain, now tell me exactly what happened. When, where, and how they hit."

Nash cleared his throat. "Well, sir, we kept seeing small bands of Indians around the area all morning. But what we didn't know was that there were five or six hundred Sioux, Cheyennes, and Arapahos hidden behind those sand hills out there.

"Ashley sent word that the people in town were getting uneasy and that he figured the Indians were up to something. A few settlers fled their farms and came to the fort, along with a number of scouts and hunters.

"Finally, a small war party of young bucks feinted an attack on the fort, taunting and challenging us. The Major—" Nash flushed, and threw Kremmling a hard glance. "Well, sir, the Major decided to teach them a lesson. He mounted up sixty troopers, ordered the gates opened, and charged the war party. They retreated and then, suddenly, hundreds of Indians came racing from behind those dunes, yelling and screaming and shooting over their ponies' necks.

"Seeing himself hopelessly outnumbered, the Major ordered a retreat, fighting off the enemy every foot of the way. As second in command, I ordered the howitzer into action. The shells caused a lot of confusion, but still they kept coming on. I saw troopers begin to fall; and then the four civilians who were with them went down." Nash paused, obviously finding it difficult to continue. He licked his lips, breathed deeply and went on.

"We kept up a brisk fire with the howitzer, lobbing shells over the troopers' heads to cover their retreat. They barely made it back to the fort. We had the gates open just enough to let them through. The Major waited until the last man was inside. Then just as he started to wheel his horse, he took an arrow straight through his heart.

"My God, the damned thing went right into the feathers, and I saw the barb tear through the back of his uniform and . . . and then a trooper grabbed his horse and got him inside before he fell. We closed the gates and poured the fire to them, but they pulled out of range of everything but the howitzer."

"What happened then?" Marlin asked.

Nash shifted uncomfortably on his chair. "About a hundred and forty of them rode away and attacked the town, while the rest—I'd say three hundred and fifty—kept us pinned up inside the fort.

"Dammit, Colonel"—his frustration erupted—"there wasn't a damned thing we could do! We'd already lost fourteen troopers and those four civilians when the Major got tricked into the open. And if those young bucks hadn't been so eager and sprung the trap too soon, we could have . . . Captain Kremmling's right . . . we could have all been massacred.

"All day, while the Indians in town raided and looted, the rest kept us busy putting out fire arrows and lobbing shells toward them with the howitzer. I watched the raid on the town through my field glasses. The Indians raced down the street, whooping and hollering and shooting down the lawmen and the few townsmen who tried to stand against them. The merchants and other townspeople fled to the residential section—all save Ed Ashley and about twenty men who holed up here in the hotel. The Indians concentrated on looting and wrecking the stores and, from time to time, charging Ashley's position. I think if they hadn't been so obsessed with overrunning him, they'd have probably burned the whole town. It was a bad thing, but it could have been worse."

Holladay, who had remained silent, suddenly brought a big hand down hard on the table.

"You're damned right, Captain," he said. "It could have been a lot worse. I've lost a home station and a few way stations, but I'll rebuild them. Meanwhile, I'm going back to Washington where I can watch that damned Conness eat crow!" He shot Marlin a triumphant "you know what I'm talking about" smile. "By God, I'd like to ram it down his throat. But listening to him try and talk his way out of this will be satisfaction enough. *God, how I hate that man!*"

"Well . . ." Marlin pushed back his chair and rose. He had but one thought in mind now—to go upstairs and find Susan Ashley. It was a deep, overwhelming desire that he could not cope with, nor did he wish to do so. "I think Ed has the situation here in town under control. And, Captain

Nash, you did all that could be expected of you."

"Not quite, sir," Nash replied grimly. "I intend to get those damned Indians yet. Captain Kremmling"—he turned to the Fort Sedgewick officer—"I'll need your help. Can we ride out to the fort and discuss it?"

Kremmling hesitated. "I suppose so," he said without enthusiasm. "We might as well get started."

Only Holladay remained seated, watching the others with shrewd eyes.

Kremmling clicked his heels, saluted, and said, "Good-bye, Colonel—Mr. Holladay."

"Thank you for your help, Captain," Marlin replied. Then, to Nash, "I'll probably see you tomorrow."

"Yes, sir." Nash saluted and left the dining room with Kremmling.

"Well, Colonel"—Ben Holladay leaned back in his chair, the tiger's claw on the gold watch chain gleaming whitely against his dark waistcoat, and smiled at Marlin with a quiet amusement—"what the hell are you standing there for? I imagine Susan's just as eager to see you as you—"

Marlin was already through the door, into the lobby, up the stairs; and Susan Ashley, just starting down, had time only to whisper, "Oh, Kurt!" before he crushed her to him, knowing that this time it was right, it was good.

The following morning, he rode out to Camp Rankin and called on Janet Beauchamp.

• • •

A half dozen officer's wives and ladies of the town emerged from the Commandant's quarters, curtsied and discreetly took their leave as Marlin approached. Pale but composed, Janet Beauchamp admitted him to the sitting room. Color flushed her cheeks and her mouth took on a bitter expression.

"You obviously didn't come here, Colonel, to console the bereaved widow," she said. "You know that I didn't love Stephen, so I'll not pretend now. But my father . . . You were the one who killed him, weren't you?"

"He gave me no choice." Marlin regarded her steadily. "Be grateful he didn't live to hang."

"I hate you!"

"And I regret that, in the interest of the nation, secrecy prevents me from sending you back to Washington to stand trial as a Confederate spy."

"Now aren't you the gallant gentleman!" Janet Beauchamp leaned back, cool, blond, and beautiful, and smiled at him. "Do you really believe you could convince a nice, chivalrous board of officers that I'm guilty of treason?"

Had he not glimpsed the fanatic, calculating mind behind the warm mask at Hamlin Weatherby's cabin, Marlin would have found the transformation in her now unbelievable. But remembering her wild outburst that day—*Damn those kinky-headed niggers! And damn nigger-loving bastards like you!*—it did not surprise him at all.

"I believe I'd have no difficulty in convincing them that you should be shot for what you did to a West Point officer." His face assumed a lean, merciless expression. "Do you have any idea of how ruthless the Army can be when its image is tarnished? Don't push me, madam, or, by God, I *will* send you back under guard and let them crucify you!"

Janet Beauchamp's smile wavered, disappeared. A touch of fear darkened her eyes. "You really would, wouldn't you?"

"I would," Marlin said. "And gladly."

She bit her lips, blinked back the sudden tears, and cried out in a genuine agony of the spirit.

"My God, what's happening to me? Why are you talking to me this way? What's happening to the whole damned world? Why is everything falling apart? Why have men gone mad over a bunch of black animals? I don't understand! I don't even understand why I feel the way I do. Why I don't feel guilty for what I've done.

"But then why should I?" The green eyes flamed with passion. "Why must I apologize for what I am? For my conscience? For having done what I thought was right? For loving the land where I was born, and for wanting to keep it the way it has always been!"

She rose to face Marlin, a slim, beautiful woman with proud, tormented features.

"Damn you, don't just stand there looking at me as if I were some sort of monster! Make me see myself and my father through your eyes, and then maybe I'll get down on my knees and beg your forgiveness! Maybe I'll even *beg* you to shoot me! But as long as I feel the way I do now . . . Don't you realize that you damn Yankees have killed the only things in the world that I've ever loved—my father and the South!"

Marlin regarded her, untouched. "I doubt that you've ever loved anything in your life except yourself. And, sometimes, I suspect you find even that difficult. I doubt it even bothers you that you're responsible for the deaths of God knows how many innocent people. Your conscience is like a red carpet; it hides the bloodstains. I would like to think that you will suffer for what you've done. But you won't; your kind never does."

Picking up his hat, he walked toward the door. There, he paused. "Captain Nash will be taking over temporary command of Camp Rankin in a day or so. You have until then to leave. Whenever you're ready, I'll see that you are escorted to Denver. From there, you'll be free to go wherever you wish."

"What about my father and my husband?" Janet Beauchamp cried. "Who's going to make the necessary arrangements?"

Slowly, Marlin came back to her. "Major Beauchamp will be buried with full military honors. For the sake of the Union, his treason will remain secret. Yet I doubt that few men have ever been punished more while living than Stephen Beauchamp."

Marlin fell silent, searching Janet Beauchamp's face for some sign of remorse, but the smooth, lovely features remained unchanged. His mouth tightened.

"I'll arrange with the undertaker for your father's funeral. If you wish a minister or anything else, you'll have to take care of the matter yourself."

"Thank you." Cool, composed. "Is that all you have to say to me?"

Marlin gave her one last intense look and said, "Good-bye, Mrs. Beauchamp."

As he closed the door behind him, he experienced a vast sense of relief. Unconsciously, his steps quickened as he crossed the parade ground, the snow crunching dryly beneath his boots. Inexplicably, he thought of Susan Ashley and, for the first time in weeks, he felt good and at peace with himself.

As ranking officer, Marlin attended Major Stephen Beauchamp's funeral the following day. Afterward, he bowed silently over the widow's hand for the benefit of those present. He did not see her again before her departure.

Accompanied by a cavalry escort, Janet

Beauchamp left Julesburg only hours after she had buried Hamlin Weatherby with no mourners at graveside save a Baptist minister and herself. Scouts had warned Marlin that although the Julesburg-Denver route was clear of hostiles, it could close any day if the Sioux-Cheyenne-Arapaho force resumed its sweeping raids.

"You want to send the Major's wife to Denver," Jerimah Henshaw advised, "you'd best do it today. That's what Ben Holladay an' his missus are doin'. Oh, almost forgot. Holladay said tell you he'd like to see you 'fore he leaves."

Marlin was on his way to pay his respects to the Holladays when Janet Beauchamp's carriage, flanked by a detail of cavalry, passed him. As she swung her head and looked straight at him, the sun struck her honey-blond hair and, despite himself, he was reminded of that first moment when he had first seen her in the hotel's dining room and the sun, flowing in the window, had glinted on her hair in just this same way. The moment held for what seemed an eternity—and then she was gone.

Bob Ridley, wearing a complete new outfit, was already on the box of the "Holladay Special," waiting while the two baggage coaches were being loaded, when Marlin arrived.

"Wondered if you'd make it in time," Ridley said, threading the ribbons through his fingers.

"Ben'll be out in a minute. Missus Holladay is already inside."

"Will you be returning to Julesburg, Bob?" Marlin asked.

The jehu shrugged. "If it's still here," he replied. "After what's happened, I wouldn't bet on it. Next time, I think they'll wipe the town off the map."

Before Marlin could answer, Ben Holladay stepped from the Overland office and came forward, his face lighting with genuine pleasure.

"Well, Colonel, I was hoping to see you before we left," Holladay said, shaking hands. "Since you'll be returning to Washington soon anyway, why not make the trip with us? We'd be glad to stay over for another day if necessary."

Marlin smiled. "You forget I'm still on Presidential assignment, sir. I can't leave until I receive my orders; and I've no idea exactly when that may be. But thanks, anyway."

"Then we'll see you in Washington." Holladay stood there a moment, studying Marlin with a quizzical expression; suddenly, he threw back his head and roared with laughter.

"An Army colonel with brains!" he cried. "If I hadn't seen it with my own eyes, I'd never have believed it! I only hope the President will believe me, since I certainly intend to recommend you to him." He stopped laughing, his mood becoming serious.

"The Overland owes you a great deal, Colonel. I owe you even more. Although I doubt you've stopped these raids, you have put an end to the Confederate conspiracy. And, for me personally, you've shown that damned loudmouth Conness up for a liar—by proving that I am not the thieving, murdering bastard he's accused me of being." He thrust out his hand.

"If the President ever runs out of special assignments for you, come around and see me. I'll guarantee you some of the most exciting battles in history are fought on the fields of big business. Good-bye, Colonel."

The jehu's whip cracked, the team of matched racers surged against their collars and the brilliant red-and-yellow Concord was gone in a spray of snow.

As he turned away, Marlin bumped into Ed Ashley, who was just emerging from the office. For a moment, Ashley stood watching the pluming snow cloud that marked the stage's passage. Then he said quietly, "Evening clothes and top hat or buckskins and moccasins, there goes a hell of a man."

"He's a special breed," Marlin agreed. "In his own way, as much of a trail blazer as the mountain man—and, like the mountain man, his time, too, will pass. Meanwhile, he'll carve himself a paragraph in history."

"Well, with him and Notley Ann gone, we're

moving back into our own house," Ashley said. "Which reminds me. Emma asked me to invite you over for supper tonight. Susan will be expecting you, and I know you won't disappoint her."

"No," Marlin's voice was suddenly gentle. "I'll be there at seven o'clock."

There was a moment's comfortable pause, then Ashley cleared his throat and spoke with obvious embarrassment.

"Kurt"—he was the only one who did not call Marlin "Colonel"—"I don't know how to put this, but—well, have you and Susan come to a definite understanding?"

"If you mean have I asked her to marry me yet," Marlin answered, smiling, "no."

A perplexed expression clouded Ashley's face. "Then would you mind telling me why she's got her trunk packed and her best traveling dress laid out to wear?"

Marlin breathed deeply. *You always could read my mind, couldn't you, Susan?*

"Why?" He looked gravely at Ed Ashley. "Because she's always known my heart, Ed, even when I didn't. But you can tell her that if she's going to Washington with me, we'll have to get married. I'll not travel across the country with a brazen hussy!"

Not speaking, Ashley laid his hand on Marlin's shoulder and, after a moment, answered with a mild challenge. "Why don't you tell her that after supper?"

"Now that you've mentioned it," Marlin said, "I will. Do you have any more suggestions?"

"Yes." A humorous gleam warmed Ashley's eyes. "Make sure you arrive on time."

He turned up his coat collar and strode away.

Marlin stood there, watching the last pluming snow spray from the Holladay Special glittering in the bright winter sunshine, and feeling a deep gratitude for Susan Ashley's special understanding of him as a man, a human being.

Straightening his shoulders, he breathed deeply of the clean, cold air and then walked briskly down the street, the snow crunching dryly under his feet.

Max von Kreisler, who was born in 1913, lived most of his life in the state of Oklahoma. He began writing Western fiction for the magazine market in 1940, primarily for Popular Publications, using the name Max Kesler. These stories frequently were set in his native state, such as "There's War in the Cherokee Strip" in *Ace-High Western Stories* (11 /41) or "Beware the Bloody Strip" in *New Western* (10/50). Oil exploitation was also a familiar theme as in "Three for the Wildcatter War" in .44 Western (10/47) or "Blood, Oil, and Bullets" in *New Western* (4/50). Later he turned to writing Western novels, beginning with *Donovan* (Zebra Books, 1975), published under the name Max Kreisler. His last novels were hardcover editions published under his full name Max von Kreisler: *Stand in the Sun* (Doubleday, 1978) and *The Pillagers* (Doubleday, 1982). The latter appeared the same year he died in Payson, Arizona. Von Kreisler was always proud of the fact that his stories and novels avoided violence and bigger-than-life characters, and in his words "concentrated more on the everyday people who gave substance and lasting character to the changing frontier both before and after the era of the trail drives."

Center Point Large Print
600 Brooks Road / PO Box 1
Thorndike ME 04986-0001 USA

(207) 568-3717

US & Canada:
1 800 929-9108
www.centerpointlargeprint.com